TIMEBLINK: FLIGHT 444

MJ MUMFORD

This is a work of fiction. Names, characters, places and incidents either are the product of the author's imagination or are used fictitiously. Any resemblance to actual persons, living or dead, business establishments, events, or locales is entirely coincidental. The publisher does not have control over and does not have any responsibility for author or third-party websites or their content.

TIMEBLINK: FLIGHT 444

Cover by
Elizabeth Mackey

First Printing July 2022

ISBN 978-1-7773362-4-0 (ebook)
ISBN 978-1-7773362-3-3 (paperback)
ISBN 978-1-7773362-5-7 (hardcover)

In memory of my dad
Alvin
who learned to fly
but wasn't much of a traveler.

Flight 444 includes content that some readers may find uncomfortable or triggering.

Please visit the **Content Guidance** page at mjmumford.com for details.

A Note Before You Board...

Flight 444 is Book 2 in The Syd Brixton TimeBlink Series.

Early readers of *Flight 444* reported being able to follow the story easily but, because of the spoilers, some wished they'd started with Book 1, *TimeBlink*, first.

Wherever you begin your timeblinking journey, the author wishes to thank you for taking a chance on her books. If you enjoy them, please consider leaving a review on Amazon, Goodreads, or BookBub to help other readers discover this series.

Chapter One

THURSDAY, APRIL 11, 2024, 10:30 A.M.

Buffalo, NY

"Honestly, Syd. Don't be so dramatic. It'll be over before you know it," Kendall said, unplugging her phone from the charging station next to our seats at Gate 34.

"Easy for you to say. You aren't being forced to babysit that sourpuss for a month," I said, nodding across the aisle at our fifteen-year-old half-sister, Lainie. "Look at her. She might as well be a street kid."

"Give her a break. She's been through so much."

"Oh, like we haven't?"

"This isn't about us. It's about helping our grieving sister through a rough time."

"*Half*-sister. And you don't have to do anything. It's all on me—for a freaking *month*!"

"Exactly. It's *only* a month. And it was Dad's final wish."

I grunted. "Still taking his side, I see."

Kendall turned to me and shook her head. "Get over yourself. After this, you'll never have to see this side of the family again."

My sister was infuriatingly forgiving when it came to our

father, who'd died nearly three weeks ago—conveniently after he'd named me as Lainie's temporary guardian in his will.

"Have you forgotten what he did to you? To *us*?" I said, lowering my voice despite the cacophony of gate-change announcements, chattering passengers, and golf carts speeding by with decrepit seniors perched on the back. "He abandoned us, Kenny. Came straight to Buffalo *on the other freaking side of the country* and set up a whole new family."

"Please, I was twenty-one. Hardly a case of child abandonment."

"But I was sixteen!"

"Hey, you two," Isla said, coming toward us with the latest Judith Wendles novel in her hand. She took her seat next to me. "You look so serious. What's up?"

"Nothing. Kendall's just making excuses for our father's terrible life choices again. Specifically, when he abandoned me."

Isla put her hand on my knee. "Remember what Julie told us after the funeral? He couldn't deal with the heartache of my disappearance and then Mom's death a year later. It devastated him."

"That's no excuse for taking off and forcing Kendall to look after my sorry, substance-addicted ass."

Kendall flicked her long brown curls over her shoulder. "Did you ever hear me complaining about it?"

I had to think about it for a moment. Sure, we'd had our share of blow-ups during that time, but she was right. She'd never grumbled about it. Not once.

"Well, no, but—"

She raised her eyebrows at me.

"Why are you sticking up for him? Don't you see? He's doing the same thing all over again. Dumping a troubled teenager in someone else's lap!"

"I can help you. With Lainie," Isla said.

"You'll do no such thing," Kendall said, wagging her

finger at Isla. "This is Syd's assignment. Dad was very specific about that in the codicil."

I shook my head. It was beyond cruel that he would ask me to help his second family now when they hadn't *once* extended a similar kindness toward me or Kendall all those years. And to boot, he'd done it from the grave, leaving me no opportunity to object.

While I stewed about the injustice of it all, Finn appeared in front of me, holding Christopher's hand. "Can I take Christopher to watch the planes, Aunty Syd?"

I looked to Isla for approval. "What do you think? Is he old enough for the responsibility?"

Finn turned to Isla. "Please, Mama? I'm not a baby. I'm almost ten!"

Isla ruffled his hair. "Okay, sweetie. But don't let Christopher out of your sight. Remember, he's still only three and wouldn't think twice about wandering away from you. And make sure you sit near Connor and Devin."

"Promise!" he said, leading Christopher toward the floor-to-ceiling windows overlooking the tarmac. They settled onto the floor next to Kendall's twelve-year-old twins, who were busy playing games on their phones. Finn leaned down and said something in Christopher's ear and pointed to a plane pulling up to the gate.

"Your kid's a rockstar," I said.

Isla beamed. "He's pretty awesome. Doesn't hurt that he absolutely adores his little cousin."

"All our boys are pretty awesome. Makes you wonder what happened to *that* particular family member," I said, nodding toward Lainie, who was slumped in her seat listening to what was probably some raunchy emo music in her ear buds. I saw other travelers stealing furtive glances at her, and I was embarrassed for the girl. And for me. Her face was slathered with three pounds of pale makeup, black eye gunk, and navy-blue lipstick. She'd topped everything off with a small gold nose ring and a curved silver barbell in her eyebrow. At least she'd ditched her usual tight black, chain-draped getup today in favor of gray leggings and an oversized burgundy hoodie. I laughed under my breath. With her neon green and black hair, she looked like a giant emo eggplant.

Kendall gave me a smug look.

"What are you staring at?" I said.

"She's the spitting image of you at that age."

"Oh, wow, you're right," Isla said.

"Seriously? You too, now?"

"Yes. I forgot to mention that when I was going through Dad's things yesterday, I almost mistook you for Lainie in one of his old photos. You even had the same haunted look in your eyes. It was so sad."

It was baffling why my father would have hung onto pictures of me from a time when he'd been so horribly vexed by my existence. But my sisters were right. Besides the birthmark on Lainie's right cheek and the green hair, she could have been my twin at that age. Everything else—the black eyeliner, tattoos, piercings, and dark clothing—was nearly identical. Lainie's body decorations were apparently new in the last few months, having appeared after her best friend, Dee, had taken her own life. And it's why my father had recently added the codicil to his will. One that asked me to take Lainie under my wing for a month.

"It's ludicrous," I said, shaking my head. "She's practically a stranger. This must be payback for all the shit I put him through."

"I don't think he meant it as a punishment," Isla said.

"Whatever."

"No, really. Who better to help Lainie than someone that's walked in her shoes?"

"I don't know. A psychiatrist?"

"Well, it's too late to change plans now," Kendall said. "They just called your flight number."

"An on-time flight? Huh. At least something's going my way today."

"That's the spirit," Kendall said.

I rolled my eyes and stood up. "Guess I'll collect my street kid and head down to our gate. Man, you guys are lucky bums. I'd kill for a direct flight."

"Don't be too jealous. Our flight doesn't leave for another two hours, and we have a bunch of rambunctious boys to keep busy. You and Lainie are the lucky ones."

"You're still going to be home literally hours before us."

"Quit being such a downer. You've got twelve hours of freedom ahead of you. And have you forgotten I'll be serving as your personal chauffeur when you land in Seattle? Sheesh. Talk about ungrateful," Kendall said, winking at me.

"Yeah, yeah. I'll go say goodbye to Christopher and be on my happy, carefree way."

Chapter Two

THURSDAY, APRIL 11, 2024, 7 P.M.

Lainie settled into her seat beside an elegant Black woman in the window seat who flashed me a bright smile. She reminded me of my sixth-grade teacher, Ms. Nnadi, for her long neck, sharp jawline, and shock of thick, shoulder-length coils. I smiled back, then slipped into the seat next to Lainie and fastened my seatbelt.

"Finally," I said as Lainie rummaged through her back-pack. She produced a pair of shiny black wireless earbuds and a phone charging cord, the latter of which she connected to a port in the seat in front of her.

"You don't mind if I zone out for a little while?" she asked, as she screwed an earbud into her ear.

"Of course not. I'll probably waste some time on Word Witch myself."

"Okay. Cool."

Flight 444 was the second leg of our journey, the home stretch from Chicago to Seattle. I hoped the flight number was a good omen. A nod from the heavens that this mission—despite being forced upon me—would go smoothly.

Almost without thinking, I reached up and took hold of my dragonfly talisman hanging around my neck, recalling the first time I'd experienced its power. One moment, I'd been sitting on my couch waiting for my tea to boil, the next I was plunging down a hundred-foot waterfall at Chapman Falls. I smiled. It seemed like yesterday that Morley had pulled me from the water, took me to his nearby cabin, and filled me in on all the mind-blowing details of timeblinking. But five long years had gone by since then. Five years since Morley had died. Five years since he told me that on every timeblink, I would be gone from my present time for exactly four minutes and forty-four seconds. And every time that number had appeared in the intervening years—on a clock, an address, the cost of my latte this morning—it always comforted me.

After saying goodbye to the rest of my family at their gate in Buffalo, it was down to me and Lainie, and by the time we boarded this flight seven hours later, we'd both had all the forced chit-chat we could handle for one day. When Lainie popped her earbuds in and cranked up the music, I breathed a silent sigh of relief.

I cinched up my seatbelt before the plane door was even closed and smiled to myself. It's exactly what Isla and Kendall would have done—buckled themselves in the minute they boarded, grabbing the laminated crash pamphlets to read as well. A couple of nervous Nellies, my sisters. Maybe it was better we'd been separated, and I wouldn't have to deal with all their fidgeting and fussing. Maybe I'd even get a few solid winks in, especially with no kids to entertain. I envied my sisters, though. They were definitely home by now. Lainie and I had four and a half hours to go.

Normally I snag the window seat, but this was a last-minute flight change thanks to Lainie's booking, and we were lucky to even have seats next to each other. The family had discussed putting her on the flight by herself, but her mother, Julie, was having nothing of it. She didn't want her emotionally wrecked daughter left to her own devices. I could hardly blame her.

Anyway, I wasn't too disappointed about missing out on the seat selection. The sky was already dark, and the first stars were glittering to life. The window would have been a wasted luxury now.

Finding my preferred channel on the in-flight entertainment system—the GPS flight tracker—I settled back into my seat. Amidst excited murmuring in the cabin, I heard the woman in the window seat say, "Peek-a-boo!" and when I glanced over, she was making faces at a little boy who'd popped his head over the seat in front of her. Cute little guy. Younger than Christopher, perhaps not even two years old. The woman pinched his cheeks, and he laughed hysterically, and it was obvious she knew the boy and was probably related to him. She didn't seem quite young enough to be his mother and was perhaps his grandmother.

The man holding the boy—the grandfather?—tried to distract him with a stuffed toy, but the little boy was far too focused on his grandmother and wasn't even remotely interested in the neon-haired teenager sitting next to her.

Pretending to watch the boy, I studied my half-sister, shocked to discover my anger with the whole situation had waned in the time I'd spent with her today. She wasn't the devil-teen I'd been expecting her to be. She had, in fact, been quite pleasant all day. All that crap she piled on designed to keep people at arms' length—the chartreuse hair, the thick makeup, the outrageous body piercings—had the opposite effect on me. It was painfully obvious she was a sheep masquerading as a wolf. Sure, her life had been bleak over the past year, losing her best friend and then her father—*our* father—but I'd gone through some heavy shit in my life too, so I wasn't about to give her a free pass. She was on *my* watch now, and she would damn well play by my rules.

As I checked my phone to see if the rest of my family had arrived home safely, a wispy, elderly woman stopped to peer at the row number above my head, then pointed at Lainie.

"I think you're in my seat, dear," she said.

When Lainie's eyes stayed closed, I said, "What seat are you looking for?"

The woman squinted at her boarding pass, then thrust it in front of me. "I think it says 24E."

"It sure does," I said, "but this is row 22. You have two more to go."

"Thank you, dear. These old eyes aren't what they used to be."

"Happy to help," I said, smiling at her.

Once she'd shuffled off, a sugary young woman's voice crackled onto the PA system and gave us a rundown of the safety procedures.

"That voice will put you to sleep, won't it?" I vaguely heard someone say when the announcement ended.

When no one responded, I looked across the aisle to see a man with short, jet-black hair smiling at me from the middle seat. At first glance, he reminded me of that hunky Spanish F1 driver Kendall is so hot after. Carlos something-or-other, though more filled out and a bit older, maybe late thirties. He wore a lilac-colored dress shirt open at the neck, indigo jeans, and a dark gray suit jacket. A patterned tie lay on the seat next to him, and a younger man with greasy brown hair occupied the window seat on his other side.

"Oh, I don't know," I answered. "I found her voice kind of comforting."

"Nervous flier?" he said, eyeing my seatbelt.

"Not at all, actually."

"A daredevil, then."

I laughed. "Hardly. It's just that flying just doesn't bother me like it does some people. How about you?"

"Not anymore. I've become immune to the bumps and weird noises. Probably because I do it so often now."

"Is it for work? All the flying?"

"Yeah. Boring stuff, though. They're always sending me places I'd rather not go."

The scruffy young dude in the window seat huffed and rolled his eyes, like he thought the man was bragging, then turned his focus to something outside the window. He was wearing a grubby gray tracksuit and scuffed white tennis shoes and had an intricate tattoo on his neck that I couldn't quite decipher. He didn't seem like a typical air traveler, but I'd misjudged people before—most notably my psycho-ex. The child abducting sociopath.

The man in the lilac shirt ignored the young guy's bristling, making me wonder if, by chatting with me, he was trying to avoid engaging with him. Maybe the kid had body odor. "Do you live in Chicago?" he asked.

"No. Port Raven. Just here on a layover. I was in Buffalo for my father's funeral." It felt strange to say that. I was no stranger to tragedy, but my dad was dead. Everything was strange right now.

"Oh. Sorry to hear that."

I smiled sheepishly and swallowed an unexpected lump in my throat. The man returned the smile, then pulled his phone out of his breast pocket. "Duty calls," he said, ostensibly answering an email or text that had just come in. Great. I had a way of killing conversation.

"So, you're from Port Raven," the woman sitting next to Lainie said. "I thought you looked familiar."

Oh boy, that could only mean one of two things.

"You're from PR, too?" I asked, trying to place her face, hoping she recognized me from the pub where I work rather than from the news stories about Isla's disappearance and subsequent discovery five years back.

"Yes. I'd been wondering how you and your sister had been faring ever since, uh..." She bit her bottom lip, waiting for me to tell her which Brixton twin I was.

"Ever since Isla was found?" I said.

"Yes! Since Isla was found," she said. "You must be Cindy. How is Isla doing, anyway?"

I didn't have the energy to correct her, that I was in fact Sydney, the less famous twin that had *not* been abducted when she was eleven. The one that spent twenty years with a dark cloud over her head fighting an urge not to end her own life. "Isla's good. Thanks for asking."

If Lainie had heard any of this exchange, she didn't show it. Her seat was reclined, her heavily made-up eyes shut, and she appeared to be asleep.

The woman must have sensed my reluctance to talk about Isla's disappearance. "How rude of me," she said. "I didn't mean to pry. Just hadn't heard whatever happened to her."

Yeah, there was a reason for that. It's called privacy. The woman *was* being rude, but I couldn't blame her. People thought our private life was their business because of the sensational news coverage that went on for months after Isla and Finn had been found *Alive and Well!*

Alive, yes, but *well?* That was a matter of opinion.

"I'm sorry to hear about your father," she said, apparently having eavesdropped on my *entire* conversation with the man in the lilac shirt.

I shrugged. "We weren't very close."

Lainie's eyes flicked momentarily toward me, probably unintentionally, but it made me wonder if she could hear the conversation going on beyond the obnoxious music in her ears.

The woman gave me a sympathetic look as the little boy popped his head over the seat again. She ruffled his tight curls, and he disappeared in a fit of laughter.

"That's Eli. He's eighteen months of pure joy and boundless energy. Like that battery bunny," she said, chuckling.

"Makes me miss my son, Christopher. He was on an earlier flight with the rest of my family. Probably home by now."

Normally it would have been awkward carrying on a conversation with a whole person sitting between us, but by way of the music blasting in Lainie's ears, she'd chosen not to take part, anyway.

When the woman didn't ask why Christopher wasn't traveling with us, I said, "Eli's adorable."

She nodded as she slid her purse under the seat in front of her. "Miracle baby, that one. Three miscarriages before him. We were about to adopt when the Lord finally shone His light on my troubled womb."

"Oh!" I said, surprised to learn she was the boy's mother—not his grandmother. "That's wonderful!"

"Thanks, Cindy, I'm Rose, by the way."

"Nice to meet you. Actually, my name's Sydney. People call me Syd, though."

"Oops, sorry about that, Syd. Pleased to meet you, too."

When the little boy popped his head over the seat again, I almost suggested that Lainie switch seats with Rose's husband but quickly came to my senses. I'd already escaped the trouble of looking after my own young family members and certainly didn't need to be seated next to someone else's squirmy eighteen-month-old the entire flight. Besides, I didn't want to ruffle Lainie's feathers—not when we'd gotten off to such a good start.

About a half an hour into the flight, after learning all about Rose's interior design company and how she'd almost lost it during the height of the pandemic, the turbulence started.

It wasn't the normal turbulence where you could collect your breath between waves of violent shuddering. It was the unrelenting, bone-jarring kind. The kind that caused me—a person who rather enjoys hurtling through the air at 40,000 feet—to wonder if we might indeed crash.

For comfort, I reached up and clutched my dragonfly talisman between my fingers. Despite it only being the size of a thick twenty-five-cent coin, it felt solid and reassuring in my grasp. Oh, Morley. Why me? Why did you give me the talisman as you lay dying in the street?

Of course, I already knew the answer. He did it because he knew its power would lead me to Isla. And, in turn, to him. Maybe one day I would figure out how to save his life, but for now, we would have to cherish our fleeting encounters in a whole other time realm.

A violent jolt interrupted my thoughts. The GPS said 38,700 feet. Nothing to be alarmed about. My shoulders loosened.

I glanced at Lainie to gauge her reaction to all the shaking. If she was scared, she wasn't showing it. Her eyes were closed, her mouth ajar, and she appeared to be asleep. Fortunately, her seatbelt was fastened, and she looked comfortable, so I let her be.

If only I could be that relaxed. Normally I was. But the plane creaked and groaned angrily every time it bounced through an air pocket, and I could almost picture bolts shaking loose. Rose leaned forward to speak quietly with her husband, whose name I'd learned was George. He was a pilot himself, but only flew smaller planes for pleasure. He was a CEO of a large grocery chain, one of those rare businesses that went gangbusters during the worldwide health crisis.

I caught Rose's attention when she leaned back. "Do you want Lainie to switch seats with your family?" The question popped out before I could stop it.

Hearing this, George craned his head over the seat. "It's okay. I don't want to give up my extra leg room," he said, winking. "However, I do have to get up," he said to Rose. "This little fella needs attention." Going against the captain's orders to stay seated, George carried Eli past the couple seated next to him and hurried off to the back of the plane for a diaper change. I relaxed a little. If George—a pilot—was confident enough to leave his seat, maybe the turbulence wasn't so serious after all.

"There's a man after my own heart," I said to Rose. "I'm a single mom. Gotta do it all myself."

"How old did you say your son was?"

"He'll be four this year. In November."

"It takes some stamina, doesn't it? Raising a toddler? I'm exhausted most days, even with George around to share the duties."

"I get a lot of help from my sisters, especially Isla. We're both single moms, so we often spell each other off. Course, it helps that Finn loves his little cousin so much."

"Oh, yes, Finn. I read about him. And about how Isla said she wouldn't have survived so long in captivity without him. That part of her story always touched me."

The plane jolted violently, sending me into anxious silence. The GPS showed that we'd climbed to just over 41,000 feet, which was probably the captain's attempt to get out of whatever system we were flying through. It was nonetheless worrying. All the bouncing was getting on my nerves. I wasn't the only one. Everyone on the plane had also gone silent, save for the odd fretful gasp.

Over the PA system, the sweet, formerly calm voice came on. Now she sounded worried, but not to the point of outright panic. "The first officer has asked that you return to your seats and fasten your seatbelts while the crew deals with an emerg—" Either she stopped herself short of telling us there was some terrible catastrophe at play or she'd been interrupted. I preferred to imagine it was the latter.

"Shit. This is the worst flight I've ever been on." It was the man in the lilac shirt. "And I've been on a few."

That's when my panic kicked up a notch. Here was this guy who'd flown hundreds of times before—maybe thousands—looking as though he might consider throwing himself out the exit door. Next to me, Lainie was now fully awake but putting on a brave face.

"This is getting annoying," she said. Her voice was a few octaves higher than normal, making me believe—despite her cool exterior—that she, in fact, was just as scared as I was.

When the plane jarred again, we grabbed for our armrests simultaneously, our hands making contact on the one between us. I left my hand there, covering hers reassuringly, even though I was anything but assured.

At once, the plane dropped and took a hard left bank, spurring a fresh burst of gasps among the passengers. Seconds later, a cold rush of air filled the cabin and the oxygen masks dropped from the ceiling. As everyone scrambled to put them on, bags and personal possessions began whirling around the cabin, hitting passengers in the head or landing in their laps. People were trying to comfort their loved ones; some were praying out loud. The plane tipped further to the left. It would only be a matter of time before it spiralled completely out of control.

There was no further word from the flight crew.

I grabbed for the talisman—there would be no better time than the present to take advantage of its power to zap me and Lainie out of there—but I fumbled and missed when the plane's nose dipped to an almost vertical angle and my body flew forward. A moment later, George and Eli tumbled down the aisle to the front of the plane where, horrifically, George slammed against the cockpit door like a rag doll and a drink cart smashed into his head. I couldn't see Eli anywhere.

Rose had also seen them fly by, and now she was screaming, unbuckling herself, crashing onto the seats in front of us as the plane continued its missile-like trajectory toward Earth.

"Rose! Sit!" I yelled. She'd ripped off her oxygen mask was clawing her way to the aisle.

She barked back that we were all about to die, and she needed to get to her family. But before she could get there, the plane jerked, then righted itself and Rose collapsed onto Lainie's legs. I wondered if the pilots had finally gotten control of the plane. It was mercifully level, and the turbulence had abated a little.

Lainie and I helped Rose to her feet, and she tried pushing past us again. "Rose, please! Sit down!"

"Eli!" she screamed. But I wasn't about to let her go. Lainie seemed to understand, too, that Rose would be safer in her seat and helped me push her back. As Rose was about to take another run at getting past us, the plane roared and banked to the right, slamming her against her window, where she slithered down into her seat and went still.

I glanced at the altitude reading: *23,200 feet.* This plane was going down. I had to act.

Around my neck was the means to get Lainie and me off the plane. I grappled at my neckline, and by some minor miracle, my fingers found the talisman. Then, before giving it another thought, I grabbed lilac-shirt's hand across the aisle. I don't know what possessed me. I just seized his hand and yelled at Lainie to grab my other hand clutching the talisman. She looked at me curiously, probably thinking I'd lost my mind.

"*NOW!*" I yelled, and she quickly reached over and laid her hand on mine.

I called out our destination.

At the exact same time, Rose launched herself over us and—

Chapter Three

MONDAY, SEPTEMBER 9, 2019, MIDNIGHT

A millisecond later, we tumbled into the dark, deserted parking lot at Chapman Falls, Washington State, on the very specific date of September 9, 2019, at the very specific time of twelve midnight. I ripped off my oxygen mask and scrambled to get up. Above us, I half-expected to see the plane continuing along its way to certain disaster yet knowing I wouldn't. It was still bumping its way through the air in 2024. A few thin clouds floated past a waxing moon, and I said a silent thank you to the stars. I'd just saved Lainie from certain death, not to mention some random dude I'd only just met.

"Are you okay?" I said to Lainie as she pulled off her mask and clambered to her feet.

"Omigod, omigod, omigod," she kept repeating. It was the most animated I'd ever seen her.

"What the hell's going on?" Lilac-shirt guy.

"Where are my fuckin' shoes?" Another voice. Male. One I didn't recognize.

And then: wailing. A woman. As though her heart had just been ripped out of her chest.

Rose.

"Shit," I said.

Apparently, I hadn't just brought Lainie and lilac-shirt with me to 2019 but picked up some hitchhikers, too. This function of time travel was news to me. Yes, I'd tandem time-blinked with Christopher a handful of times before, but I'd never had the occasion to bring along a third, let alone a fourth, person. Here was evidence that multi-person time-blinking was possible, and it seemed none of them were the worse for wear. Apart from their sheer terror, of course.

As my eyes adjusted to the moonlight, my entourage came into view. What had I done?

"Okay, everyone, calm down," I said, putting my arm around a convulsing Rose, who seemed the most upset. This made her cry even louder, but I didn't retreat.

"Jeez, lady!" It was the young punk who'd been sitting next to lilac-shirt. "Wouldya shut up already!" he shouted, getting right up in Rose's face.

"Zip it, asshole," lilac-shirt said, yanking the young guy away from Rose. That's when I noticed they were attached to each other by handcuffs. I pretended not to notice.

"Where are my fuckin' shoes?" the young guy said again. His shoes were indeed missing, as were mine and lilac-shirt's. Lainie's and Rose's slip-ons had made it through.

"Like I said, let's just all take a breath. I can explain, but not if everyone is shouting at each other."

"This is messed up," Lainie said, shivering.

Even though she was technically family, Lainie didn't know I was a time traveler. No one did, apart from Kendall. I had taken Christopher to visit Morley a few times, but that's when he was still a baby and too young to understand what was happening. As for this group, so much for keeping the phenomenon under wraps now.

"I'll tell you everything, Lainie. Promise. But we have to take a little walk that way first," I said, pointing across the highway to a neglected looking side road that disappeared into the darkness.

At this, Rose quieted. She pulled away from me and wiped her face with the sleeve of her cardigan and seemed to understand it would be helpful to remain calm.

"Where are we?" Lainie said, scanning the parking lot, spotting the sign at the entrance. She gave me a quizzical look. "Chapman Falls? How did we get to the West Coast so fast?"

It was an odd question when the more obvious one was: *How did we get off the plane?*

At that moment, the faintest glow of headlights appeared at a bend in the road, signalling an oncoming car. "Shit!" I yelled, grabbing Rose's and Lainie's hands and heading to the dense cover of trees. "Everyone! Come with me!"

The guys followed, and a police cruiser passed just as they ducked into the woods after us.

Once the car was out of sight, I stepped back into the parking lot. "We can't risk being seen, *especially* by cops. Let's go."

Lilac-shirt stepped in front of me. "We're not going anywhere until you tell us what's going on and why running into cops would be a problem."

I sighed. "Look, uh, what's your name, if you don't mind?"

"Jarett Cooper . . . *Officer* Jarett Cooper, Seattle PD. People call me Coop."

I laughed.

"What's so funny?"

"Nothing. No disrespect, officer, but I'm calling you Jarett. I'm Syd."

"Well, nice to meet you, Syd, but I'd really like to know what the hell's going on."

"This is messed up," Lainie said again. She wrapped her arms around her middle and shivered despite being dressed in her cozy purple hoodie.

The kid attached to Jarett said, "We're dead! Don't you get it?"

"Quiet. We're not dead," Jarett said. "Right, Syd? You seem to be the authority here. Are you going to fill us in?"

Officer Jarett's questioning was beginning to irritate me, but since his entire job centered on getting the facts, I decided to cut him some slack. The most important thing right now was herding everyone up the hill where a comfy, warm haven awaited us. And I was betting Morley would be there, too.

"You'll just have to trust me. I've got a cabin at Sandalwood Lake. It's a five-minute walk from here."

Jarett let out a defeated breath. "Guess we have no other choice," he said, tugging his young charge's hand and brushing confidently past me. But he wasn't fooling me. He was terrified. And he seemed suspicious of my intentions, despite our friendly banter on the plane earlier.

The group fell into tense silence as we crossed the highway and started up the winding gravel road to the cabin with nothing more than the moonlight to guide us. A mild breeze whistled through centuries-old cedar branches, and a lone owl hooted in the distance.

Sandalwood Lake was Washington State's elite summer playground for two dozen well-to-do families, most of whom lived in the nearby city of Port Raven, where I was born and raised. Almost all the lake residents would have had set their security alarms after Labor Day last weekend, locked up their cabins, and headed back to the city. I was an anomaly in the community, having received the property as a gift. Even Sparkles—the eccentric lottery winner who lived at the lake year-round and served as the community watchdog—had died years ago, making me the only property owner who hadn't come from generations of old money.

"Fuckin' gravel," the young man said when we reached the long driveway to the cabin.

"Quiet," Jarett said, yanking him along.

The three of us hotfooted it over the sharp gravel in our

sock feet while Lainie and Rose followed behind in their comfortable footwear.

My heart fell when we reached the cabin a few moments later. Morley's driveway was empty, the house dark, illuminated only by a dozen path lights at our feet and the shadowy moonlight overhead.

"Welcome to Sandalwood Reach," I said with forced cheerfulness, echoing Morley's words the first time he brought me here. The group gathered silently around me, stunned, it seemed, by the beautiful structure in front of us.

To think, right here, right now, September 9, 2019, my past-self didn't even know this cabin existed, let alone that I would own it outright in a few short days. The thought of it made my heart hurt. Morley. My soul mate, the father of my only child, would be dead in less than a week. Why on Earth did I pick this date for a timeblink? I must be a glutton for punishment. At its root, though, I knew this was one of the few dates I wouldn't run into some past—or future—version of myself.

"I thought you said *cabin*." Officer Jarett was gawking at the grand log building stretched out before us.

I smiled. "Hard to believe there are houses much bigger than this on the lake. And most of them will be empty until May."

"And you own this place?"

"I will on Friday."

"Who owns it now?"

"A friend. Morley." It felt strange referring to him as a friend when we'd become so much more. "He's not here right now, so we'll have to let ourselves in."

Lainie narrowed her eyes. She knew Morley had died back in 2019 and that he'd left the cabin to me in his will. She'd even been here before. A couple of summers ago, when domestic air travel had resumed a somewhat normal schedule, Kendall coerced me into inviting the whole family to celebrate my father's birthday here. While I'd been dreading every single day leading up to the event, the weekend had been tolerable. Healing, even. Dad and I talked a lot, and we both came out understanding each other a little better. Not friends, but not adversaries, either. It had been a start.

"We're dead," the young guy said under his breath.

"Enough." Jarett gave the handcuff another quick yank, like he was correcting a dog's bad behavior.

"Fuck, man! Don't you see? The plane crashed, and we're dead! But it sure don't look like Hell to me! Shit! Maybe there is a God after all!"

"We're not dead," I said, irritably. "But keep talking and you might end up that way."

I saw Jarett smirk as I stepped up to the door and punched in the code (my birthday), hoping Morley hadn't changed it in the meantime. I held my breath, sinking into a brief panic before I heard the familiar beep and click. "We're in."

My relief was short-lived. As I pushed the door open, a shrill, unexpected ringing screeched in the foyer. The security alarm.

"Damn it!"

"Oh, you are so busted!" the young punk said, laughing. "Want me to bash it?"

"Shit, shit, shit!" I said, flying over to the control pad, entering my birthday again. I'd never had to disarm it before. God, I hoped it was the same number as the door code!

But after I punched in the numbers and hit Enter, the screeching sound continued. I tried Morley's birthday next. Nothing! What was it? At a loss for ideas, I entered Morley's death date, but still no change.

"Everyone, get inside," I said, switching on lights to make the place look hospitable instead of a playground for criminals. "Go upstairs and stay there until further notice. Except you," I said, gesturing to Lainie. She rolled her eyes but stayed put.

"I'm a cop," Jarett said. "And can probably help when my cohorts show up."

I threw my gaze to the handcuffs and the wiry, tattooed delinquent he was towing around. "How are you going to explain that?"

Jarett opened his mouth to object, but he knew I was right.

"Get going! Please!" I said, glancing outside. There were headlights in the driveway already. "That was fast."

"They were in the neighborhood. Remember?" Lainie said, unhelpfully.

"Go!"

"Maybe she should come with us," Jarett said, nodding at Lainie, and I looked at her as if for the first time. Her green hair and piercings would probably put us at a disadvantage.

"All right. All of you. Split."

Jarett pulled the kid along and Lainie followed without objection. Rose was already halfway up the stairs. I shivered. She looked like she was floating.

Just as everyone got to the top of the stairs, the squealing alarm slowed to one short beep every five seconds, and my nerves instantly calmed.

"Syd! You might need these," Lainie said, tossing her black leather flats over the railing. I caught them and gave her a thumbs up.

"Thanks. Great thinking. Now get outta sight," I said, wrestling my feet into the tiny shoes. I hobbled to the doorway and gave a friendly wave to the approaching vehicle, hoping to look as harmless as possible. As the door clicked shut behind me, a spotlight blazed to life from the roof of the car. It hardly seemed necessary. The crew on the International Space Station could have seen the house for all the feature lighting I'd flicked on. I shielded my eyes with both hands.

This was so degrading. This was *my* house. At least it would be soon.

A tinny voice crackled over a PA.

"Stay where you are, ma'am. Keep your hands where we can see them."

Ma'am? That description was for retired schoolteachers and wrinkled bingo players, not a fit and healthy thirty-six-year-old runner like me.

The passenger door opened, and an officer got out, strategically positioning himself behind the door. Or was it a woman? I couldn't tell. The spotlight was blinding. The whole scenario took me back to the night we found Isla—the night Coop, or rather *Viktor*, was arrested for his part in her abduction.

My stomach churned at the thought of it.

"State your name and birthdate," the cop behind the door called. Definitely a male voice. Deep and gravelly. I could hear static inside the car. The CB radio.

"Sydney Anne Brixton. October 10, 1987," I said, my voice cracking.

An eternity passed before anyone spoke again.

"Okay, Ms. Brixton," the officer behind the door said. "We're going to come and have a chat. Stay where you are."

They must have run my name through the system, which was fine by me. The only priors they would find—if they were even still on record—were a string of misdemeanors I'd committed as a teen. Drunk driving. Petty theft. Disturbing the peace. The latter offence occurred when I cornered a young girl in a Denny's bathroom believing she was my missing twin. I'd been drunk, which was one of the reasons I'd finally cleaned up my act.

The big light on top of the police cruiser winked out and the car's engine switched off, and now the only sounds were the cooling engine and the muffled beeping inside the house. Damn. It looked like they were going to stay a while. After another minute, the driver emerged from the car and slammed the door. When he reached his full stance, my jaw dropped. He must've been seven feet tall and as wide as a fridge.

"This is my hous—" I began to say. But it wasn't true. Yet. On September 9, 2019, Morley was still very much alive and still very much the legal owner.

"This is my friend's house. Morley. Dr. Morley Scott. Wouldn'cha know it? He gave me the door code but forgot to tell me the one for the alarm," I said, shrugging my shoulders.

The walking fridge approached me on the stoop while the other officer, an equally tall but slender young guy who didn't match his big, booming radio-announcer voice, crept off to scan the property with his flashlight.

The giant cop's scruffy, gray beard and droopy eyes made him look more like a tired Santa than a feared member of our local law enforcement team. He flashed me his ID. "I'm Officer Charleson. He's Fiera," he said, gesturing to his wispy partner who'd disappeared into the dark.

I nodded.

"Can you tell me where Dr. Scott is right now? The alarm company hasn't been able to reach him. Neither have we."

"I, uh, don't know? He was supposed to be here."

"May I see some ID, ma'am?"

The ma'am thing again. It was pissing me off.

Then the bigger issue hit me. I had no ID. It was on the plane. Wherever that was right now. I shuddered.

"Ma'am? Your ID, please."

"Can you try calling Morley again? I'm sure he can straighten all of this out in a jiffy."

"I'm sure he can. But I need to see your ID first."

Then an idea struck.

"Oh, no!" I said, patting my body frantically, feigning panic. "I left my purse in the taxi!"

It was a plausible story, considering the only vehicle in the driveway belonged to the cops.

Regardless, Officer Charleson narrowed his eyes and

peered past me toward the cabin's front door. He seemed to be thinking about going inside, maybe to look for a body. Was he allowed to do that? To go inside without a warrant? In his eyes, I was a former teenaged delinquent with no ID who'd just broken into a luxurious lakeside cabin in the middle of the night. And the homeowner was suspiciously absent.

The scrawny cop walked up beside him. "All clear, sir."

Officer Charleson returned his attention to me as he produced a notepad and pen from inside his bomber jacket. He sighed. "Which company did you use?"

"What?" Oh no.

"The taxi that brought you here? Maybe we can get your purse back. It can't have gotten too far."

"Oh! It wasn't a taxi," I said, flustered.

His eyes narrowed again. I felt like running off into the bush. Surely, I could outpace him. Maybe not the younger cop, though.

"You said you left your purse in a taxi, did you not?"

"Yes. I meant LimeLift. That new ride-sharing company?"

Shit! LimeLift was a real company, but it didn't start up until 2023.

"LimeLift?" He began writing. "Never heard of it. Is that one word or two?"

At that moment, his phone rang. "Excuse me," he said, walking away, tucking his notepad back into his jacket. The other officer—Ferrero, was it?—stayed put. He yawned and looked up at one of the top-floor windows. For a crazy minute, I thought he'd spotted one of my fellow timeblinkers, but he returned his attention to me, smiled wearily, and bounced on his heels a few times with his hand resting on the butt end of his gun.

Charleson's voice: "The intruder says she knows him . . . uh huh. Yep . . . Brixton . . . blue eyes, blonde hair . . . thirty-one. I understand. We'll stand by."

Charleson came back to the stoop, and he eyed me with

what I thought might have been pity, maybe thinking how old I looked for being "thirty-one." My vanity momentarily made me want to fess up. To tell him I was a thirty-six-year-old time traveler.

"Dr. Scott's been located. He should be calling any minute."

The relief that raced through my body made me want to pee.

The cop's phone rang.

"Officer Dan Charleson here," he said, eyeing me. "Yes . . . says she came here in a LimeCar." He shook his head and pulled out his notepad. "A LimeLift, sorry. Uh huh . . . yes, she's fine. Just a little shaken . . . Oh, of course."

Charleson handed me his phone.

"Hi sweetheart," Morley said on the other end, and I burst into tears.

"Shh. Shh. It's okay," Morley assured me. "I'll be out there lickety-split. The code is Christopher's birthday. Hang tight, love. Can't wait to see you."

I squeaked out a goodbye and handed the phone back to Charleson, then went straight to the alarm control panel and punched in the code. Why hadn't I thought of Christopher's birthday? He was Morley's son, too. The beeping stopped immediately, and I let out a huge breath.

"Good grief. I'm sorry you had to trouble yourselves with this," I said, stopping in the doorway, willing them to leave.

As if reading my mind, the younger cop said, "We'll be on our way. But we'll need to file a report on this, Ms. Brixton. If we have any questions, we'll be in touch, but everything seems in order."

Charleson shrugged. "It's the job. Sorry for scaring the bejeebers out of you."

"It's okay. I appreciate your watchfulness," I said.

"Oh, and just so you know, we patrol this neighborhood

regularly at night. You can feel safe out here, considering you're all alone."

I smiled.

"Do you want us to contact that ride sharing company? See if we can't help get your purse back?"

Crap, no. The company didn't exist yet. Why the fuck had he written it down?

"No, no. Don't worry. I can manage. Honestly. You've got way more important things to worry about than a stray purse." And then I had a thought: "May I ask a favor, though?"

He raised his eyebrows. "Fire away."

I nodded toward the little notebook in his hand. "May I have the page you wrote on? You know, for a souvenir?"

The two officers exchanged amused looks. "That's a new one," Charleson said.

He inspected both sides of the page, reciting the things written there: the cabin's address, my name, my date of birth, and the word LimeLift. It was all information they'd already called in. He tore it out and handed it to me, still amused, perhaps even flattered. "Nothing exciting here. But whatever floats your boat."

As they walked back to the cruiser, I thanked them again and closed the door, thinking how close I'd come to blowing everything. If Charleson hadn't given me the paper, he might've looked at it later and been intrigued enough—even on a personal level—to do some digging about this new company, LimeLift. But he would have been met with a dead end. At least now there was no physical evidence of it, and I could always say he must have misunderstood. One problem averted. Now I had to focus on a much bigger catastrophe: getting my ragtag group back to the present time in one piece.

Chapter Four

MONDAY, 12:33 A.M.

I closed the door behind me and called up the stairs. "They're gone!"

A moment later, Lainie, Jarett, and the punk emerged from the front bedroom and clambered down the stairs to join me.

"Shit, that almost went sideways," I said. "Where's Rose?"

"She's laying down," Lainie said.

It was understandable. The poor woman had just lost her husband and son in what was no doubt a horrific air disaster.

"All right, come on. Time to bring you up to speed." I headed into the living room, switching on all the table lamps along the way.

Once everyone was seated, I asked if anyone needed anything. A drink? Something to eat?

"Ya got any beer?" said the punk.

Jarett yanked the cuff and told the kid to shut up.

"Lainie, how about you get everyone a glass of water?" I said.

She got up and plodded through the stone archway into the kitchen.

"So," Jarett said. "What the serious F is going on here?"

"It's a little hard to explain."

"Try me."

"I will. But first, two rules. One, promise you won't breathe a word of this to anyone when we get back."

"Get back? From where?"

"And two, you'll need to keep an open mind."

"What choice do we have? We were on a plane that was about to smash to the ground, and two seconds later, we were stumbling around in the dark at Chapman Falls."

"We're dead, asshole! Don't ya get it?"

"For shit's sake, Gus! Shut up and listen for a change."

"Calm down, guys. We're not dead. It's just that we've. . ."

"We've what?" Jarett said impatiently.

"Okay." I took a small breath. "We've time traveled. To September 2019."

"What the f—?" Lainie said, walking back into the room clutching four glasses of water precariously in her small hands.

"I can't elaborate on *how* we got here, but I can tell you I am surprised by the number of people that came through. I was only expecting you, Lainie. And Jarett. Rose and . . . *Gus* were completely unexpected."

"Well, shit!" Gus said, shooting a look at Jarett. "If it's 2019, you have no reason to detain me!"

"Dial it back, buddy. You're not getting out of my sight. Syd, do you have some stiff wire? Or a paperclip? I seem to have lost my key to these damn handcuffs somewhere along the way."

"Give me a minute."

I went to Morley's desk in a small alcove off the dining room and found a paperclip in the top drawer. Jarett used it to jimmy his handcuff open. After a brief scuffle, he wrangled Gus's free hand into the cuff, then pushed him onto the couch. "Don't try anything stupid."

Gus raised his cuffed wrists in the air in front of him.

"Sure thing, boss."

Lainie distributed the water to everyone, then settled on the loveseat, pulling a fleece blanket over her shoulders. While Jarett took a seat next to Gus on the couch, I went to the thermostat and bumped it up a few degrees. Not too much, though. Didn't want everyone getting too comfortable and groggy when they needed to be alert for what I had to tell them next.

"The problem is getting back. To 2024," I said, choosing a spot in front of the fireplace to deliver the bad news.

Jarett gave me a look that seemed to say *this has all got to be a joke*, but he stayed quiet to hear me out. Lainie looked as though she'd been awake for three straight days.

"Would you rather get some sleep, Lainie? I can catch you up in the morning."

She flipped the blanket off her shoulders and stood up. "Thought you'd never ask. Anyone got a cell phone I can borrow? To listen to music?"

"Nope," I said. "If your phone wasn't in your hand when you timeblinked, it stayed behind."

"Timeblinked?" she said.

"Morley gave it that name when he discovered the phenomenon, and it's stuck ever since."

"*Morley?* As in, Christopher's dad?"

"Yeah," I said, smiling.

"Isn't he like . . . dead?"

"Not in 2019, he isn't." My spine tingled. Morley was going to meet one of the half-sisters I'd complained to him about before. Talk about worlds colliding.

She shrugged apathetically and yawned. "Which room should I use?"

"Morley and I will be in the master bedroom, the one facing the lake. You can take whichever room Rose isn't using." I looked at Jarett. "You two will have to be couch dwellers, I'm afraid."

"Beats sleeping on a lumpy cot," Gus said.

Lainie gave him a curious glance, then grabbed her water and headed to the stairs. Despite her punk-rock exterior, she looked so vulnerable, so young in that moment, and I was grateful she wouldn't be there for the next part of the conversation: the part where I elaborated on my concerns about all of us getting back to 2024 in one piece.

When she was out of sight, Gus said, "That's a hot little package. Can't wait to roll her."

Before I even realized what I was doing, I flew over and grabbed him by his grubby, gray sweatshirt. "You so much as *look* at her again, I'll stab your eyeballs out with a fork."

He flinched away from me. "What? Is she your daughter or something? Shit, man. You musta been her age when you got preggers."

"Enough!" Jarett warned. He turned his focus to me. "You got a place to lock him up for the night? A shed? An outhouse?"

"There's a crawlspace."

"Fine! I'll shut up. Just get on with it, will ya?"

To keep Gus from knowing too much, I just covered the basics. That, yes, we had time traveled to 2019. That, no, I wasn't at liberty to tell them how it all worked. And finally, that anyone with whom they'd had physical contact in their natural time wouldn't be able to see them in this timeline. Morley and I had dubbed that feature *cell swapping*, since all it took was the slightest brush against someone else's skin to set the whole thing in motion. This seemed worrying for Jarett, who'd been planning on contacting his fellow police officers for help. I was quick to head him off, forbidding him to contact anyone he knew. Then I swore them both to secrecy, explaining that the power of time travel could be extremely dangerous in the wrong hands. Gus threw his head back and laughed, and I instantly regretted telling him anything.

"I gotta use the can," Gus said, struggling to his feet awkwardly.

Jarett got up and guided him to the bathroom down the hall—where we would be able see him when he came out—then shuffled back to the living room.

"How'd I get stuck with that asshole?" he said under his breath.

"I've been wondering that myself. What did he do to warrant a fancy police escort like you?"

"Sorry, but it's against policy to say."

I nodded. "Hey, is there any possibility you could get rid of him for a little while? I have more details to share with you, and I'd rather keep them between you and me. For now, anyway."

"Yeah, sure. How about the deck?"

"Perfect."

When Gus came out of the bathroom, Jarett ushered him outside, then handcuffed him to the railing where we could monitor him through the French doors.

"That was nice of you, giving him a blanket," I said when he came back inside.

Jarett smiled. "I'm not a complete jerk. Which reminds me. Sorry for yelling at you earlier, down at the park."

"I get it. It's not every day you escape a plane that's about to crash and get zapped into an alternate time realm."

"Damn, that sounds like something straight out of a sci-fi movie. Can you prove the date?"

I went over to the TV and switched it to a 24-hour news channel where a story was running about a fourteen-foot alligator being caught in Georgia, allegedly the biggest on record for that state.

Jarett shook his head. "Wow. It's just un-fricken-believable."

"Right? That's a huge gator," I said, smirking.

"Very funny, but I was talking about this time-traveling business."

I went on to explain why none of our cellphones or other personal possessions came through with us: because we hadn't been touching them at the time.

"But my keys were in my pocket."

"I know. It's weird, but again, skin plays a huge part. You must be touching anything you want to bring through . . . so coins and other items in your pockets won't make it. On one of my timeblinks, I'd been wearing a purse on my shoulder, but on the other side, I found it empty."

"Why?"

"Because none of the items inside were part of the handbag itself. It makes sense if you imagine a continuous line. If an object isn't *part* of the item you're bringing through—"

"The line is broken."

I nodded. "It will be an important detail to remember for when we go back. It's why some of us lost our shoes."

He looked at his socked feet with amusement. "Because they weren't touching our skin."

"Yep. Rose and Lainie weren't wearing socks, so their shoes made it through."

Jarett seemed receptive to everything I was telling him. It helped that he'd had other witnesses to corroborate the events of the last hour, making it hard to dispute. Not like the first time I'd timeblinked. One minute I was sitting on the couch next to my dog, the next, I was tumbling down Chapman Falls, and even when Morley pulled me out of the water a few minutes later, I was sure it had been an elaborate practical joke.

"Listen. As I started to explain earlier, our return trip to 2024 is going to be tricky."

"I kind of figured that, considering we're still here. What's the problem?"

"There are two of them, actually. First of all, we need to make sure we're all together when it's time to return, or no one will be going back."

"Really? Like, if I took off today, *all* of us would be stuck in 2019?"

"Yes."

"Do you know this for certain?"

"Sure do. I stumbled across the issue on one of my time-blinks with my kiddo, Christopher. The moment we were about to return to our present, he let go of my hand. I nearly had a heart attack. For a split second, I thought I'd accidentally stranded him in the past. But that didn't happen."

Jarett leaned forward in his chair. "What did happen?"

"Nothing. We both stayed put."

"Because he wasn't touching you?"

I nodded. "When I took his hand and tried again, poof. We went back. It makes sense, right? You have to be touching the people you bring over, so naturally, you'd have to be doing the same thing on the way back."

"That shouldn't be a problem. This is 2019, right? None of us would be crazy enough to stay and relive the pandemic years over again."

I laughed.

"So, what's the second problem? Someone spotting us when we beam back?"

"It's much worse than that. When you go back, it's always to the same place."

He narrowed his eyes. "Back on the plane?"

"Worse."

"What could be worse than that?"

"The plane will have kept going."

I let that sink in a moment.

"Oh, shit," he said.

"Oh shit is right. When we go back, we'll be thousands of feet above the ground. In midair."

His eyes went wide. "You're joking."

"I'm still trying to come to terms with it myself. It's one of the weird nuances of timeblinking. You're always gone from your present time for exactly four minutes and forty-four seconds. Every time. And every time you come back, it's to the exact same spot."

Jarett rose from the couch and crossed the living room to grab an armful of logs from the bin next to the fireplace. He arranged the wood in a pile on the grate, then crumpled up some newspaper and lit it on fire with a long match. He did all of this without a word.

I waited until the fire was burning vigorously before speaking again. "Morley will be here soon. We'll figure something out."

Could he be thinking the same thing as I was? That there was only one way for a person to survive a 20,000-foot freefall? If so, he wasn't voicing it.

When his gaze stayed on the fire, I tried to lift his spirits with the story about how Christopher had been conceived during a timeblink. After humoring me with a few polite questions about how Christopher was doing now and whether I had any other kids, he eventually snapped out of his funk, and we were talking about everything from where we'd grown up to favorite pets to shocking events that had happened on our jobs (I left out the most shocking of all: the night of Morley's grizzly death right outside the pub's front door, which, I was now reminded, would happen in a few short days.).

"So, how did you stumble on this power in the first place?"

My hand spontaneously went to the talisman, but I stopped myself from actually grabbing it, pretending to scratch my chin instead. The last thing I needed was Jarett putting two and two together. "I wish I could tell you, but the fewer people that know, the better." I wrinkled up my nose. "You get why, right?"

"Sure. I guess. But there's something I don't understand

about the skin thing. If what you're saying is true—that we're invisible to anyone we've had physical contact with in our real time—what's the deal with Morley? You guys had a kid together. Going out on a limb here, but wouldn't you have had to touch each other for that?"

I laughed. "Yes. But remember, we conceived Christopher when I was on a timeblink, and for whatever reason, cell swapping isn't an issue when one of the parties is on a timeblink."

"So, it's only a problem if you've touched someone in your real time?"

"Yes. Your mother wouldn't be able to see you, nor your dentist. Not even your fellow officers. And listen, it only takes one tiny skin cell to trigger it—not a roll in the hay."

"Okay, I get that. But how is it you and Morley never touched in real time? You said he was a regular at your pub for years."

"Your sleuthing skills are admirable, Officer Jarett."

He shrugged. "I've always been a curious sort of guy."

"Well. It's a long story, but in a nutshell, Morley has a history of losing people he cares about and began to think of himself as a sort of modern-day male Medusa, but instead of looking at someone and turning them to stone, he believed he could sentence them to death with a touch."

Jarett shook his head slowly. "That's some heavy shit."

"Right? The last straw was when his wife, Collette, died from cancer. It nearly broke him. And as irrational as it was, he vowed never to touch anyone he loved again. That's when he started wearing gloves pretty much full time."

"Wow, poor guy. Reminds me of a woman I met in college who wore gloves all the time, too. I used to think it was weird until we became friends and I learned she had a huge germ phobia. But who knows? Maybe she was really a time traveler in disguise."

"Maybe. I definitely look at people differently now. What

secrets are they keeping?"

"Lots. I didn't even tell you half the weird shit I've encountered on the job."

When our conversation stalled, I studied Jarett's profile in the dancing firelight. Back on the plane, I remember thinking he was attractive, but in a "someone else's man" kind of way. Yeah. I remember thinking he was definitely hitched, what with that exotic Formula 1 race-car driver thing he had going on. I'd even looked for a ring and had been secretly delighted to find his finger bare. It hardly mattered. Even now, five years after my disastrous relationship with a child-abducting monster, I rarely thought about men in a romantic way (at least ones who weren't Morley). So, why here? Why now? When the real love of my life was about to walk through the door? Maybe it was the sheer exhaustion of the past few hours.

Still. I couldn't help it. A flicker of pleasure stirred inside me as I watched Jarett's broad shoulders rising and falling reassuringly. I found my attention wandering down to his crotch and not being disappointed by the way he filled out his dark jeans. I jumped when he unexpectedly turned to me and yawned widely. "You okay?" he said.

I nodded, letting out my own small yawn. "Just tired."

"I hear you. It's been a crazy day."

"I don't mind if you try to get some sleep until Morley gets here."

"Nah. Don't want to be crashed out and drooling all over the doctor's toss cushions when he arrives," he said.

"I'm sure he'd forgive you."

"I'd rather not take that chance. Besides, I'm too wired to sleep," he said, standing and grabbing our empty glasses off the coffee table. "More water?"

"Oh, sure. Thanks."

I pulled a blanket from the back of my chair and spread it over my body as he headed to the kitchen.

There was that feeling again. He might have been a little abrasive at first, but who wouldn't be in the same situation? Now, in the quiet of the night, warmed by the impressive fire he'd built for us, I felt protected. Safe. In another life, another time, I might have entertained the idea of flirting with this attractive, apparently single, law enforcement officer. But Morley was my one true love. Why, oh why did he have to die?

I must have dozed off.

Morley's voice jolted me awake, but he wasn't talking to me. He was hovering over Jarett, grilling him about who he was and what he was doing there. When Jarett threw off his blanket and rose to defend himself, I sprang from my chair. "No, no! He's with me!"

"Syd!" Morley said, surprised. "I didn't see you there."

I realized I hadn't told Morley about my little entourage. I'd been too flustered when we'd talked on the phone earlier.

I ran into his arms.

"Hello, love," he whispered into my ear.

We stood there for almost a full minute before I heard Jarett clearing his throat.

Reluctantly, Morley and I unraveled ourselves from each other. Jarett smiled at us cautiously.

"I take it you're the rightful owner of this property," he said, stretching his hand out. "I'm Coop."

Morley shot me a startled look.

"Officer Jarett Cooper," I said. "We'll be calling him Jarett. For obvious reasons."

Jarett looked at us sideways. "You guys got something against my name?"

"Don't take it personally," I said. "We once knew someone with the same name. Which actually turned out *not* to be his real name at all."

"Someone you didn't like, apparently."

"That's an understatement. Morley, want to help me make a pot of tea?" I said on my way to the kitchen. "I need caffeine. How about you, Jarett? Tea?"

"Just water, thanks," he said, sitting back down, taking the hint that I wanted some privacy with Morley.

When we were tucked into the corner of the kitchen out of Jarett's sight, Morley said, "Where's his car?"

"Car?"

"Yeah. Cops tend to use them to get around. How else did he get here for the security call?"

"No, no, no. I told you. He's with me."

Morley raised his brows. "Really? Another man in uniform?"

"No, it's not like that! We just met. On a plane that was about to crash. And I decided at the last second to bring him along."

"Who on Earth is *that*?" Morley said, looking over my shoulder out the window, apparently noticing Gus asleep on the lounger. "And why is he handcuffed to the deck?"

"I'll explain everything soon. He's with me, too."

"Oh boy. This should be interesting."

After I'd given Morley the rundown of the events of the last few hours and assured him that Christopher was safe and had been on a different flight, we carried our cups of tea and shortbread biscuits into the living room.

"So, let me see if I've got this straight," Morley said as we settled onto the loveseat together. "You zapped out of a plane with four other people as it was about to crash."

"Yes. Flight 444, Chicago to Seattle."

Morley cocked his head. "Really? That was the flight number?"

"Crazy, right?"

Jarett said, "What's so crazy about it?"

Morley cut in before I could answer. "And now we have your half-sister and another woman asleep upstairs, a cop hanging out in my living room, and a criminal handcuffed to my deck."

"Yeah. That pretty much sums it up," I said, grimacing. "But you're making it sound weirder than it needs to be."

"Is he, though? It's straight out of the Twilight Zone." Jarett said, raking a hand through his short, dark waves. I wondered if he was of Italian descent or maybe Spanish. I was useless at guessing people's ethnic background and generally avoided the embarrassment of guessing wrong. Spanish, I decided. Definitely Spanish. Or Portuguese.

"Everyone got here in *one* timeblink?" Morley said, snapping me out of my thoughts.

"I could barely believe it myself. All five of us, alive and well, some of us missing our shoes."

Jarett kept his focus on Morley. "Has Syd told you about the potential disaster awaiting us in 2024? About how we'll be plummeting to the earth like human missiles?"

Morley nodded solemnly, and when he saw the terror in Jarett's eyes, he said, "Look, we'll sort this out. I like Syd's idea about the parachutes."

"*Parachutes?*" Jarret practically shouted.

I scrunched up my nose and nodded.

"You're joking. Surely."

"I'm not, but if you can think of a better idea, I'm all ears," I said, putting my head on Morley's shoulder.

"That plan assumes we can get our hands on five parachutes and that we can learn how to use them in less than ten seconds."

"Who says we have to learn on the fly?" I said. "No pun intended."

"How else?"

"I'm pretty sure there's a skydiving club out at the Port Raven airport. And if not, there's definitely one at Snohomish."

"Umm, okay. But how are we going to sign up for skydiving lessons with no ID? And even if we do, how long will it take? Weeks? Months?"

"Hell, no. We have to get back as soon as possible," I said.

"Okay, so, we should bank on being here for at least a few days, then. To learn how to skydive. With no plane to jump out of."

"Probably. Yes. I don't know. We'll figure it out tomorrow. I'm too tired to think about it right now."

Morley drank the last of his tea and stood up. "Why don't we get some sleep? It's two-thirty. We'll have a fresh perspective on it in the morning. I'll get you some pillows. You'll find more blankets in that trunk in the corner," he said to Jarett before disappearing upstairs.

I went to the kitchen to get a glass of water, and when I came back, Jarett was pulling cushions off the back of the couch to make room to lie down.

"I panicked," I said. "My goal was to get me and Lainie off that plane, and at the last second, I brought you along. I guess I'm trying to . . . I don't know, apologize?"

Jarett's shoulders slumped. "Don't. I'd rather be taking my chances with this whacky parachuting idea than burning up in a fiery plane crash."

I gave him a weary smile as Morley bounded into the room with an armful of pillows, which he put on the coffee table. "This should be plenty for you and your buddy out there on the deck. Help yourself to whatever you want from the kitchen."

"Thanks, man."

"Good night, Jarett," I said, grabbing Morley's hand, pulling him up the stairs with me.

Chapter Five

MONDAY, 7:43 A.M.

I woke up to gentle sunlight warming my face, and for a few seconds, I didn't know where I was. Through bleary eyes, I glimpsed a misty lake so picturesque it could have been featured on a postcard, and beyond that, a dark, jagged line of pine and cedar trees outlined by the burgeoning pink light of day. Much closer to me: a retro blue alarm clock. Morley's alarm clock. Right. This was Sandalwood Lake, seven-forty-three a.m., September 9, 2019—five years in the past—and I was instantly very much awake.

The memory of last night flooded back to me now in a pleasant, euphoric rush. Morley and I had fallen into bed in the wee hours of the morning and reveled in the frenzied, urgent sex a couple of horny twenty-year-olds might enjoy.

As happy as I was to be back in Morley's world, though, it was impossible to push the looming disaster out of my mind: the challenge of getting me and my fellow timeblinkers back to our present time unharmed. Make that *two* looming disasters. By the end of the week, whether or not I was still here, Morley would be dead.

I found his arm, lean and warm, wrapped around my waist.

"G'morning, sunshine," he said over my shoulder.

I rolled over and tried to put on a bright face. "Hi, you."

He kissed my forehead. "Are you okay?"

"Yeah," I said. "Just taking it all in. It's been a while. God, I must look ancient to you."

He smiled. "You're silly. You're still as beautiful as the day we first met. At least now you're more my age. People won't be so quick to accuse me of being a dirty old man."

"Ahh, I hadn't thought about that. You, perpetually forty-nine. Me, getting older every time I drop in on you."

"Well, I'm glad you're here, love. On this date, especially. It'll make Friday easier to handle."

"Must you remind me? About *that*?"

"What? About my death date?"

"Honestly!" I said. "Let's not talk about it."

He brushed my hair back from my face. "Sorry, sweetheart, but you chose this date. Not me."

"I've always intentionally left the week before your accident off-limits because, selfishly, I couldn't bear the pain it would cause me. But I panicked, and here we are."

"It was a natural reflex. We run to people who can help us when we're in trouble."

"Yes, there's that," I said, with tears pooling in my eyes. "But also, when the plane was going down, I figured I might as well spend my remaining days alive with the love of my life."

He smiled. "Who says you're going to die?"

"I don't really think that. Not yet, anyway. As far-fetched as this parachuting proposal is, it's our best bet at surviving this thing."

"That's the spirit," Morley said.

"Ugh. I absolutely hate that our precious time together will be spent figuring out how to get me and my group of misfits back to 2024."

"Don't give it another thought. You caught me at the perfect time."

"Perfect? Hardly. Are you forgetting my run-in with the cops last night? Where were you, by the way? I thought you were taking this week off?"

"That was the plan. Until one of my little patients needed emergency surgery. His parents called me in a panic and asked me to be there, which is why the alarm company and the police couldn't find me right away. I'd turned off all my devices."

"How's the patient?"

"Stable when I left. The little guy has osteosis imperfecta and fractured his tib-fib when he fell out of bed."

"His leg?"

"Ha, yes, sorry. His tibia and fibula. Broke them clean in half, but it was a straightforward fix."

"Ouch, poor little guy. When I hear about stuff like that, I thank my lucky stars that Christopher is so healthy."

"He's still doing well? What is he, three, now? The last time you brought him—even when I told you not to—he was eighteen months."

"He'll be four in November. I wish you could see him agai—"

Morley brought his finger up to my lips, and I pushed it away, "Yeah, yeah. I know. He's at the age where he would start remembering timeblinks. But would that be such a bad thing? Being able to remember the time he spent with his dad?"

"Already too many people know about it. You, me, Kendall."

"And my four hitchhikers," I said, wincing.

He rolled onto his back. "Right."

"I think they can all keep a secret. Well, all of them but Jarett's little friend."

"Speaking of the illustrious Officer Coop," Morley said, smiling mischievously, "he's quite the looker."

I play-punched his bicep. "Jealous?"

"Now that you mention it, yes. I'm gonna be dead in four days. He's a lucky guy."

"How so? We still haven't figured out if we're going to get back to our present time alive. Unless you know something I don't know."

He rolled back to me and took my hand. "Even if I were privy to that information, I wouldn't tell you."

"I know, I know. It would take all the fun out of learning it for myself."

"You took the words right out of my mouth."

"You're a stubborn one, Dr. Scott. Come on, let's get up. I'll introduce you to the rest of the misfits."

After a quick shower, I knocked on the middle bedroom door, Lainie's room.

"Come in," came her muffled voice.

She was sitting on the bed against the headboard, looking bored out of her skull. It was strange to see her without her ear buds in; she wore those things constantly. It surprised me she hadn't complained about that, but she'd just escaped a catastrophic plane crash. Maybe she was realizing the world wasn't all about her. She gave me a weary smile.

"Everything good?" I asked.

"Sure."

"I know how weird this is. But you seem to be handling it a lot better than I did the first time it happened."

"You've done this before?"

I remembered she hadn't been in on most of the debriefing, which, in retrospect, was probably for the better.

"Yes. That's how I knew I could bring you along."

She nodded absently. "What's going to happen now?"

"Morley, Jarett, and I were up late last night brainstorming, and we've got a tentative plan in the works to get us back."

"Back? Like, to 2024?"

"Yeah." I pictured Christopher's giggling little face, and my heart seized. Instinctively, my hand went to my belly; if my obstetrician's calculations had been right, Christopher was merely a fertilized egg in this timeline.

"I'd rather just stay here," Lainie said, studying a chip in her navy-blue nail polish. "If you aren't shitting me that it's really 2019."

"I shit you not," I said, trying to lighten her spirits. "But I can't imagine you'd want to go through the damn-demic all over again."

She shrugged. "It wasn't that bad. Can I take a shower?"

"Of course. Morley's already downstairs making breakfast for everyone, so you can use the master bathroom. Help yourself to towels and a hairdryer—whatever you need—and come on down when you're ready. In the meantime, I'm going to check on Rose."

"Is she gonna, like, go bonkers?"

"I don't know. She just lost the two people she loves the most."

Lainie nodded knowingly. "So, why is she here? Why are any of us here?"

"It's a long story. I'll fill you in, but right now, I've got to help Morley with breakfast. Oh, and if you need a change of clothes, you can borrow some of mine, kiddo."

Kiddo? That came out of left field, but she smiled and walked past me into the hall. I instantly wished I could take it back.

"There are leggings and t-shirts in the bottom right dresser drawer in the master bedroom," I said, following her into the hallway.

"That's okay. I'll just use my own."

Once she'd disappeared into the master suite, I knocked on Rose's door. There was no answer.

"Rose," I said. "Are you okay?"

Still no answer.

It was worrying, considering my own family history of my mother taking her own life, which also had to do with the loss of a child. Rose had just lost her child *and* her husband at the same time.

I knocked once more. "If you don't say something in ten seconds, I'm coming in."

When she didn't respond, I opened the door.

"Rose?" She was lying on the bed, facing away from me. My nerves tingled. The covers hadn't been disturbed. She lay motionless on top of the duvet.

"Will you come downstairs for something to eat?" I said, trying not to panic.

She didn't move.

I waited a few seconds before noticing her shoulder rising and falling—almost imperceptibly, but enough to reassure me. I chastised myself. Rose had been holed up in this room since our arrival and hadn't had the means to harm herself. I let out a quiet breath.

"You must be in terrible pain, Rose. Just know that I'm here for you. We all are."

Nothing.

"Morley's making breakfast, and we'd love for you to join us."

I realized she had no idea who Morley was, let alone how we even got here. She hadn't asked a single question, and it was worrying.

"Okay, I'm going to give you a rundown of our situation, and it's going to sound impossible, but I think you should know what we're up against."

When she didn't move, I spelled it all out: that Morley was

the owner of this cabin; that he was the father of my son I'd told her about on the plane; that our little ragtag group had time traveled back to the year 2019; and that I was working on a way to get us back to our natural timeline.

None of this information seemed to register.

"Anyway, I'll bring you something to eat and a cup of tea if we don't see you downstairs by nine o'clock. Do you take milk?"

When she didn't answer, I stepped out and closed the door, knowing I'd be back soon with a tray of food.

A few minutes later, Morley heaped a stack of pancakes onto a platter, and I ferried them into the dining room. Jarett and Gus were seated across from each other at the table.

"I really appreciate all this trouble, but who the hell can eat right now?" Jarett said.

"Speak for yourself," Gus said, jabbing his fork into two steaming cakes before I'd even set the plate down. "I'll have summa that bacon when it's done, too."

The handcuffs, I noticed, were suspiciously absent, which made me a little uneasy. Jarett seemed to sense this. "Don't worry about him. I've secured his ankles."

"Somebody has trust issues," Gus said, winking at me. My heart leapt, and I was instantly ashamed. The kid must have been half my age, but he was a dead ringer for a twenty-year-old Robert Pattinson with the edgy bad-boy vibe of a young Christian Bale. I could picture him sweet-talking some innocent girl into going home with him and doing all sorts of kinky things to her. I blushed and headed back into the kitchen.

"What do you think Gus did?" I whispered to Morley. "To need a police escort?"

"Coop wouldn't say but assured me the kid is no threat to us."

"His name is *Jarett*. If I didn't know better, Dr. Scott, I'd say you were jealous of our new friend."

"Who me? Impossible," Morley said, sliding the bacon onto a plate next to the stove. "And to prove it, I'll stop teasing you now."

"Impossible."

He leaned over and kissed my forehead, then handed me the plate of bacon. "Go on, feed the animals."

Lainie was sliding into a chair next to Gus when I entered the room.

"That was fast," I said. She smiled thinly. I almost didn't recognize her. She was devoid of her usual heavy, dark makeup, making her look twelve rather than fifteen. I hadn't seen her birthmark so clearly in years and wondered if she'd chosen to sit to Gus's right so he couldn't see that side of her face.

As I sat down at the far end of the table, Morley walked in carrying a bowl of diced fruit, stopping dead in his tracks for effect. "Be still my heart! If it isn't the infamous Lainie Brixton. Fruit salad, my dear?"

Lainie actually giggled. I smiled inwardly as Morley set the bowl down and took a seat at the end of the table.

Maybe my father's harebrained assignment had its merits after all.

Chapter Six

MONDAY, NOON

Three hours later, when Rose still hadn't emerged from her room, I went up to check on her.

My delivery of toast and tea after breakfast had gone untouched. The only difference was that she'd moved from the bed to an armchair in front of the window and was staring at a couple of gray squirrels bouncing around in the manicured grass. I'd forgotten how sunny the weather had been leading up to the night of Morley's death, when an apocalyptic West Coast rainstorm had blown in.

"Pretty, isn't it?" I said.

She didn't answer.

I took a small breath. "Oh, Rose. I wish I could make everything better. But I can't. My only goal right now is to get us back to 2024 safely. Morley and I are going for a paddle in the canoe to hash it all out, if you'd like to join us."

The offer came out of nowhere. I'd been looking forward to spending some time alone with Morley and in no way wished to have a third wheel tagging along. Especially one that was obviously in a great deal of pain. But her utter stillness confirmed her intention of staying sequestered in this room—not going for a quaint little canoe ride.

"There's a trail circling the lake that takes about an hour to walk if you want to get some fresh air. Help yourself to the bottled water in the fridge, though. It's getting warm out there already."

It was so nice, in fact, that after breakfast, Lainie had taken one of Morley's Stephen King novels, *Misery*, and curled up on a lounge chair on the deck a small distance away from Gus, who'd been secured to the railing again. The two of them were in the same positions when I came downstairs after my chat with Rose.

"Ready?" Morley said behind me at the dining room window, making me jump.

"Should we, uh, leave them alone?" I said, nodding toward the younger members of our group, who seemed completely uninterested in each other.

"Jarett will be out of the shower any minute. But if you want to wait, no problem."

"We'll wait."

Going for a paddle wasn't as important as keeping Lainie safe. We still didn't know the nature of Gus's crime.

"I have an idea," Morley said, bounding off toward the living room. When he returned, he pushed through the French doors and tapped Lainie on the shoulder. I saw him hand her his phone and a pair of earbuds. Her face lit up. They exchanged a few words, and just as Morley came back inside, Jarett was coming down the stairs, ruffling the water out of his hair. Some people look extra sexy with wet hair. Jarett, who'd also grown a faint shadow of facial hair in the last fourteen hours, was one of them. If Morley could read my thoughts, he'd be saying, "See? I told you he was hot!"

Jarett joined us at the window overlooking the deck where a perpetually dusty glass railing obscured the view of the lake.

"You guys seem awfully calm," Jarett said. "Have you figured out how we're getting our doomed asses back to the future yet?"

I felt Morley bristle next to me, but his answer was measured, probably from his years of working with children. "Not yet. But Syd and I are about to go for a paddle to kick some ideas around. Hoping the fresh air will give us some perspective."

Jarett's brows went up momentarily. I waited for him to say something like, "Seriously? Are you going to pick daisies to put in each other's hair, too?"

Instead, he nodded toward Morley's desk in the corner of the dining room. "Mind if I noodle on your computer?"

Morley shrugged his shoulders. "Only if you don't try contacting any friends or relatives."

"Why is that such a big deal?"

"Timeblinking is still an enigma to us. We don't know if tampering with the past might affect the future."

I noticed Morley didn't say that as far as we knew, we couldn't change the past, but I wasn't about to call him on it. Better that Jarett stuck to surfing funny cat videos or monster trucks or whatever he was into.

After Morley set Jarett up on his computer, we finally headed out for the paddle I'd been dying to take all morning.

Most property owners at Sandalwood Lake would tell you there is no better place on Earth to spend the summer. They wouldn't be wrong. The weather is never too hot nor too chilly and the lake is clean and the perfect temperature for swimming. At the height of the season, it's alive with swimmers, kayakers, and canoers. Some residents have small outboard boats to shuffle their kids around in or to fish for rainbow trout; fortunately, the lake isn't big enough for noisy jet boats or waterskiing. And best of all, the residents are friendly without being nosey or overbearing.

However, I've always found their disdain for this slice of

paradise in the off-season to be misplaced. They describe it as a rainy, gloomy place they'd just as soon avoid the rest of the year. I'm the opposite. I embrace the cool season here. In fact, it's one of the main reasons I didn't sell the cabin right after I inherited it from Morley. The air is resplendent with the scent of pine and fir in the cooler months, especially after a quenching rain. It's wonderfully rejuvenating. Our family comes here to recharge and snuggle together on a stormy weekend in the middle of winter just as well as romp and play under a bright summer sky.

I reached the dock twenty steps ahead of Morley.

"Hey, hey!" he said, jogging to catch up. "I thought we were going canoeing, not running!"

"Sorry, sweetie. My feet must be on auto-pilot."

"Do you run here often?"

"Sounds like a pickup line."

"Not the worst one I've ever used," he said, winking at me.

As we untied the ropes tethering the canoe to the dock, I said, "Yes, I run here often. In fact, if Christopher is on a play date and I have some extra time on my hands, I'll often drive all the way out here for a quiet off-season run. It's soul-cleansing."

"You do seem happiest out here. Not that you aren't happy at the condo, but you absolutely shine when you have fresh air in your lungs and sun on your shoulders."

"What a sap," I said, laughing.

"This sap is glad you're here. Although, I wasn't expecting it to be under such dire circumstances."

"Neither did I. But it's kind of fitting, isn't it?"

"How so?"

"That your upcoming death may coincide with mine. And Lainie's. And the other poor folk who escaped a fiery plane crash only to freefall from several thousand feet to a whole other horrific death."

Just as he was about to board the canoe, he stopped and

came over to me. He tilted my chin up and made me look at him. "Shush, my love. That is not going to happen."

"I thought you weren't going to tell me about my future."

"I'm not. What good would that do? I'm just saying you shouldn't lose hope. You need to focus all your energy on getting back to our little boy."

"Oh, Morley. I don't want him to grow up without me."

"That's why we need to get moving on a plan."

"I'm so sorry," I said, grabbing his hands and holding them to my heart. "You shouldn't have to spend your last few days worrying about me."

He brought my hands to his lips and kissed my knuckles. "As I already told you . . . I would have it no other way. It gives me a sense of purpose."

"Morley! The boat!" I said, watching helplessly as my rope slithered into the water and the canoe drifted away from the dock. He calmly pointed down to his foot, which was firmly planted on his end of the rope, then picked it up and pulled the canoe back to the dock.

"I learned my lesson after having to swim after the darned thing a few too many times. Come on, jump in. I'll take the stern."

"As usual," I said, happy to let Morley sit at the back and do most of the work. I'm not exactly an experienced paddler. In 2024, this canoe is hanging on the garage wall collecting dust. I should really get rid of it, but like many of the things that remind me of Morley and our time together, I haven't been able to bring myself to part with it.

We pushed away from the dock and Morley maneuvered the canoe past the swimming buoys and got it pointing toward the north end of the lake. It got me wondering why we always chose the same route: counterclockwise. But I supposed it was like anything else people do. Habit. Like when you take a certain path around the grocery store every time. Or when you habitually visit your soulmate in another time dimension.

The lake's surface was as smooth as polished glass, spoiled only by gentle ripples fanning out from the boat's hull. We paddled in silence for the first little while until we reached the house where Sparkles used to live, and I stopped rowing.

"Remember when Sparkles took me hostage?"

"That's a little dramatic."

"How else would you describe it? He found me alone in your house and forced me to sit in your living room until you came home."

"I'd say he was taking his duties as the community watchdog seriously."

"A little too seriously."

Sparkles wasn't the brightest bulb on the marquee, but his heart was in the right place, and Morley had always maintained the guy was just a big pussycat. Anyway, it was water under the bridge now; Sparkles died from a horrific fall down his stairs not long after I inherited Morley's cabin.

So, naturally, I nearly jumped out of the boat when he appeared in his window and waved at us.

"Oh, my goodness," I said, staring at the man in disbelief. Of course. Sparkles was still alive in 2019.

"You still afraid of harmless old Sparkles?" Morley said, returning the wave.

"No, it's . . ."

I didn't want to tell him about what had become of the poor fellow. About how his cousin, having not been able to reach him for several days, found him at the bottom of his grand staircase with a broken neck. Morley had been friends with Sparkles. Or at least pretty good acquaintances. Did he really need to know what had become of him?

"Sweetheart," he said. "You look like you've seen a ghost."

"I kind of have," I said, quickly resuming my rowing.

"What does *that* mean?"

Morley had an uncanny ability to sense a troubled heart. Especially mine.

"Ugh. I don't want to tell you."

"Good grief, you're going to have to tell me now."

I slowed my paddling. "Are you sure?"

He nodded.

"All right." I pulled my oar out of the water and laid it across the bow. "A few weeks after learning I inherited your property, I finally came out here. It wasn't easy. I was still in shock about your accident and about Coop's involvement in Isla's abduction."

"Understandable."

"Anyway, I went for a run while I was here. To clear my head. It was November and all the summer people were gone, so it surprised me to run into Helen Withers, who was out for a walk. You know, the cute little old lady who lives in that big blue house at the end?" I said, pointing to the northernmost property on the lake.

"Of course."

"She said your accident had devastated her, particularly the way it happened."

"The poor dear," he said, pulling his oar through the water to keep us on course. "You're stalling."

"Okay. I'm just going to say it. Sparkles died from a fall down his stairs."

Morley stopped paddling and took his gaze back to Sparkles's house, where his friend had already disappeared from the window. "Shit. Poor guy. When?"

"Coincidentally, right around the time of your accident."

Morley's eyebrows went up.

"Right? What's worse is that his body wasn't discovered for almost two weeks."

"You could've spared me *that* detail," he said.

I wanted to throw my arms around him, but I was too far away to even hold his hand. "I'm so sorry to break it to you."

"That's okay. People die."

"Wow," I said.

Morley brought his oar aboard and laid it in front of him. A raven squawked in the distance.

"What I mean is, it's unfortunate what happened to Sparkles, but we all gotta die sometime."

"There's the doctor talking. You must be immune to the idea of it by now."

"It's certainly helped me come to terms with my own imminent death."

"I still don't understand how you can be so casual about it," I said, wishing he had more fight in him. I still believed with all my heart that I could use the power of timeblinking to save him, and that we just hadn't figured it out yet.

He shrugged. "I've known about it for months. It's had time to sink in, and there's nothing either of us can do to change it," he said, plunging his oar back into the water, gesturing for me to do the same.

When we resumed paddling, I was glad he could only see the back of my head, where he wouldn't be able to see the tears running down my cheeks.

Behind me, he said, "But you, my dear, have full control of *your* future."

I could only nod.

"A future that includes seeing our son graduate and get married and have kids of his own."

I wiped my face and took a big, sweeping stroke. Morley was right. I had to move forward.

After a twenty-minute paddle halfway around the lake, we trudged up a sandy beach where Morley had pulled the canoe ashore, then spread out a blanket for us to lie on and enjoy the sun. As expected, we were the only ones there.

We stared up at a few lazy wisps of clouds as they floated by.

"Is Christopher still collecting rocks?" Morley said, rubbing my forearm.

I laughed. "It's an out-and-out obsession. He's got three shoeboxes filled with them. But his latest thing is sea glass. It's like he's won the lottery every time he finds a piece."

"Impressive."

"He barely has a jam-jar's worth of those. I must admit, I don't mind this new obsession and have started looking for them, too. Maybe we'll do an art project when we get enough of them. That's if I ever see him again."

"Hey, where did all your fiery resolve go?"

"Sorry. It's just terrifying, the skydiving thing."

"Darned right it is."

"But it really is our best option, isn't it?"

"It's your only option, love. You're just going to have to put all your doubts aside and get on with it."

"Ugh! I don't want to think about it."

I rolled over and kissed him behind his ear, where I know it drives him crazy. He pulled me on top of his chest and began kissing me slowly at first and then with abandon. I surrendered to him without a care about who might be watching.

"Dr. Scott, are you seducing me?" I said, running the tips of my fingers through wisps of gray at his temples.

"Mmm, I think it's the other way around? You're on top of me," he said, rubbing my ass. That did it for me. I stood up and tore off my clothes, then knelt down and tugged his off, too. Then I pulled the other half of the blanket over us, attempting to be discreet, but by the time I took him fully inside me, I was only vaguely aware of the sun beating down on my back. And I didn't care.

As we found each other's rhythm, I leaned back and plowed my fingers into the warm sand, my face to the sky, my bare breasts exposed for the whole world to see. It didn't matter. Nothing mattered when Morley was inside me. Nothing.

When we finally rolled apart, sweating and out of breath, I instantly wanted to do it again, but Morley was already reaching for our clothes.

"This is so unfair!" I screamed at the sky.

"You're telling me, love. I could do this all day."

But instead of pulling me on top of him for more, he handed me a small pile of sandy clothes. "As much as I was enjoying the view," he said, "you never know when Sparkles is doing his rounds."

"Good point."

We quickly dressed, then Morley shook the sand off the blanket and spread it back out on the ground. I was glad he wasn't ready to go back to the cabin. After he sat down, he grabbed something from the sand. It was a flat, purple-tinged stone, which he held up for me to see.

"Christopher would love that one," I said, taking it from him, joining him on the blanket. "I wish you could experience being a dad. I mean, you know . . . like, for longer than a year." Talk about a buzz kill. No sooner had the words come out of my mouth than I wanted to retract them. But there they were, hanging between us.

"Do you feel like talking about Kaylee?" I said. Might as well go for broke now that it was out in the open.

He sighed.

The one and only time we'd ever talked about his daughter—the daughter who'd drowned in infancy—had been right here on this beach. Eons ago, it seemed. For me, it was five years. For him, it was perhaps only a few weeks. He hadn't wanted to talk about it then, and I certainly wasn't expecting him to discuss it now, so it surprised me when he cleared his throat and began talking.

"She was only eleven months old. Collette had had terrible postpartum depression. I'd seen it in patients' mothers before, but until you're living with it, you can't even imagine the toll it can take."

"Oh," I said. "Did she, um . . ."

Morley didn't make me finish the question. "No. She didn't hurt Kaylee on purpose. She was just so out of sorts. Walked away from the bathtub to answer her phone in the next room, then got to talking with her sister. And . . ."

"Oh, Morley." I didn't want him to go on. It was obvious what had happened next. We sat silently for a good two or three minutes.

"We weren't sure if we wanted to have any more children after that, though we were plenty young enough. But about two years later, after a ton of counselling and healing and soul-searching, Collette announced she wanted to try again."

"That's great," I said. But something must have changed their minds because he didn't have any children after that. I waited for him to explain.

"She thought it would be best if we tried foster parenting for a little while, you know, to get our feet wet. And that's when Tristan came to live with us."

"Tristan?"

"He was almost four. His mother had developed a massive drug problem, so he ended up in the foster care system."

"How come you never told me?" I should have known better. He barely talked about his life before me at all. He'd always said it was too painful. That he'd lost too much. I knew the feeling.

"Tristan was only with us eight months, but by that time, we'd become really attached to him. Unfortunately for us—and fortunately for him, I suppose—it took his biological mother hitting rock bottom and having her child taken away to motivate her to clean up her act. And that was it for us. One day he was there. The next, he was gone. That's foster parenting for you. It rarely has a fairy-tale ending."

"Awe, I'm so sorry, hon."

"Me too. Shortly after that, Collette got her cancer diagnosis. Annnd . . . you know the rest of *that* story."

I did. She'd fought a hard battle.

I wrapped my arms around Morley's shoulders and kissed him on the cheek. "Thank you for sharing that with me. It means a lot."

He reached up and held my arms and actually cried. I held him tight and cried right along with him. When he composed himself enough to speak, he said, "It's part of the reason I don't want you bringing Christopher on timeblinks."

"Not because you're worried that time travel could affect his health? Or that he'll tell people he's been visiting his father in a whole different time realm?"

Despite himself, Morley chuckled. "Those are two reasons, yes. But moreover, it's that . . . that I can't bear the pain when he leaves."

I put my head on his shoulder, willing myself not to cry.

"The rock thing. Tristan had a strange fascination with rocks, too," he said.

"I think all little boys do. And dinosaurs," I said, trying to lighten the mood.

"And the word *poop*."

"Oh, yes. *Poop, poop-potty-poop pants* is Christopher's favorite saying right now. He says it at the dinner table, the grocery store, swimming lessons. Everywhere. It's so embarrassing!"

"That's completely normal for his age. He'll grow out of it."

"Not soon enough, Dr. Scott. Not soon enough."

Morley laughed. "Anyway, shall we go?"

"We shall. As much as I'd rather stay here forever, I've got a little boy with a feces fixation to get home to."

Chapter Seven

MONDAY, 2:30 P.M.

Lainie

I awoke, drenched in sweat, sprawled out on a lounge chair on Morley's deck. For a minute, I believed it was still the abnormally hot spring day in 2024 where I'd just attended my father's funeral and Dee had been dead almost a year. But no, it was 2019, and my father and Dee were alive.

They were both *still alive.*

Now to figure out a way to get back to Buffalo to be with them.

I shielded my eyes against the sun to get a look at Gus, but he was gone. Damn. I hoped my mouth hadn't been hanging open when that cop came out to grab him. Or worse, that I wasn't snoring like a trucker, which, according to my family, is the reason I always get my own room on holidays.

I sat up and checked my face in Morley's phone. Ugh. A crusty drool line stretched from the corner of my mouth all the way to my ear, and my face was the color of the inside of a watermelon. With my green hair, I might as well have *been* a watermelon.

I picked up *Misery* where it lay open, face-down on the

deck. I couldn't believe I'd made it all the way to page eighty-nine before I'd drifted off to sleep. People weren't exaggerating when they said the author was the "master of horror." For a book that came out more than twenty years before I was born, it was surprisingly interesting. And disturbing as hell.

I pulled the borrowed earbuds out and wrapped the cord around the phone. Morley was cool to trust me with it. But should I trust him? Until last night, I only ever had a vague idea how he fit into my half-sister's life. All I knew is that he was the stinking rich friend who'd left this cabin and his kajillion-dollar penthouse to Syd in his will. Oh, and that he was Christopher's dad. Aside from that, I'd heard nothing more about him, either from my parents or Syd's side of the family. And then, in the wee hours of the morning, I witnessed the two of them going into Morley's room together. Hand in hand. I wished I hadn't cracked my door open at that precise moment, but at least now I knew their relationship had been more than a one-night fling.

But right now, I didn't care about any of that. The only thing that mattered was getting back to Buffalo, and I would get there with or without Syd's blessing. I'm a planner. A doer. I'd been on the honor roll every single month of my high school career until eight months ago. The day I came home with my first straight-C report card, I was this low-life piece of shit in my mom's eyes. Oh, the fights we had. I nearly ran away from home at one point. Then the fights stopped, and the spotlight turned fully on Stoopid Sarah (if only she could appreciate the irony of that spelling), the golden child, the rising internet celebrity, giving my mom yet another reason to brag to her friends about her one amazing daughter.

But wait. It was 2019 right now. Maybe things didn't have to turn out that way. Maybe I could lob a brick at Stoopid's face and change the trajectory of her life altogether. I shuddered. How could I even think about doing something so wicked? And then I remembered a true story I'd watched about an Olympic figure skater who'd been involved in wounding a fellow competitor's leg. The story ended horribly for the accused, whose stunt earned her a lifetime ban from professional skating. But I wasn't an important person like that. What would I have to lose by breaking my sister's perfect face? Diddly squat, that's what. I'd already lost everything that really matters.

But then a bigger idea hit me: Forget Sarah. I could use the power of time travel to save my dad's life! And to stop Dee from being humiliated in front of the entire school. Dee would still be alive in 2024.

Oh wow. I could change the past. And in turn, the future.

With a lighter heart, I gathered up my things and headed into the gloriously air-conditioned cabin where the cop dude, Jarett, was busy at the computer and didn't hear me walk in. I peeked around the corner into the living room and spotted Gus, who was tethered to the couch, clumsily flipping through the pages of a *Cottage & Cabin Life* magazine in his lap. It was deadly sexy.

Yep. Gus was hot. Hotter than hot. A freaking inferno.

I'd known it the first moment I saw him on the plane yesterday—even when I thought he was this small, wiry thing under his grubby oversized sweatshirt and track pants. He'd proved me so wrong. Today, his biceps were on full display, bulging out from the sleeves of his simple white t-shirt, taunting me, inviting me to touch them. It took all my willpower not to do just that.

Oh, if only he wasn't under lock and key all the time. We could go for a walk to Chapman Falls together. Or swim naked under the moonlight. It didn't even matter what crime he'd committed. In fact, knowing he was a badass made him all the hotter.

One problem, though. He hadn't said a single word to me the entire time we'd been here. We'd literally spent the entire morning together on the deck—him tethered to the railing against his will; me glued to my chair by choice—and he just sat there the whole time, like a statue, watching the lake, pretending I didn't exist. Or maybe he wasn't pretending at all. Maybe he really didn't give a shit about me. I needed to change that, but how could I make him notice me? I'd only come with the clothes on my back, which were the baggiest, comfiest ones I could find for traveling, never mind that this morning I'd washed off the remains of yesterday's makeup. Yesterday being April 11, 2024, which was freaking weird.

With some effort because of his bound wrists, Gus flipped a page in the magazine. What crime had been so serious that he needed restraints and a police guard? He looked more like a rock star than a criminal. On his face and ears was evidence of what had definitely been some pretty sick piercings, and his forearms were covered in tattoos. One of them was a cupid holding a banner with the name "Ruby" printed across it. His mom's name? God, everything about him was sexy. Those plump lips. The five-o'clock shadow. His ice-blue eyes and messy brown curls. I wished everyone would just leave, and I'd free him, and he could do with me whatever he wanted. Wouldn't *that* be a memorable way to lose my virginity. As a time traveler! And in that moment, I wanted to save him, too.

But, to save him—and my dad and Dee—I would need Syd on my side. She held the power, not to mention the knowhow, to flip all these injustices upside down.

"Need something?" It was Jarett, jolting me out of my thoughts.

"What? No. Just seeing where everyone was."

"Good idea. Especially *that* one," he said, tipping his head toward the living room. "We gotta be careful not to let him slip out on us."

"What did he do, anyway?"

"You don't wanna know."

"Try me."

He swiveled his chair around to face me fully. "It's Lainie, right?"

I nodded.

"Well, Lainie, there are people in this world worth thinking about. That guy in there? Not one of them."

"Who said I was thinking about him? I'm only curious."

He sighed. "For shit's sake. Girls sure love a bad boy. Don't waste your time on that piece of garbage."

If it was even possible in my boiling-hot state, I felt heat rising in my cheeks. "I was just wondering if I needed to be concerned. You know, like if he was going to kill me or something."

"As long as I'm here, you've got nothing to worry about."

I glanced at Gus, who tossed the magazine onto the coffee table and flopped backwards, fixing his gaze on a lazily rotating ceiling fan. He looked bored stiff.

"Sounds like they're back," Jarett said, getting up and stalking over to the patio doors. "I hope they figured out how the hell we're gonna get back to 2024. Crazy, isn't it? Yesterday at this time, we were blissfully ignorant about plane crashes and time travel."

I joined him at the window when Syd and Morley were halfway up the yard. "How do you think it all works?" I asked.

"I have no idea. We were on a plane, and then we weren't."

I wasn't about to divulge my suspicion that Syd's dragonfly necklace had had something to do with it. She'd grabbed it right before we zapped off the plane. Right before we ended up at Chapman Falls.

"Hello, hello," Morley said as he and Syd pushed through the French doors. They hurried to the kitchen where they filled glasses with water and chugged them down.

Jarett approached them, rubbing his hands together. "Did you make any headway?"

"We sure did," Syd said, wiping her mouth with the back

of her hand, giving Morley a playful smile. "We're going to the city tomorrow morning."

"Who is?"

"Us three," she said, pointing to Morley, me, and herself. "Got some chores to do."

"Chores? Like what? Picking up milk and eggs? Shouldn't we be focusing on getting back to 2024?" Jarett said.

"Yes, we will. After we've prepared properly."

"Which involves getting skydiving gear, I assume?"

"Eventually. But first, we're going to the condo to grab Morley's other vehicle, then he and Lainie are going on a shopping spree."

"We are?"

"Shopping for what?" The cop was clearly getting impatient.

"Well, we're going to be here a few days. Tell me you won't appreciate a clean pair of tighty whities."

In the living room, I saw Gus chuckle. Sweet. The dude had a sense of humor.

Morley winked at me. "Don't worry. I won't make you pick out the men's underwear."

I smiled weakly. An unexpected picture of Gus's bare butt popped into my mind, making me blush all over again.

Syd rubbed Morley's shoulder. "Dr. Scott, don't be such a tease."

"Can I talk to you a minute?" I said to Morley.

"Sure, sweetie. What about?"

"Privately? About medical stuff," I said, glancing at Syd, who was looking at me curiously. I didn't mean to offend her. I just needed a minute alone with Morley.

"How about we go outside? On the deck. I'll catch up with you in a bit," he said to Syd as he opened the door for me.

Once we were seated on a couple of Adirondack chairs in the sweltering heat, I said, "This is kind of embarrassing."

"What's up?"

"I . . . uh. Well," I said. "I shouldn't be bothering you."

"You're not bothering me at all," he said, looking concerned. But he didn't push and instead waited patiently.

"I'm on some medication, but it didn't make it off the plane."

"What kind?"

"Fluxipram."

He didn't even flinch at this news. "How long?"

"Almost a year," I said after a quick calculation of how long ago Dee died.

"And you've been taking it regularly ever since?"

"Yeah."

"So, it's been helping? Your mood's been good?"

I nodded.

"Well, you did the right thing coming to me. I'll take care of it lickety-split."

"Thanks," I said. "It's just that my doctor told me not to quit cold turkey."

"Wise advice."

"Um, Morley? Can we keep it between us? I really don't want Syd to know I'm on happy pills."

Morley smiled. "Of course. It's nobody's business but your own."

Chapter Eight

TUESDAY, NOON

Lainie

I could see why Syd was so hot for Morley. He wasn't just rich, charismatic, and handsome for an older dude, he was ridiculously *nice*. He'd gone out right after our chat yesterday and hooked me up with my antidepressants, and then this morning when we got to the mall, he gave me one of his credit cards and told me to "go crazy."

I held off buying too much, though. Just picked up a few days' worth of clothes for me and Rose. Syd already had plenty of clothes here, which was fortunate, because I'd been dreading having to figure out what she liked. I also grabbed a sweet new nose stud, some makeup, deodorant, toothpaste, and a pack of toothbrushes. I thought about buying a phone, too, but it would be too much of a hassle because I would need an adult's signature. Besides, Morley's phone was working fine for my needs.

Back at the cabin, Morley handed Jarett two of the shopping bags from our trip. "For you and Gus."

"Thanks man," Jarett said. "I feel useless without my wallet. I'll repay you someday."

Syd and Morley gave each other weird looks, as if they didn't trust Jarett to hold up his end of the promise.

I tried giving Rose's bag to Syd, but she pushed it back. "Do you mind running it up to her?"

I wasn't exactly overjoyed about having to deal with the troubled lady who hadn't emerged from her room since we'd arrived. However, it *would* give me an opportunity to slip away and hang out in my room afterwards.

When I opened the door to Rose's room a couple of minutes later, the smell of unwashed hair and sweat hit me in the face. A half-finished cup of coffee sat on the nightstand next to an uneaten bran muffin. Rose was sitting in an armchair facing the window, humming a tune I recognized but couldn't quite place. A nursery song, maybe.

"Morley and I picked up a change of clothes for everyone. Here's yours," I said, setting the bag on the bed.

She didn't reply. Didn't even move, in fact. Man, it was worse than I thought.

"I told the salesclerk what you're wearing now, and she helped me pick out something kind of the same," I said. "Sorry if we got it wrong."

Nothing.

"There's some makeup in there, too. I'm kind of known for my way around a cosmetics counter."

Her head moved. A nod, perhaps.

"Anyway, I thought you might appreciate having it. I told the lady you kind of look like that actress, Nathalie Emmanuel. You know, from *Game of Thrones*? Missandei? Anyway, she helped me pick out a few things. Hope you like it."

I wasn't worried about offending Rose by comparing her to a TV star who was probably twenty years younger than her and twenty pounds lighter. The comparison wasn't far off, though. I recall being a little intimidated sitting next to Rose on the plane because she *did* seem like a celebrity, so elegant and put together. And it was for this reason I knew she would want to freshen up sooner or later. She hadn't showered or even washed her face in two days.

"I feel terrible about your family," I said, nervously.

She didn't move. I thought I might have offended her and was about to leave when I remembered something. The stories. I remember being so grateful when people talked about Dee and Dad in the days after I'd lost them and didn't pretend they'd never existed.

"Your little boy, he . . . what a sweetie."

At this, Rose stopped humming.

"Eli, right? Great name. He reminded me of a little guy I used to babysit down the street from us. Tavis. He was so curious, you know? He was constantly asking me about my birthmark and wanted to know why everyone didn't have one. I love that about little kids. No filter."

I sat down on the bed. She turned her head—slightly—to acknowledge that she was listening. When she stayed silent, I said, "At my dad's funeral a few days ago . . ." I swallowed. It had seemed like months ago. "My three-year-old nephew—Syd's little boy—was obviously getting bored near the end of the service. When the memorial video came on, he appeared at the front of the chapel and started bouncing around like a pop star. The music was the most depressing stuff on the planet, but that didn't matter to Christopher. I think that's what made it so hilarious. Only a cute little three-year-old could get away with twerking to a funeral ballad. And by the time Syd rounded him up, the whole room was laughing. Even my mom. Which says a lot. I hadn't seen her smile since my dad died."

Rose turned to fully to face me. "I'm sorry about your father."

I choked back a lump in my throat. "Thanks."

We sat in silence for a few moments before she spoke again. "I keep thinking. Maybe they're not dead, George and

Eli. What if the crew got the plane under control and landed it safely, after all?"

"Omigod, right? We don't know what happened after we . . . beamed outta there."

"So, what about us?" she said. "Are we stuck here forever?"

"Apparently my sist—*half-sister*—is trying to figure out a plan."

Rose gave me a sympathetic look, the same look people give me when they notice my birthmark. "Syd is still your sister, sweetie, no matter who your parents are."

I smiled awkwardly. She must have picked up on my underlying bitterness toward Syd, who'd been this mysterious distant relative I'd always done my best to ignore. Huge credit to my parents, who'd never tried to force a relationship between us. Until now, of course.

I sighed. "Would you like some lunch?"

"No thanks. I'm not hungry right now."

"Okay. Everyone's doing their own thing this afternoon, then meeting for dinner at six-thirty. I hope you'll join us."

"I'll think about it."

"Sure," I said, getting up. "Oh, and there's a house meeting on the deck after dinner tonight, too."

She nodded.

"I hope you're right about the plane landing safely," I said, stepping into the hallway.

"Me too, sweetie. With all my heart."

After leaving Rose, I took a long, luxurious shower and spent a good forty-five minutes putting on my new clothes and makeup. I'd splurged on a sweet new stud for my nose—a sparkly blue topaz (my birthstone)—to replace the gold nose ring I'd been wearing the past six months. I won't lie. At first, I thought the topaz clashed with my hair, but the combination was starting to grow on me. Besides, it matched my eyes perfectly and went way better with the silver barbell ring in my eyebrow.

My leggings and burgundy hoodie lay in a heap on the floor, and I was glad to be rid of them. Back at home, I'd dragged them from the back of my closet knowing I had a long travel day ahead of me and that I wouldn't likely be running into anyone I knew. It was comfort over style. But looking at them now, it was hard not to feel a little sentimental. That was my old look. Boring. Plain. A way to blend in with the crowd and attract as little attention as possible. And when Sarah's lame-ass influencing gig started taking off, it made me want to disappear even more.

Until Dee died, that is. Then something clicked in my brain that said, *fuck it, I'm not gonna hide anymore*.

Dee had always told me I could be "smokin' hot" with a bit of effort. She was so sure that my frumpy clothes were doing the opposite of what I wanted—drawing *more* attention instead of hiding me—and that with a few dabs of makeup and clothes that didn't look like a potato sack, maybe I'd fit in a little more. Fuck, I missed her. She was a nerd like me, but she had style and could get away with just about any look, everything from leggings and a cute tee and faux leather jacket to her favorite black skinny jeans, cropped tank, and faded jean jacket. Her style was neither flashy nor slutty, but it was *something*.

So, in her memory, I found my style. One that makes people stop and take notice almost as much as they notice Stoopid Sarah and her fake fairy-princess beauty. They may not be the same *kind* of looks, but in the big scheme of things, who really cares?

I decided on an all-black outfit today. Head to toe. Wait till Gus got a load of me. If only that Jarett dude would let him off his leash for a little while. We could hang or go for a walk around the lake. Who was I kidding? The cop just about popped a nut when Morley presented him with a shiny new set of handcuffs from our shopping trip this morning—complete with a working key.

When I went downstairs to look for Gus, I found Morley sitting in the dining room, staring out at the lake. Poor guy. He looked so sad. As I came closer, I caught sight of what he was looking at: Gus, who was sitting on the dock, shirtless, muscular in all the right places, and *hot AF*. His back was covered in a ton of sick tattoos that I couldn't wait to see up close.

It did surprise me that he was sitting out there all alone without his trusty cop friend cramping his style. But that wouldn't have mattered much—not with the new handcuffs tethering him to a sturdy O-hook on the dock.

"Hey," I said. Morley's head snapped around.

"Yikes, you shouldn't sneak up on an old guy like that."

I smiled. "You're not that old."

"You think not? Care to take a guess?"

"Ummm . . ." I said, unexpectedly nervous. He was a good-looking man. Fit. Not an ounce of extra weight on him. A few faint wrinkles around his eyes. The tiniest bit of gray above his ears. ". . . thirty-seven?"

He laughed.

"I'm sorry! Thirty-two?"

He laughed even harder. "You are officially my favorite person of the day."

"Well, how old are you?"

"I've always been told I look young for my age, but never *that* young. Thank you, my dear!" he said, before fluttering his eyelashes and pretending to primp his hair. "I'm forty-nine."

"Wow! I never would have guessed. No wonder Syd snagged you!"

My eyes went wide. What a dumb thing to say. I could feel the heat flooding into my cheeks.

"What are you up to this afternoon?" he said, mercifully changing the subject. He must have thought I was such a loser in my badass clothes, blushing like a stupid little schoolgirl.

"Dunno. I was thinking I'd go down there," I said, nodding toward Gus.

He flashed me a surprised look. "Really?"

"Yeah. He looks bored out of his skull."

"He does, doesn't he? Or maybe he's plotting his escape," Morley said, winking. "But sure, if you have nothing better to do, go ahead. Keep it brief, okay? Before your sister gets back from her run. She'll have my head on a platter if she finds out I allowed you a visit."

"He'll probably ignore me, anyway."

Morley shrugged. "His loss."

"Right?"

"At any rate, it'll give me something interesting to watch. I've given Jarett the afternoon off."

I flashed him a weary smile. All this extra security detail seemed so unnecessary. They'd handcuffed Gus to the dock, for shit's sake. How would he get himself out of that?

"Wish me luck," I said. Morley gave me a thumbs up as I swung the French door open and stepped into the warm afternoon sun.

My tummy did a little backflip when I was halfway across the yard, and if Morley hadn't been watching, I would have turned around and run back inside. Instead, I whispered, "*Don't be such a chickenshit. He's just a dude.*"

When I was close enough that there was no turning back, I let out a small warning cough. Didn't want to startle the guy and have him slip off the dock, although it wouldn't have been so bad. It would've given me the opportunity to pull him to safety and get my hands on his hard, wet body.

He glanced at me over his shoulder as I approached, then took his gaze back to a gigantic white house across the lake that practically glowed in the bright daylight.

"Sweet pad, hey?" I said, dropping a patio cushion at my feet. I tossed a second one toward him, which nearly flew into a canoe tied to the dock, but he caught it in midair and set it down without speaking. Without looking at me.

"I've been here a few times with my family. Well, my *real* family," I said, hoping to pique his interest, but he just sat there, one foot in the canoe, lazily pushing it around in the water.

It gave me the chance to check out the ink covering his back, which mostly featured dragons, tribal patterns and skulls, but instead of being a random mishmash with no thought to design, they all seemed to go together perfectly. One of them in particular caught my eye, and not because it emphasized the ripples of his left deltoid. The design was stunning. It showed a motorbike from the perspective of the rear wheel, as if the artist had been sitting on the ground behind the bike. I was mesmerized by both the detail and the unusual angle.

"What kind of motorbike is that?" I said.

"Huh?" he grunted, casting me a surprised look that I'm sure he instantly regretted.

"Your ink. What kind of bike is that? It's dope."

"Doesn't matter."

My heart! Of course, it mattered. He'd committed the design to his body forever.

"Sorry, I was just curious."

When he didn't reply, I took the hint and focused on the twittering of unseen birds—sparrows, probably—while gentle waves lapped on the shore. I heard a dog bark in the distance.

"When were you here?" he said without looking at me.

I was shocked into momentary silence. He *had* been paying attention.

"A couple of years ago, with my family. They're all a bit whacked."

No response.

"You've met Syd. She's just my stepsister. Well, technically, she's my half-sister since we share the same father, but stepsister sounds more menacing, right? Like those bad bitches in Cinderella?"

He cleared his throat like he was going to say something but stayed quiet instead.

"My dad—our dad—died a few weeks ago and forced us to hang out together. Look where that's gotten us."

I brushed my fingers over a plank in the dock, and my heart clenched when I realized my dad's bare feet had probably once touched it.

I took a breath. "And then there's my *real* sister. Stoopid Sarah. She's an influencer on the internet. Hah. Wait till people discover she really has nothing to contribute to the world. Well, apart from dumb makeup and fashion bullshit."

He gave me a quick glance, as if to say, *Oh yeah? You're fuckin' drenched in makeup and fashion.*

"Well," I said testily to his unspoken comment. "At least I'm not a sheep like all her followers. I have my own style."

I saw his eyes roll, even from this angle, slightly behind him.

"Want me to steal the key?" I blurted. "To your handcuffs?"

"Sure," he said in a tone that hinted I was crazy. But was it so crazy, the idea that I could help him? If he thought I was on his side, maybe he'd stop being such a grump. Hell, maybe he'd even start being civil to me.

"No, I mean, for real. I know where Jarett keeps it."

"Ya. In his pants. You really wanna go there?"

"Hey, a guy has to take his pants off at some point."

"Whatever."

He still hadn't laid his eyes on me for any length of time. Maybe he wasn't into exposed belly buttons. Or maybe he didn't like girls.

"What did you do, anyway?" I said. "To deserve a cop on your ass all day?"

"None of your fuckin' business."

"Umm, it's *all* my business, dude. I'm living under the same roof as a guy with a police escort. Don't you think I deserve to know what you did?"

"Nope."

Oh, he was annoying. Why wouldn't he just look at me?

"If you stop being such a piss-ass, I might help you get out of here."

"Sure," he said again. "Look, I've been in custody long enough to know when I'm totally fucked."

He was right, of course. And besides, how far would he get, even if he managed to break free? What was he going to do? Steal Morley's Tesla and drive off into the sunset like the Lone Ranger? I giggled under my breath.

"The fuck are you laughing at?"

"Yikes, who peed in your corn puffs this morning?"

He sneered at me, then took his gaze back to the lake. I scrambled to my feet, grabbing the cushions along the way. "Okay. Well, nice chat," I said, lingering for a moment to give him one more chance to drop the sourpuss act and talk to me nicely, but he just grunted.

I looked up to the house where Morley was still watching and shook my head. He smiled and raised both hands in a gesture that said *What did you expect?*

Chapter Nine

TUESDAY, 6 P.M.

I was at the stove stirring a pot of gravy when Lainie emerged from her room and came downstairs. She looked like a completely different person. Apparently, Morley had given her free rein to buy whatever her little heart desired at the mall. Her face was covered in what had to be thirteen different types of makeup products, ranging from almost white foundation to heavy, dark eye shadow and maroon lipstick. Her new duds were no less menacing: skinny black jeans and a black hoodie which she'd left unzipped to expose, no surprise, a tight black cropped t-shirt. She'd bought some new jewelry too, if that's what you'd call it, consisting of a half a dozen chains in varying thicknesses, one with a chunky black cross that tinkled against her belly-button ring as she walked. I was embarrassed for her. She looked like a homeless punk rocker whose family had failed her on every level.

She wandered into the living room and flumped down on the couch as Gus snoozed on the loveseat. When she caught me looking, she raised her eyebrows in my direction before popping her earbuds in and adjusting the volume on Morley's phone, which she'd practically adopted as her own in the short time she'd had it. She picked up a magazine from the coffee table and set to flipping through its pages with what looked like false interest.

Jarett was upstairs having a nap in Morley's room—having had a near sleepless night worrying about our impossible situation—and had asked us to wake him for dinner, which would be soon. Rose was doing her usual Rose thing, and Morley was busy cutting potatoes and dropping them into a pot of water when I spoke to him.

"Do you think you'll ever get your phone back from Lainie?" I said.

He laughed. "Who cares? She might as well keep it at this stage of the game. I'm not going to need it where I'm going."

"Geez, you're morbid."

"I'm a doctor. I come by it honestly. Besides, I've set my phone to Do Not Disturb. Got my trusty pager if anything happens with one of my patients."

I shook my head. "Why are you still on-call, anyway?"

"I have to be. For optics. It would be out of character for me to go dark."

"But you're on holidays this week."

"Technically, yes. But I haven't done that in years—shut everything down completely, even on holidays. Not since Collette died, anyway."

I wasn't in the mood to talk about his dead wife. Not when we were enjoying each other's company so thoroughly. "Well, thank you for lending Lainie your phone. She'd be crawling the walls right now without her music. It's a good thing you don't want it back. Your algorithm is going to be so screwed."

"I think that's the least of our worries right now," he said, tilting his head toward the living room.

Gus was still asleep, half upright, half reclined on the loveseat, completely unaware of Lainie's laser-beam focus on him behind the safety of her magazine, which she held amusingly upside-down.

"Holy moly," I said.

"And that's not the first time. The pair of them were hanging out on the dock earlier while you were out for your run. That girl has it bad."

"What? They were together? Alone?"

"Don't worry, I had my eye on them."

"*You* were watching them? Where was Jarett? And what was that little punk even doing outside?"

"Relax. Your cop friend seemed antsy, so I let him take one of my bikes out for a burn."

I shook my head. "Seriously? You guys figured leaving Gus alone was the safe move?"

"It was my suggestion. I thought some fresh air would do him some good, so I suggested putting him out there to contemplate life. Jarett was happy to oblige when I showed him my motorbike collection."

"Oh, Morley, you're such a trusting soul. Must be from working with innocent little kids all day."

"Relax, love. I didn't let him out of my sight. And besides, Lainie was only out there for fifteen minutes before she gave up and came in."

"Gave up?"

"From my vantage point, it looked like she was having a tough time getting his attention."

"Really? He didn't even bat an eye? Belly-button ring and all?"

"Nope. Only gave her the odd glance when he was answering her questions. But remember, you did threaten to poke his eyeballs out at one point."

I laughed. "Ooh, yeah, like this big, scary, thirty-six-year-old mom would really act on that threat."

"Hey, scary moms are the most threatening creatures on the planet—especially when they're trying to protect their young. Trust me on that one."

I handed Morley my whisk. "You're on gravy duty."

Lainie was still hiding behind her magazine, ogling Gus

when I approached her from the side, just out of her sight line. "Dreaming of cottage life?" I said.

She jumped. "What? Uh, pardon?" she said, snatching an ear bud out.

"The article you're reading. Is it good?"

She glanced at the magazine she was holding to her chest, embarrassed, it seemed, to discover it was upside down. "Oh, not really."

"Can I bother you to set the table? The roast will be ready in about twenty minutes."

She seemed to appreciate the change of subject and tossed the magazine on the coffee table, then went into the kitchen ahead of me. I heard Gus rousing behind us, and I had the urge to tell Lainie to zip up her hoodie. I was thankful she was wearing it at all, considering how warm the day had been. Anyway, it was none of my business. I wasn't her mother.

Jarett came downstairs looking fresh as a daisy just as everyone was gathering in the dining room at six-thirty.

"Thanks, my good man," he said to Morley, who was busy seating Gus at the table and securing his ankles with a plastic tie. Gus swung his legs under the table, grabbed a fork, and speared two slabs of beef, pulling them onto his plate. Lainie lowered herself to the seat directly across from him, trying, it seemed, to ignore his lack of table manners. She might look like a street kid, but at least she'd been taught proper etiquette.

"It was thoughtful of you to set out a place for Rose," I said, sitting down next to Lainie. "Did she like the clothes you picked out?"

"Not sure."

"She's still not talking?"

Lainie shrugged. "Not really."

It was like pulling teeth with this girl.

I watched Gus closely. He seemed to pay little heed to Lainie, as much as she was trying to get his attention. Maybe my threat had sunk in after all.

As I laid my napkin on my lap, I heard a door creak open upstairs. A moment later, Rose appeared at the top of the stairs and carefully made her way down. She was wearing her new clothing, which fit her perfectly, and she'd obviously taken a shower and put on some of the makeup Lainie had picked out for her. When she reached the bottom, Morley jumped up to guide her into the dining room, introducing himself along the way. Oddly, we'd been here almost two full days, and they were just meeting.

"It's great to see you, Rose. We were just about to start," he said, pulling out the empty chair at the end of the table.

Jarett looked sideways at Gus. "Some of us have already started."

Rose slid into the chair and scanned her surroundings. "You have a lovely home. It looks so much different in the daylight. Bigger."

"Dude, this is just his summer home," Gus said, inadvertently spitting out a small chunk of meat.

Rose lifted her eyebrows in Morley's direction. "This is your second home?"

He explained that his principal residence was a condo in the city but that he preferred living out here in the woods.

"Well, thank you for your hospitality. I understand there's a plan afoot to get us back to our own time?" she said, as everyone dug into the food.

"We're having a meeting after dinner to hash it out. But for now, I'd like to propose a toast," he said, picking up his glass of wine. Apart from Gus, everyone picked up their drinks and waited for Morley to go on.

"To friends, both old and new, and a safe return to 2024. Cheers."

Rose sighed as we all clinked glasses. "I'd be happy to stay here in 2019, to be honest."

A hint of a smile formed on Lainie's lips, as if she, too, had been considering that idea.

As twilight gave way to a cool, clear night, I volunteered Lainie's services to clean the kitchen while Morley, Rose, and I filed out to the deck for the house meeting. Jarett joined us after fastening Gus to the couch and grabbing a beer on the way out.

"The less Gus knows about the plan, the better. I'll fill him in when it's absolutely necessary," he said, helping Morley drag five Adirondack chairs around the gas fire table in the middle of the deck. Morley flipped the switch on the wall next to the French doors, and a gentle blue-orange flame sparked to life in the center of the table. I smiled to myself. I've never told Morley that I gave the big, ugly thing to a neighbor soon after I inherited the cabin. He loved its ambience, but as a heat source, it was utterly useless. Rose and I set our glasses of water on the wide ledge surrounding the fire and settled into our chairs.

As Jarett cracked his beer and sat down, he asked the first —and most pressing—question of the night. "So, what exactly *is* the plan?"

I was quick to answer. "Same as before, but now we have more of a strategy. It's going to be risky. And scary as hell."

"Scarier than smashing to the earth in a tin can and being incinerated on impact?" Jarett asked.

I glanced at Rose across the circle. Fortunately, she appeared not to have heard him. "Here's the thing. The plane will have traveled a further four and a half minutes by the time we go back, leaving us—"

Jarett grunted. "I know, I know. In midair. Hence, the parachutes."

Rose gasped. "Did he say *parachutes*?"

I wrinkled my nose apologetically.

"Is this a joke?" she said, wide-eyed.

"I wish it were. Unfortunately, there's no other way."

Hearing this, Rose seemed to turn into herself. I couldn't blame her. The whole idea was terrifying.

Jarett grunted. "Maybe we were better off staying on that plane. At least then it would've been quick. Like ripping off a Band-Aid."

Rose shook her head despondently. I wanted to reassure her that everything would work out, but my own doubt kept me silent.

Jarett turned his attention to Morley. "I hear you'll be footing the bill for the skydiving equipment."

Morley nodded modestly.

"Are you sure about that? When I was puttering around online, I found a place that sells the stuff. You got to be a millionaire to take up that hobby."

Morley shrugged and winked at me. "I've been meaning to sell the Range Rover, anyway."

Jarett took a swill of his beer and raised it to Morley. "Well, thanks, my good man. That's very generous of you."

When the dazed look on Rose's face went on unabated, I said to her, "I'm so sorry about all this. You're not afraid of heights, are you?"

She laughed. A chuckle at first. Like she'd just recalled a funny joke. Then she erupted into deep, hearty, side-splitting laughter.

The rest of us exchanged amused looks before reaching an unspoken agreement to wait it out. She would let us in on the joke soon enough. But when her laughing intensified to where she could barely take a breath, Morley sprang from his chair, grabbed Rose's water, and offered her a drink. After several gulps, her breathing leveled off, and she slumped back in her chair.

"Whooh. You almost lost me there," she said, dabbing tears from the corners of her eyes with the sleeve of her new cobalt-blue cardigan.

"Are you okay?" I asked.

A ghost of a smile crept across her lips. "My husband is—my husband *was* a U.S. Army paratrooper before he retired and went into the grocery business."

Everyone's eyebrows shot up simultaneously, and when no one spoke, she went on. "In fact, we were both avid recreational skydivers before Eli came along. I actually met George when I took lessons at the Drop Club. He was an instructor there."

"You're kidding," Morley said, sitting back down next to me.

"Crazy, right? Who would've thought my extremely indulgent hobby might one day save my life?"

"And several others' too," Morley said.

"So, let me get this straight," I said. "George was a CEO, a pilot, a paratrooper, *and* a skydiving instructor? Was he a secret agent, too?"

Rose laughed. "Only in his mind. He was totally obsessed with James Bond."

I smiled. "So, what do you think of our plan? Will it work?"

"It's not impossible. And I know where we can get some gear. For free."

"Rose, you are amazing," I said, shaking my head in utter disbelief at our good luck. "Honestly, though. Do you think a bunch of rookies like us will really be able to pull it off?"

"I won't lie. It's not going to be easy," she said, sizing everyone up. "We have the right amount of people for three tandems. Much easier to control than six separate jumpers."

"Five," Morley said.

"Oh? You're not coming?"

Morley flashed me a wry smile. "Just can't get enough of 2019, I guess."

"Actually," I said, rubbing Morley's back, "It's because 2019 is Morley's natural time. *His present.* We're the time travelers. Not him."

Rose shook her head wearily. "I still feel like I'm dreaming."

"It takes some getting used to," Morley said.

Jarret wrapped his arms around his chest. He seemed nervous, though, rather than cold. "So. What do we need to do, Rose?" he said.

And just like that, Rose became the leader of the entire operation. Not that I minded. Quite the opposite. It was an immense relief to hand the reins to an expert for the most dangerous and complex part of the mission.

"Can we be ready to go by Friday?" I said to her.

"*This* Friday? Have any of you jumped before?"

Jarett and I looked at each other hopefully, but we both shook our heads.

"Maybe Gus has," I said. "Or Lainie. Though she's never mentioned it."

As if we'd summoned her, Lainie emerged from the house carrying a trayful of coffee mugs and the pastries we'd picked up in town. She approached the circle and offered Rose the first pick.

Jarett said, "Hey, kid. Have you ever parachuted before?"

She gave him a startled look and shook her head. "Nuh-uh."

"Damn. I doubt Gus has ever done it, either."

After Lainie finished distributing the coffee and dessert, she set the tray on a side table and said, "Anybody need anything else? I'm heading up to my room."

"Are you sure you don't want to stick around to hear the plan?"

"Can you fill me in tomorrow? I'm kinda tired," she said, zipping her hoodie up to her neck and burying her hands in its tiny pockets. She looked as cold as I felt, making me shiver in turn. If only the fire weren't purely decorative.

"You bet, kiddo," Morley said. "Before you go, would you mind grabbing a couple of blankets from the living room?"

"Sure."

Lainie came out a few moments later carrying a pile of fuzzy throws. "Gus says he's never skydived before. But he did go BASE jumping with his uncle twice."

"Figures," Jarett said under his breath.

"BASE jumping. Isn't that when people parachute off buildings?" I said, accepting a blanket from Lainie.

"Also cranes, cliffs, and bridges," Rose said.

Jarett shuddered. "I don't know about you, Syd, but I'm worried I'm gonna pass out from sheer terror."

"Has that ever happened, Rose? Someone fainting during a jump?"

"Haven't encountered it firsthand, but I've heard of it happening. And in those cases, the divers either hadn't slept well the night before or hadn't eaten anything all day. Or else showed up with a wicked hangover. When it's time for our jump, we'll be in tip-top condition. We *have* to be. Especially with all the unknowns at play."

"The unknowns?" Jarett said uneasily.

"Our physical locations in the air. Our velocity. Altitude. I mean, we can make some educated guesses, but it's still a crapshoot." She looked at me. "I take it you've never time traveled from a plane before?"

I shook my head solemnly.

"So, regarding whether it's possible to be ready by Friday: absolutely. But you'll need to work hard."

"We'll be ready," I said.

"Why is it so important we go on Friday?" Jarett asked.

Morley stood and wrung his hands together. "Because after that, I won't be able to help you."

"You going on vacation?"

"You could say that. A permanent one."

Rose and Jarett exchanged puzzled looks as Morley strolled over to the railing and looked out at the glittering moonlit lake. I could have finished his story but allowed him to collect his thoughts instead. After a few moments, he turned around to face all of us.

"Through the magic of timeblinking," he said, putting air quotes around *magic*, "I discovered that in three days—Friday, September 13—I will be unceremoniously squished to death between a 2013 half-ton pickup truck and the stone wall of The Merryport pub."

"Oh my God," Rose said, her eyes wide with disbelief.

Morley tried to smile, but his bottom lip quivered, and he seemed on the verge of tears. I threw off my blanket and dashed over to him, wrapping my arms around his middle.

We swayed together without speaking. Out of the corner of my eye, I saw Rose get up from her chair and nudge Jarett and Lainie toward the house. After they'd gathered their mugs and plates and went inside, I let out a huge, loud sob.

"I love you," I said into Morley's neck. "So much."

"I love you too, sweetheart. And I'm so sorry."

I knew what he meant. He was sorry he couldn't be there to help raise his son. He was sorry that he could never marry me. He was sorry he wouldn't be going on family vacations with me and Christopher or attending parent-teacher interviews. Or celebrating birthdays. Christmases. He was sorry he involved me in his life. A life that would be snuffed out in a few short days.

It would do no good to ruminate on all those stolen moments. I had to make the most of our next few days together. Days Morley would be devoting to getting my fellow time travelers back to 2024. And making sure I made it home to our son.

Chapter Ten

WEDNESDAY, 3 A.M.

Lainie

Morley's phone buzzed under my pillow. I whipped it out and silenced it, hoping the noise hadn't woken anyone up.

When the house stayed quiet, I got up, dressed, and crammed all the stuff I'd bought at the mall into a black canvas tote bag, then cracked the door open. A bright moon streaming through the skylight gave me just enough light that I wouldn't need the flashlight on Morley's phone to guide me.

The top floor of the house was built like a loft, with the master bedroom positioned at the end overlooking the lake. Next to that was a small bathroom, then two more bedrooms—mine and Rose's. I peered down both sides of the hallway, which was more like a big open landing surrounded by a sturdy railing made of smaller, crooked logs in a style Morley's magazines called "rustic." The railing opened to a gently curving staircase leading down to the dining room and kitchen in one direction and the living room, a powder room, and the front entrance in the other.

Through the rungs, I could make out two figures nestled

under blankets in the living room—Jarett facing the back of the couch, Gus arranged awkwardly on the floor on a row of loveseat cushions. One ankle was zip-tied to a couch leg, making any attempt at escape nearly impossible. His hands were bound at the wrists—also with a plastic tie—so even if he did end up freeing his leg, there was little hope he could fend off Jarett. Besides, even if he miraculously got past Jarett, he almost certainly wouldn't make it out the door without tripping the security alarm.

It was time to make my move. As I stepped into the hall, a floorboard creaked. I froze. That was the problem with wood floors. People loved them, but damn, they were noisy.

When the light snoring from the living room went on interrupted, I hurried to the stairs and tiptoed down them as quietly as possible. The only sound was the soft *schk, schk, schk* of my clammy feet on the wooden stairs, but even that sounded loud to me. I wished I was wearing my flats, but I'd left them next to the patio door with everyone else's shoes. At the bottom of the stairs, I waited again, resuming my mission only when I was sure no one had stirred.

In the front hall, I found everything I needed in one convenient spot next to the door: the security system control panel, the garage remote, a motorcycle key fob, and Morley's wallet. From the wallet, I withdrew three credit cards and a healthy wad of cash, leaving him two other credit cards and a hundred bucks for emergency. I stuffed my haul into the canvas bag along with the fob and remote and then deactivated the security alarm. It was easy, seeing as how Morley had given us all the code. Well, all of us except Gus.

I punched in the numbers quickly and held my breath. The soft beeping might as well have been an air horn in the quiet of the night, but when I peered around the corner and saw that the guys hadn't budged, my whole body relaxed.

With the first part of my plan completed, I dug through my bag and produced a twelve-inch chef's knife I'd scooped from the kitchen earlier. My gaze went to the front door. I could walk out this very minute and find my own way back to Dee. But logistically, it felt impossible. I didn't even know how to ride a motorbike, let alone drive a car, so before I could change my mind, I took another breath and tiptoed into the living room.

I'd gone over the plan a gazillion times in the last twelve hours, but now that it was actually going down, I felt my dinner bubbling in my stomach and worried it might end up all over the floor. But after a couple of slow, deep breaths, I found my courage and crept further into the room. The cop's snoring had deepened to a disturbing level. How could someone make that much noise and not wake up? More shocking was that Gus could sleep through it.

I lingered next to the couch for a moment, then started toward Gus.

But I was only halfway there when Jarett mumbled something unintelligible and flipped over. If he'd opened his eyes, he'd have seen my dark silhouette an arm's length away, holding a rather menacing kitchen knife in my hand.

But his eyes didn't open.

I rushed over to Gus. As I leaned down to nudge him awake, the floor creaked, and his eyes flew open. Before he could cry out, I thrust my hand over his mouth and clamped down hard. Even in the dark, I saw his fear. Who could blame him? It was a rather rude awakening. I glanced at Jarett, who somehow still hadn't woken.

"Shhhh," I whispered. He nodded slowly when I showed him the knife. "We're getting out of here."

His body went lax. He seemed to understand I wasn't there to stab him to death but to help him.

The knife made easy work of the zip ties, which I sliced off his wrists and ankle in quick upward thrusts, then I helped him to his feet. We both froze on the spot when Jarett made some disgusting smacking sounds with his lips before resuming his snoring. I pointed toward the patio door. Without a moment's hesitation, Gus headed over to it, grabbing his hoodie from a dining room chair on the way. We slipped into our shoes and hurried outside.

The night was cool and cloudless, and the moon was bright, once again making the need for a flashlight unnecessary. As I closed the door behind me and turned to join Gus on the stairs, we were met with a bright light in our faces—like a floodlight—shining up from the bottom.

"What do you think you're doing?" came a man's voice. I shielded my eyes with my hand but couldn't see who it was.

Gus and I backed away from the stairs. We probably should have carried on down, but we didn't know who this person was or if he might be dangerous. I wished I hadn't already put the knife back in my bag.

Gus, who was standing to my right and slightly behind me, spoke firmly but quietly. "What's the problem, dude?"

The man started up the stairs without replying, and we took a couple more steps backward. I bumped into a chair, making it scrape loudly on the wood deck. "Shit!" I said under my breath, glancing at the house to see if someone woke up. I almost welcomed the idea of being caught, but the house stayed quiet.

The man was out of breath when he reached the top of the stairs and had to hang onto the railing for support. When his flashlight beam strayed for a couple of seconds, I finally got a look at him. He was a dorky looking beer-bellied guy, maybe in his fifties, who didn't seem capable of violence. But that didn't mean he wasn't.

"What're you doing here?" he said, flooding our faces with light once again.

"Dude," Gus said with his hands up, showing the man he was unarmed. "There's no need to get upset. We're visiting a friend."

"What's his name, then?"

I volunteered the information, desperately wanting this man to leave us alone. "Morley. He knows we're here."

"Morley *what*?" the man said.

Shit. I couldn't remember Morley's last name. "He's a doctor. Works at St. Barney's? Drives a Tesla."

"I didn't ask you where he worked. I asked you what his last name was."

"I have no idea. We're here with Syd. His . . . girlfriend."

"Does Dr. Scott know you're sneaking around in the middle of the night?"

Dr. Scott! Of course, that was his last name. I cursed at myself for forgetting.

"Look, buddy," I heard Gus say over my shoulder. "This is getting annoying. We were just leaving, so if you'll step aside, we'll be on our way."

"I don't think so," the man said before abruptly lunging at Gus, who jumped out of the way. The man stumbled, dropping his clunky industrial flashlight on the deck. Surely the noise would rouse someone in the house, an outcome I secretly hoped for, despite the deep shit I'd be in.

The man was closest to me when he regained his balance. Without warning, he reached out and latched onto my arm and twisted it behind my back. Gus was on him. With a couple of quick tugs, he wrestled the guy off me. But the man whirled around and swung at Gus, who caught his arm in mid-punch. The man wrenched his arm free and backed up a few steps, panting, wiping his forehead with the back of his arm. Then he charged, throwing his full weight at Gus. The two of them scuttled backward, narrowly missing the stairs. But Gus hit the railing with a dull thump, and the man used his sheer size to pin him down. Gus was no match for the giant, and he began gasping for breath under the weight.

I had to do something. I spotted the guy's big green flashlight a short distance away and snatched it up. Not even thinking twice, I ran over and smashed the back of the head with it. Hard. So hard that the lid flew off and the big square battery went sailing over the edge of the deck. He took a couple of unsteady steps backward, then turned and lunged toward me, but before he could get there, Gus was on him, spinning him around. He gave the man one swift push backwards.

What happened next will probably haunt me forever.

The giant man fell back—not against the railing or onto the deck, but into the open space at the top of the stairs. Back he fell, his beefy arms flailing, as if in slow motion, reaching for something to stop his fall. There were about five sickening thuds in the darkness before everything went quiet.

"Oh my God," I said, trembling.

Gus plucked his hoodie off the deck and headed down the stairs. I followed behind robotically. At the bottom, the man lay in a twisted, motionless heap on the last two stairs. Gus had to crawl over him to get by. I stopped short.

"Come on. We gotta get out of here," he said, walking away.

"We should do something!" I said. But in my heart I knew he was probably dead—*dead!*—given the impossible angle of his neck and his absolute stillness.

Gus turned around and sighed. He trudged back to the man and placed two fingers on his neck. After a few seconds, he stood up. "Well, that's a fuckin' shame."

"Is he dead?

"Yes. Let's go," he said, waiting for me to join him.

"Are you sure?"

"Yes! I'm sure. Come on. We gotta go before someone wakes up."

I looked up at the dark house, wishing I could run upstairs and jump into the cozy bed. Then, out of the blue, Dee's face flashed in front of me, and I remembered why I'd broken Gus out of there in the first place.

"Can you please?" I said, reaching my hands toward him.

He took the hint and lifted me over the dead man's body. As heartless as it seemed, Gus was right. There was nothing we could do for the poor guy now.

We scurried around the side of the house, and I led Gus to the detached garage at the far end of the driveway.

He spoke quietly, as if that mattered now. "I'm guessing you have a plan?"

I whipped my bag open and began digging around for the garage remote.

Since arriving in 2019, I'd been wondering why Morley didn't park his car in his enormous garage, but when we got back from our shopping trip, it had become clear why.

We'd pulled up in front of the garage and Morley asked me to help him unload the cases of water and soft drinks. When he raised the door, my jaw dropped. It was no ordinary garage. The whole thing was white and sparkling, and there were five shiny motorcycles lined up looking every bit like they belonged in a Hollywood showroom. They ranged from slick-looking speed bikes to those big, heavy kind people used for touring the country. After we chatted about them for a few minutes, I'd learned that the glitzy black Suzuki was the fastest one but that the candy-apple red Goldwing was the most comfortable for two riders, especially for long distances. It was then that I began formulating a plan.

It started as a tiny flicker of an idea when I'd followed Morley into the house and saw him drop the garage remote into the hall table drawer—right next to five motorbike key fobs—and had grown into an elaborate, multi-part escape plan by the time I saw Gus's kickass motorbike tattoo.

I fished the garage remote out of my bag, and I swear Gus nearly crapped himself when the door lifted and he saw all that color and chrome against the glossy white backdrop.

"Holy shit!" he said, hurrying in. He hopped onto the sparkly black bike whose speed Morley had described as "almost illegal". Time was wasting, but I let Gus pretend to ride the sexy bike for a few moments.

"Dope! A Hayabusa!"

I produced a key fob from my bag and dangled it in front of him before tucking it into my bra for safe keeping.

"You fuckin' rock! I've always wanted to ride one of these!"

"Sorry, but we're taking *that* mean machine," I said, pointing to the sturdy looking Goldwing at the end of the row. "Come on. Let's go before they find us missing."

"Where's the key for this one?"

"In the house. Let's get moving."

"Fuck." He dismounted the slick bike and stalked over to me like a moody ten-year-old.

"Wheel it out and I'll lock up. What are you waiting for? *Go!*"

Scowling, he obediently pushed the bike down the driveway toward the road while I grabbed two helmets and closed the garage, leaving the remote on the hood of Morley's Tesla. When I caught up to Gus at the end of the driveway, I stuffed my canvas bag into the bike's storage compartment and handed him the bigger of the two helmets.

"Fire it up. We should be far enough away from the house now," I said. "Although, if no one's woken up by now, who knows if they ever will?"

"Where're we going?" he said.

"Let's just get to town where we can blend in a little better. Then I'll tell you how we can help each other."

He grunted, then slipped the shiny blue helmet over his head. His compliance was peculiar. But if he was as exhausted as I was, he was probably thankful someone else was calling the shots.

As I hopped onto the bike and wrapped my arms around Gus's middle, I cast a final glance at the sleepy house. My heart dropped. That poor man. How could we have just left him lying there in the dark? All by himself!

Because it was an accident, that's why. We did not mean for him to die, even if he *was* threatening us.

By the time we got to the highway a few seconds later, the whole horrible encounter felt like a dream. A nightmare, actually. But instead of obsessing about all the ways I could have prevented it, I let it go. Saving Dad and Dee was my only mission now.

As the cool air numbed my fingers and we'd put some distance between us and the nightmare back at the cabin, I landed on another troubling thought: Syd's reaction when she found us missing in the morning. She was going to lose her mind.

Or would she?

Syd, of all people, knew how hard it was to lose people she cared about. She also knew the joy of having them back in her life.

Almost an hour later, somewhere near Everett, Gus shouted over his shoulder, "We need gas, but we gotta find a station that lets you fill up without paying first."

I realized he had no idea about the credit cards and the couple hundred bucks in my bag. "Don't worry about that. I have some cash."

"No shit? Well, in that case, I'm hungry, too. You got enough for food?"

"Yeah."

"Cool. We'll find a place to eat after we fill up."

It was four-thirty in the morning, and I was anything but hungry, but stopping for a break would give me a chance to let Gus in on my plan, which so far had only been to go south on

Interstate 5 where we could eventually get on I90 heading east toward Buffalo.

We coasted into the parking lot of the Good Grub All-Night Diner twenty minutes later. I hopped off the bike and waited for Gus to ease it behind a big green dumpster out of view from passing traffic. Good. The dude was using his noggin.

"Damn. We gotta get rid of this thing," he said. "We don't exactly look like your typical Goldwing cruisers."

"I did the best I could."

He reached over and tousled my hair. "You did good, kid. Sucks about the Hayabusa, though."

Kid? What a jerk. Look how far I'd gotten him in the last hour and a half! Not exactly the handiwork of a child.

"Let's eat!" he said.

Inside the diner's washroom, I dug through my bag for my happy pills, which I couldn't honestly remember grabbing from under my pillow at the cabin. Sure enough, they weren't there. Damn! This was Syd's fault. If it wasn't for her, I wouldn't have had to hide them. Now I was on my own with the withdrawal symptoms. Maybe I'd get lucky and wouldn't experience any. Or maybe I'd be one of those disaster cases you hear about. And there was nothing to do now but wait it out.

After I'd freshened up and we were seated in a booth with a mountain of greasy food in front of us, I began rolling out my plan to Gus in small, digestible chunks.

"So, remember how I went into the gas station when you were filling up back there?"

"Yeah," he said, stuffing his face with hash browns.

"And remember how I asked you to stop at two more because I had to pee?"

"Ya. It was pissing me off."

I pulled out a stack of cash from my bag and placed it proudly between us. He immediately grabbed it and shoved it into his lap under the table.

"Hey!" I yelled.

The scruffy old dude behind the counter glowered at us and muttered under his breath, "Stupidi delinquenti."

Gus lowered his voice. "Cool your jets. I'm not taking it from you. Y'just shouldn't be flashing that kinda money around, especially in a dive like this."

He passed it back to me under the table and I slipped it into my bag, then turned my attention to the man behind the counter. "Non siamo delinquenti , signore," I said.

Gus's eyes went wide. "You know Spanish?"

"Yeah, I do. But that was Italian. I'm just learning, but I'm pretty sure he called us a couple of troublemakers. I told him we're not."

"You fuckin' rock!"

That was the second time tonight he'd said that. I tried not to smile.

He stabbed a sausage with his fork and crammed the whole thing into his mouth. After he'd finished chewing, he said, "So, smarty-pants, why'd ya bust me outta Jarett Jail? I mean, we've only known each other, like, two days."

"Know each other? You've barely even looked at me this whole time."

He put his fork down to take a swig of Coke, ignoring my comment.

"Hello? Are you there? Why have you been avoiding me?"

"Your handler laid out the rules when we got to the cabin."

"Handler?"

"Your sister. She said she would make my life hell if I even laid an eyeball on ya."

"Seriously?" I said. "For fuck's sake, I'm not twelve." Yet, I had to admit, I was a little shocked that she'd stuck up for me, and I wondered what would've caused her to give Gus such a sharp warning. He must've said something to show his interest in me.

"You didn't answer my question," he said. "Why'd ya bust me out?"

"I need to get to Buffalo."

"Buffalo? The fuck? Do you know how far that is?"

"Sure do."

"And you picked a stranger in police custody to get you there? Seems like a pretty weak plan if y'ask me."

"Hey, give me some credit. Look where we are."

He grunted and stuffed more food into his mouth.

"In fact, I knew right from the start we could help each other get what we wanted."

He rolled his eyes and kept chewing.

"So, are you with me?"

"Maybe. Where'd you get all that cash, anyway?"

"As I was trying to tell you, I used Morley's credit cards. Figured I'd better take out as much as I could before he discovered them missing. I doubt he'll report it, though. Did you hear? He's supposed to die in a few days."

"Yeah. Shitty for him."

"It works for us."

"Look at you, kid, thinking of everything."

"Quit calling me that. I'll be sixteen in December."

"Ha. Like I said . . . *kid*."

"How old are *you*? Seventeen?"

He stuffed another whole sausage into his mouth before answering. "Twenty-three."

"You're full of shit."

"Whatever. Look, can't you find someone else to drive you across the fuckin' country? Or are ya just after my body?" he said, flashing me a devious smile.

My face turned so red I could feel it all the way to the tips of my ears.

"Oooh, somebody has the hots for Gus!"

I balled up my napkin and threw it at him. He dodged it, knocking his plate of toast off the table. When the plate finished spinning, he said, "Now look whatcha did!"

"This was a bad idea," I said, scooting off the bench to pick up the mess. I gave the scruffy Italian a tight smile. "Mi dispiace. Partiamo presto," I said. *Sorry. We're leaving soon.*

Gus didn't even bother to ask what I'd said. "Okay, okay, all right. I'll be serious. Why Buffalo, kid?"

"A couple of reasons."

"It's so damn far."

"Only forty hours. I checked."

"*Forty hours?* Are you high?"

I sighed. "Look, I know it's a lot to ask, but there's something in it for you, too. *Something huge.*"

He looked at me skeptically. "What's huger than being free? In fact, I could just leave right now and do whatever the hell I want."

"You could, but you'd still be in trouble—maybe even more so, now that you've stolen a motorbike and killed that guy at the cabin."

"Fuck that! He started it!"

"I know. But the police will see it differently."

He grunted.

"What if I said I had the power to prevent you from landing in trouble with the law in the first place?"

He lowered his utensils without setting them down and leaned back on the ripped vinyl seat. "I don't need you for that. This is September 2019. I haven't done my crimes yet."

"Crimes? Plural?"

"Yeah. So what? You don't seem to be the purest egg in the carton."

"What does that even mean?"

He ignored my question. "Yeah. I'll know better this time around. I won't be such a fuckup. D'ya think I want to go to prison all over again if I don't have to?"

"Here's the thing. Syd filled me in on how this time-blinking power works." Which was an out-and-out lie. I'd only heard bits and pieces about how it worked, but I had to convince him otherwise. And if it meant making stuff up, then so be it.

"You can't change what you've already done," I said. "You're still going to get busted for drugs or theft or whatever you did. There's no way to change it by staying in 2019. Sorry."

"Seriously? So, you mean I'd still go to prison?"

I nodded. "Unless you take me to Buffalo."

He narrowed his eyes. "What's the big fuckin' deal about Buffalo?"

I looked over my shoulder, then leaned into the table. He followed my lead. When I had his full attention, I spoke quietly, "Syd left a special ring at my house when she came out for my dad's funeral. A *magic* ring. It has the power to change the past. So, when we go back to 2024, it's as if your crimes never happened. You'll carry on. Get a job. Marry someone nice. Eat sausage and hash browns at four in the morning any time you want. You'll never even see the inside of a jail cell."

I could almost hear the cogs in his brain click into motion. A magic ring didn't seem so far-fetched to someone who'd just time traveled. To someone in desperate need of a life do-over.

Chapter Eleven

WEDNESDAY, 5:29 A.M.

Morley was in the habit of leaving the bedroom curtains open, even at night. I wasn't worried about privacy, though. The cabin didn't follow the traditional rectangle-shaped floor plans that generally included a full-width deck on the lake-facing side of the house. Instead, the layout was more of an L-shape, with the master bedroom cleverly jutting out past the rest of the house, providing an unobstructed view of the lake through a massive picture window. I mentioned to Morley once that with a fairly decent telescope on the other side of the lake, a person could probably get an eyeful of this bedroom, especially with the lights on at night. But Morley was unfazed. He'd always contended that if Bob and Mildred in the executive cottage across the lake wanted to see him walking around in his birthday suit, then all the power to them.

Curtains would have been helpful tonight. The extra bright moon was shining straight in my face, making sleep almost impossible. It had also been a particularly busy night for weird noises outside—one of the charms of sharing your home with nature. It wasn't uncommon for groups of deer to trot across the yard or for families of raccoons to scale the side of the house and run around on the roof, I swear, just to annoy me.

As I was drifting off for probably the tenth time, an unusually loud thump jolted me awake. And then three or four more. I glanced at Morley. He was out cold, so I left him sleeping, then threw off the covers and dashed over to the window. I instantly felt very exposed standing in front of the window in my silk champagne camisole, and I shivered.

Shadows from the towering pines to the right side of the property stretched across the yard and shoreline, making it difficult to find the source of the sound. I strained to see something—anything—that could have made a noise loud enough to penetrate the dense log walls that Morley had always been so proud of. He was famous for getting all technical on me and blathering on about the cabin's state-of-the-art soundproofing thanks to its thick log walls and triple-paned windows. Having owned the cabin myself for almost four years, I'd occasionally caught myself nerdily bragging about those features, too.

I pressed my forehead to the window and cupped my hands around my eyes.

My breath faltered when I saw it. Something that rocked me to the core.

A deer.

A deer so big it might have been mistaken for a moose.

In the moonlight, I could barely make it out, but I knew one thing: it wasn't one of those cute little mama deer known around town as the evil "garden gluttons" but a remarkable black-tailed buck. His huge antlered head flicked toward the house, where his eyes locked on mine for a fraction of a second before he bounded off into the trees.

I sighed, equally in relief and awe, then crawled back into bed and curled myself around Morley. He took my hand from his belly and sleepily kissed it, then held it to his chest. Within a few minutes, he was dozing again.

If only I could settle my mind enough to do the same. It was Wednesday, I just realized, and in two days, this warm, solid, beautiful human asleep in my arms would be gone. This got me thinking about the deer. That in my own time, like Morley, the buck was probably long dead. I'd met plenty of hunters over the years, mostly customers at the pub, and felling that giant buck would've been a career highlight for most of them. It was only a matter of time for the deer. And for Morley.

After what felt like a mere ten minutes later, there was an urgent rapping at our bedroom door. Both Morley and I sat bolt upright in bed. I snatched the sheet up to my chin and glanced at the clock: six ten. It seemed I'd finally gotten to sleep, but only for a few minutes, and I was more than a little irritated that someone was waking me up now.

Jarett's muffled voice came through the thick wooden door. "Sorry, guys, but we have a situation."

"Come in," I said, flicking on the bedside light.

Jarett stepped into the room. His eyes were wild. "He's gone. Gus is gone."

"What?" I shouted. "How?"

"No idea. I woke up and saw the remnants of the restraints on the floor. He must've hidden some scissors somewhere. Or a knife. I don't know, but he's AWOL now."

"Well, that's not good," Morley said unhelpfully, leaping out of bed and grabbing a pair of jeans off the back of a chair.

"Wouldn't the alarm have gone off?" I said, immodestly throwing the covers off me. I didn't care that Jarett could see me in my skimpy lingerie.

Morley chucked me my shirt. "Have you checked the whole house? The crawlspace?" He said to Jarett, who'd respectably retreated to the hallway to let me dress.

"Yes. I checked everywhere. And both vehicles are still there."

"Well, he couldn't have gone far then," I said.

As we were assembling at the bottom of the stairs a few minutes later, Rose emerged from her room. "What's going on?" she said, peering at us wearily over the railing.

"Gus is missing," I said. "Can you stay here? With Lainie? We don't know where that punk is, and we need to find him, or none of us will be going back."

"Absolutely," she said.

Jarett brushed by me out the front door as I joined Morley at the security panel in the front hall.

"I was sure I'd set the alarm," Morley said, fiddling with the controls, simultaneously wiggling into his shoes.

"You did. I saw you do it."

Abandoning the control panel, he opened the drawer of the small table directly beneath it. "Shit. That's not good," he said for a second time.

"What?"

"Garage remote's gone. Uh oh. And the Goldwing key, too."

"Oh, no!"

We dashed out to the driveway just as Jarett appeared from the other side of the Tesla, holding something up to show us. It was the garage remote. "Found this on the hood of your car."

Morley snatched it out of Jarett's hand, and we all rushed over to the garage. The door lifted.

"That's not good," I said when the door was halfway up, revealing the missing motorcycle.

At that moment, Rose rushed out of the house, pulling on her cardigan.

"Is Lainie out here?" she asked me.

"No, she's in her room," I said dismissively, more concerned about Gus's whereabouts.

Rose grimaced. "I'm sorry, but her room's empty."

"What?"

Within milliseconds, I understood the implications of Lainie's absence and turned all my energy on Jarett. "What the fuck? Now he's kidnapped Lainie!"

"This ain't exactly San Quentin," he said.

"Actually," Rose said carefully, "She may have gone with him by choice. All her things are gone, too."

Morley emerged from the garage, scratching his chin and reporting two missing helmets.

"That little bitch!" I said. "Do they have any idea what this means for all of us?"

"What does it mean?" Rose said innocently. I realized she'd missed this part of the story.

"We all have to go back together. All five of us. If even one person is missing, *none* of us can go back."

Rose took a deep breath, then started toward the house. "Come on then, let's go inside and figure this out."

"Are you insane?" Jarett shouted. "I'm not going inside. Morley, give me your keys. I'm going to look for them. They probably went into town."

"Probably?" Rose said, stopping halfway to the house. "Even if they did go there, where would you even look?"

"Rose is right. We need a plan first," Morley said.

"Look, buddy. In my line of work, if you hesitate, you're toast," Jarett said.

"In my line of work," Rose said, "if you don't have a plan, you're toast."

Left with little choice, we followed Rose back into the house. Jarett included. He wasn't happy about it, but I think he realized it would be futile to look for Gus and Lainie without at least having an idea about where they might be headed.

Once we got inside, Morley went to the kitchen to make coffee while the rest of us gathered at the dining room table. A thin pink band had risen over the treeline, signalling the start of a new day. One horrible day closer to Friday.

I grabbed a pen and notepad from the desk and took a seat across from Rose. Jarett sat next to me.

"Okay. Let's think. Would they have gone to the bus station? The airport?" Rose said. I realized just then how much I liked her. And how much I appreciated her calm presence.

"I doubt it. Not without money or credit cards."

Out of the corner of my eye, I saw Morley dart out of the kitchen toward the living room as if suddenly remembering something.

Rose gave me a fetching look. "Is there a chance they'd go to Buffalo?"

"What? No. Why would they?"

She licked her lips. "Lainie and I had a pretty revealing heart-to-heart chat yesterday. She told me all about her dad—*your* dad—and about her best friend's suicide last year."

I rolled my eyes.

When Rose's eyebrows went up, I realized how insensitive that must have seemed, and I shrugged apologetically. At the same time, I was annoyed. Rose didn't know about my family's history. How spoiled Lainie had always been. How she'd taken advantage of my father's guilt about abandoning me to get whatever she wanted.

"Yes. It's been a trying year for Lainie," I said instead.

"No offense, but what does any of this have to do with where they might have gone?"

Rose took a small breath. "I think I might've planted a seed. When Lainie and I were talking, I mentioned how nice it would be to stay here in 2019—specifically to see George and Eli again. And it was looking like a darned good idea. That is, until fifteen minutes ago when you told me we would all be stuck here forever."

"Lainie knew we all had to go back together," I said. "And she took off anyway."

"I wouldn't be so sure," Morley said, entering from the

living room. "She wasn't around for most of our meetings, and when she was, her music was blasting in her ears at four hundred decibels. I'll bet you a million bucks she doesn't know. And I'm sure she doesn't know that even if she made it to Buffalo, her parents and friends wouldn't be able to see her anyway."

Rose looked at me, shocked. "Is that true?"

I nodded. "Even if you wanted to see your husband and Eli right now, you'd be invisible to them. It's the main drawback of timeblinking."

Morley flipped his worn leather wallet onto the table, where it landed with a thud. "They might just make it to Buffalo after all," he said. "With the help of some cash and three of my credit cards."

"You gotta be KIDDING ME!" I yelled.

Morley scooted around to my side of the table. He crouched down and hugged me, talking softly in my ear. "They left me some cash and two credit cards. Besides, Lainie knew I wouldn't be needing any of this stuff after Friday, sweetheart."

I burst into tears and pulled away. "That makes it even worse! If I ever get my hands on her—"

Morley pulled me into his chest again, and in the comfort of his embrace, I heard Rose's buttery, calm voice. "I know exactly how we can find them."

She had our attention now.

"And Dr. Scott," she said carefully, "It might be the trickiest operation you've ever performed."

Chapter Twelve

WEDNESDAY, 6:05 A.M.

Lainie

"Stop worrying, wouldja?" Gus said as we wheeled the Goldwing behind a rickety single-car garage next to a modest 1960s bungalow. It was an impossible request. Every nerve in my body was zinging.

"I'm freezing," I whispered, scanning the small, well-tended yard where a raised vegetable garden was on its last hurrah of the season. "How long are you going to be?"

"As long as it takes," Gus said irritably, popping the side compartment on the bike open, pulling out my canvas bag.

"Hey!" I protested, locking my fingers on the straps. He yanked the bag away.

"Relax! I need hush money," he said before disappearing behind the house, leaving me to pout next to the cooling bike.

Everything about this little side trip was suspicious, but I was beyond exhausted and more than ready to let Gus take over. At least for a little while.

I leaned against the garage, thinking back to our conversation at the restaurant where Gus rightfully suggested we'd be sitting ducks if we rode the Goldwing all the way to Buffalo.

He'd called it a "heat magnet." Not that he'd said it outright, but I'm sure he pegged me as an idiot for picking the flaming red bike. He'd insisted we needed to "trade down" and that he knew a guy who would lend us his car. "Fine," I'd said, hotly reminding him I'd done the best I could, and that the Goldwing seemed like the best choice at the time. And the most comfortable for a long journey. "Smart thinking, kid," he'd said.

But now, as I stood shivering in a stranger's dark yard, I believed my thinking had been anything *but* smart. Nobody back at the cabin knew where we were going. The warmth and comfort of the Range Rover would've made way more sense, despite its splash and flash and its potential to be a "heat magnet." I sighed. Damn Gus, anyway. Had he forgotten he would still be hitched to the couch if it weren't for me? Shit, that's right! I'd convinced this smoking-hot guy to drive me all the way to Buffalo, and he genuinely believed I could help him erase his criminal record, too. Good for me.

I looked up, taking comfort in the twinkling stars against the slowly brightening sky. Soon, the residents of this sleepy suburb would begin pulling themselves out of bed to brew their morning coffee or take their dogs for a walk or start getting ready for work or school. Or look out their windows to find a green-haired teenager lurking in their neighbor's yard amongst a bunch of weather-beaten garden gnomes.

Gus didn't seem like the sort of guy who kept company with gardening enthusiasts, but stranger things have happened. Like time traveling to 2019 and running away with a known criminal, for instance.

As I reveled in the beauty of the starry sky, I nearly jumped out of my shoes when a robin burst into loud, urgent chirping to ring in the new day. To me, it sounded more like a warning.

"Come on, come on," I whispered to myself, trying not to bolt off down the street.

When the robin still hadn't quieted a few minutes later, I crept around the back of the house and tiptoed over to the porch, where a cluster of tiny bugs flittered in the light above the door. I gathered my nerves and pulled the door open. A tsunami of smells whooshed into my nostrils—cinnamon, drug-store perfume, Tiger Balm—instantly reminding me of my grandmother and the warmth and comfort of her 1890s heritage home in Syracuse. We hadn't been there since she died five years ago, and all of a sudden, I missed her terribly.

As I was about to step inside, Gus came flying around the corner at the top of the stairs and barreled down them like his feet were on fire. "We're in!" he said when he reached me, pushing the canvas bag into my chest, jingling a set of keys in front of my face before taking off toward the garage. I followed.

As Gus tried various keys in the garage handle, I noticed he had some bloodied toilet paper wrapped around his other hand.

"What happened to your hand?"

"I cut it on the fuckin' knife when I reached into your bag."

"Oops, sorry about that."

As usual, he ignored me and kept wiggling keys in the garage door, finally having success on the fourth or fifth try. He lifted the door and pushed it back, exposing a silver minivan that looked about twenty years old but in apparent good repair.

"Well, this sure isn't a cop-magnet," I said, scooting toward the passenger-side door.

"It's perfect. No one will be looking for us in this heap."

Inside, the van was the furthest thing from being a heap, and was, in fact, immaculately clean and smelled like vanilla and looked as though it had just undergone a bumper-to-bumper detailing job.

"Your friend rules! Did you tell him we're driving all the way to Buffalo in it?"

"Pffff, yeah, of course," he said, rolling his eyes.

I gave him an incredulous look.

"He's got the Goldwing now," he said. "Who *wouldn't* be stoked about that?"

"Won't he have the same problem as us? You know, riding a fancy stolen bike and all?"

"He's got friends, kid. That bike won't be recognizable in about twenty-four hours when they're finished with it."

This was the coolest adventure ever. I might as well have been in a mafia movie.

The minivan's engine hesitated for a second before chugging to life, and we were on our way. Soon I'd be warning Dee and my dad about things to come, and the world would be right again.

Chapter Thirteen

WEDNESDAY, 6:33 A.M.

"Do you have a better idea?" Rose said.

"It's totally crazy," I replied from across the dining room table.

"Is it though? How else are we going to find them?"

I opened my mouth to suggest another idea that didn't involve sending Morley on a timeblink of his own but couldn't think of one.

Jarett said, "What do you think, Morley? Ready for a trip six hours into the past?"

Morley, who was standing next to me with his hands on his hips, shrugged as if to say *Why not?*

I beseeched him. "Is it even possible with both—" I nearly blurted out my concern about both talismans being present and how it might affect a timeblink. "—with both of us here at the same time?"

Morley rubbed at his stubbled chin for a few seconds before his eyes lit up. "Of course it's possible. We already performed a simultaneous timeblink before. Remember San Fran?"

I shook my head.

"It was during your first blink. We were in the living room, and I accidentally zapped myself to the San Francisco airport in the middle of our conversation."

I did recall that. He'd been explaining how timeblinking worked when he'd vanished into thin air. Both talismans had been present that day, and while this revelation should've calmed me, I was still leery. "Are you sure about this?"

"If I thought there was even a slight chance it wouldn't work, I wouldn't risk it."

"But what if you get stuck? What if it disrupts everything that's supposed to happen from now on?"

Morley set his gaze on me. "Love. Have you forgotten everything you know about timeblinking?"

"It's just so scary," I said. "Mind you, it wouldn't be the worst thing if you didn't actually make it to The Merryport on Friday."

Jarett clapped his hands together. "All right. Let's do this."

I glowered at him. "Wait just a damn minute."

Jarett's face dropped. I hated being so hard-nosed, but he was only responsible for one other person, whereas I was responsible for four. And if none of us made it back to 2024—if we all ended up dying of old age here in this realm—it would spark a huge investigation that had no chance of being solved. Ever. Five people will have vanished from Flight 444, and our families would be stuck in a lifelong limbo. I simply couldn't do that to them.

"Look, sorry," Jarett finally said. "It's just . . . you don't know what that punk's done."

"What *has* he done?" Rose said.

Jarett ran his hand through his hair, and I chastised myself for thinking how sexy it looked. He licked his lips.

"Have you ever heard of Gus Knox?"

Rose and I exchanged confused looks and shook our heads.

"How about Baby Face?"

I shot Jarett a surprised look. "*The* Baby Face? The guy who killed all those college kids?"

"Yeah, him. AKA Gus Knox."

"He *murdered* people?" Morley asked, stunned.

"Oh, no!" I said, suddenly terrified for Lainie's safety. I vaguely remembered hearing about Chicago's notorious Baby Face, the troubled delinquent who'd shot seven ex-high-school classmates at a party. Sadly, it had been one of those familiar tragedies that tended to be forgotten soon after, especially here on the other side of the country. For the people of Chicago, though, it was a story that would never go away.

"Yes," Jarett said to Morley. "He's a cold-blooded murderer, times seven. Possibly eight now. He's been extradited to Washington State to stand trial for the murder of an elderly woman from Everett, and it was my job to transfer him here."

I shook my head in disbelief. Lainie was with that monster right now. "Are they sure it was him that murdered the woman?"

"They wouldn't be going to all this trouble otherwise. In fact, the case was cold until a few months ago when a sharp-eyed investigator found a DNA match on the blood found at the woman's house: Gus's. It was all over the murder weapon left at the scene."

"What was the murder weapon?" I asked.

"A twelve-inch chef's knife."

Morley dashed into the kitchen and returned a moment later, setting a wooden knife block on the table in front of us. "Well, now we know where Gus got the knife," he said, pointing to the empty slot.

Jarett's eyes widened. "Ah, this is all making sense now! Investigators found three sets of prints on the knife but could never identify them. I'll bet at least one set is yours," he said to Morley.

"And another set was obviously Gus's," Rose added. "But if Gus killed all those kids, wouldn't his prints and DNA have been in the system?"

"Remember," Jarett said, "We're in 2019 right now. He didn't kill those kids until early 2020. So, when that investigator took another run at the case recently, I bet he just about shit himself when he stumbled on all Gus's data."

"That's insane," I said.

"What's even more insane is the date the woman was murdered: September 11, 2019."

"Today!"

Jarett leaned back in his chair and said, "I'd been hoping to prove—if only to myself—that Gus hadn't been responsible for the woman's death because he would have been with me this whole time. But now that he's gone AWOL, it looks like he committed the murder after all."

Rose said to Morley, "Can't you go back in time and stop him?"

"Unfortunately, no. What's already happened cannot be changed in a timeblink. That's one of the rubs of this power. You're powerless to change the past. Or the future."

"The investigators are certain he's guilty, but there's one hiccup they haven't been able to explain. The age of the DNA collected at the scene. Extensive testing showed Gus's age to be more in the range of 21 to 25, not 18 as he was in 2019."

Morley said, "The Horvath Clock."

I gave him a questioning look.

"It's a test that measures DNA methylation levels to estimate a person's biological age. Horvath found th—"

I interrupted him before he went into a long, drawn-out scientific explanation on the merits of Dr. Horvath's work. "And my sister is with him now."

My *sister*, I'd said. Not half-sister. Not my dad's other daughter. *Sister*. Damn Lainie, anyway.

Morley nodded. "All right then. It's settled. I'll blink back to the wee hours of tonight and find out where they went. I'll take the Kawasaki. They won't even know I'm following them."

"Thanks, man. I appreciate your help," Jarett said, standing up briefly to give Morley's shoulder a couple of vigorous pats.

While Morley ran upstairs to change into his motorcycle gear, Rose refilled her coffee mug and headed into the living room. When it was just the two of us left at the dining table, Jarett said, "Look, I'm really sorry about all this. But I don't think you have to worry about Lainie's safety. Gus had a bone to pick with the kids he murdered. All jocks who bullied and ridiculed him in high school. Lainie doesn't fit the demographic."

"You're forgetting the murder of that poor old woman in Everett. Pretty sure she didn't bully Gus."

"Yeah, I don't know what happened there."

I sighed. "This is so messed up."

"Listen, I want to apologize for my insensitivity earlier."

"Insensitivity?"

"When I was so quick to volunteer Morley's services. I didn't even think about the danger involved," he said sheepishly.

I shrugged. "You're just eager to find Gus. Don't worry about it."

"Still, I must've come across as a grade-A jerk. Does time traveling make a person extra high-strung?"

"I don't know. Maybe," I said, smiling, despite myself.

"Well, again. I apologize," he said, raising Morley's *I SEE LITTLE PEOPLE* mug to his lips, his second coffee in twenty minutes. We'd all woken up far too early. No wonder everyone was resorting to caffeine to stay alert.

"Don't worry about it. We're all on edge."

Jarett's eyes narrowed, as though remembering something.

"Hey, I've been meaning to ask you. I couldn't help but overhear you and Rose talking on the plane. Is it true someone abducted your twin sister?"

I sighed and took a sip of coffee, making a face when the bitter liquid hit my tongue.

Jarett winced, mistaking my scrunched face for heartache. "Oh, no. I didn't mean to—"

"No, no! It's the coffee. Hate the stuff. How on Earth do you drink this battery acid?"

In the light of the rising sun, Jarett flashed me the broadest, whitest, most mesmerizing smile I'd ever seen, and I felt my cheeks go hot. I wanted to crawl under a rock.

Instead, I crossed my arms and leaned back in my chair. "Yes. You heard right. My ex and his lecherous father snatched my twin from a park in broad daylight right before our twelfth birthday. I finally found her five years ago, thanks to Morley. And timeblinking."

It was strange to discuss the ordeal with someone outside my family, yet oddly liberating at the same time. I'd obviously withheld the truth about how I'd found Isla, telling the police only that I'd followed Coop (or rather, *Viktor*) to his secret hideaway in the country and discovered Isla and her little boy in the basement. If only we could explain away our survival of the Flight 444 crash so easily.

Jarett pulled me out of my thoughts. "Let me get this straight. Your *ex* abducted your sister?"

"I'm surprised you don't know the story. Didn't you say you live in Seattle?"

"Now, yes. Born and raised in SoCal, though. Moved up here a couple of years ago."

I was thankful for the change of subject. "Why'd you move?"

"Two reasons. One, to escape the chaos and danger of LA police work, and two, to get a fresh start after my divorce." He raised his brows briefly, looking almost embarrassed about that last part. "Turns out the Seattle job is even more treacherous than the LA gig."

"Really? Seattle is scarier than LA?"

"I was referring to *this* crazy adventure," he said, twirling his finger in the air between us.

I laughed. "Yeah. Sucks losing your perp in a whole different dimension."

He smiled again. Tiredly this time. "Anyway, that's why I didn't know about your sister. But your *ex*? That's a story I want to hear one day."

"Deal. If we get out of this thing in one piece, I'll tell you how Coop and his father destroyed my family's lives. And how we rebuilt them."

"Wait, did you say *Coop*?"

I smiled wearily. "Secret's out now."

He struck his forehead with the heel of his hand. "No wonder you guys have such an aversion to my name."

"Turns out it wasn't even his real name, so—"

"Well, well. Glad to see you two getting along," came Morley's voice behind me, making me jump. I hadn't heard him come downstairs. But there he was, dressed head to toe in his sleek black leather riding gear, thrusting the sexy-factor needle way past Jarett's. I smiled. Order had been restored.

While Jarett followed Morley into the living room, I went to the kitchen to rinse my mug and get some water. The sun had risen just enough to give the lake a postcard-perfect orange glow, but I spotted something on the deck that didn't look right. A flashlight. Dark green. The kind that takes one of those big square batteries. It was missing the lid. And the battery.

I put my cup down and opened the patio door tentatively.

When I stepped outside, the trees were alive with twittering birds. Sparrows, I think. It was a cheerful sound that put me at ease. But when I stooped to pick up the broken flashlight, my gaze settled on a horrific sight at the bottom of the stairs, and I screamed.

Chapter Fourteen

WEDNESDAY, 6:40 A.M.

Lainie

I'd been exhausted from trying to stay awake all night waiting for the right moment to help Gus escape—so tired, in fact, that I'd dozed off soon after we'd grabbed the van and gotten back on the road. The van was warm and comfortable, and the day had still been dark. A perfect combination for inducing sleep.

When I woke up, the sun was just peeking over the horizon, and the freeway was humming with traffic. I glanced at the clock on the dashboard: six-forty. I'd only been out for about a half an hour, but I felt refreshed and ready to tackle the day. Gus, on the other hand, looked beat. The makeshift bandage on his hand was nearly soaked through with blood, and I wondered if minor blood loss could cause a person to pass out.

"Maybe we should pull into a rest stop so you can change your bandage."

"Nah. I'm good."

Of course, he would say that. I would keep my eye on

him, and if his head started bobbing, I would suggest it again later.

He punched the gas to get past a giant moving van.

"So, what did you do, anyway? To need a cop escort on the plane?"

He made a noise in his throat that was half-groan, half-growl. "You're not gonna leave this alone, are ya?"

"Well, since we're going to be together for the next forty hours, don't you think you owe me the truth?"

When he ignored me, I took my gaze to a white minivan traveling in the lane beside us where a little boy about Christopher's age was pushing a toy car around the back window. He caught my eye and waved his pudgy little hand at me. It was the sweetest gesture. But instead of waving back, I stuck my tongue out at him playfully, and he burst into a fit of laughter. I found myself wondering if he, too, would end up committing some terrible crime in the future that he was too ashamed to talk about.

"I was framed," Gus said, startling me out of my thoughts.

"Framed? For what?"

He lurched into the next lane without signaling. "Murder."

He let that information sit with me for a moment, and before I could ask another question, he said, "I robbed a bank, but a dumb security guard got shot in the confusion—by a cop—and I took the heat for it."

"*What?* You robbed a bank?"

This guy was getting more and more interesting by the minute.

"Tried to."

"So, the security guard died?"

"No shit, Sherlock. I said I was charged with murder."

"That's awful. What about the security camera footage? Couldn't that prove your innocence?"

Gus sped up again, making the minivan shudder as he

passed two giant transport trucks in the right lane. He veered in front of them without slowing down. The lead truck blew its air horn.

I reached for the plastic handle above the door and was reminded of a conversation I'd once had with my dad. He'd said if I'd ever had the urge to use one of those handles, I should ask to be let out of the vehicle immediately. Dee used to call it the *oh-shit handle*, and now it made sense why.

"Enough questions already. How 'bout ya just zip it so I can concentrate?"

Speed normally didn't bother me, but I'd never been in a car with such an aggressive driver before, let alone one who was obviously agitated. Even Dee's older brother was much more cautious.

To keep busy, I opened the console between the seats. Inside was a plastic cup filled with coins, a packet of tissues printed with ladybugs, and a stack of coupons held together with a rubber band. There was also a half-empty package of big, round chewy mints, to which I helped myself. They were a welcome find, considering I hadn't thought to grab my brand-new toothbrush from the cabin. I popped a mint in my mouth, stuffed two more in my hoodie pocket, and was reaching for the tissues to offer to Gus when he slammed the lid down, narrowly missing my fingers. "Quit snooping," he said. "Show some respect."

"Whatever. How old is your friend, anyway? Ninety-seven?" I said, mumbling around the giant mint in my mouth.

He ignored me.

I wished I could fall back to sleep—if only to pass the time more quickly—but every nerve in my body was on alert from Gus's erratic driving. Instead, I distracted myself by surveying the rest of the minivan, which I had to strain to see in the low morning light. Behind me, a knitted multicolor blanket was spread across the seat. On top of that was a pink nylon bag with "Keep Calm and Yell Bingo" printed on it. And at the very back of the van in the cargo area was one of those wheeled walker thingies that old people pushed around for balance.

The sight of it gave me a sinking feeling in the pit of my stomach. I swept my gaze past Gus to the busy road in front of us, trying not to worry about the implications of this discovery, but it wasn't easy. I cranked the window down and spat out the mint and took a few deep breaths of the chilly wind.

Gus barked at me to roll up the window. I wasn't about to argue with him. If he'd lied about the owner of this van, chances were he'd also lied about the nature of his crime. Come to think of it, he never did answer my question about the security footage at the bank and how it could've potentially proven his innocence.

Which led me to the next natural conclusion: that he was definitely lying about his crime and that we were cruising down the freeway in a stolen minivan belonging to a gray-haired bingo buff—probably a grandma with ten grandkids.

Gus never had a buddy in the first place.

Acid rose in my throat when I thought back to the house. We'd left the Goldwing there. Surely the old lady would report her van stolen, exposing the stolen bike. Which would be traced back to Morley. But I wasn't ready to confront Gus about it yet. I needed to think.

"We should switch cars again," I said to him a few minutes later.

"Wouldja stop freaking out? You're getting on my nerves."

I sighed and glanced at Gus out of the corner of my eye. Despite his grouchy mood, there was no doubt about his sex-factor. Dee was going to lose her mind when I showed up with this smoking hot twenty-three-year-old badass, and I couldn't wait to get home to her.

I grabbed my black canvas bag off the floor. But when I picked it up, my finger grazed a sticky substance on the hem that hadn't been there before. Honey from my tea at the diner? I brought my finger into the passing light to have a look and nearly screamed when I saw the dark red smear.

Blood.

Gus's, obviously.

Disgusted, I wiped my finger on the bag and glanced at Gus, whose attention was still on the road. As I studied his profile, I found my mind going places I didn't want it to go, and now I couldn't shake the main thought that kept popping up: *I really hope the blood is his*. But why wouldn't it be? The cut on his hand was serious enough to have soaked through the wadded-up toilet paper, so it made sense that a drop would've landed on my bag. Yes, the blood belonged to Gus. For sure.

I let out a long breath and continued rummaging through the bag, looking for nothing in particular, but my relief was cut short when I made a troubling discovery: the knife was missing.

My head swam. Gus said he'd cut his hand on it. But why would he leave it at his so-called "friend's" house? Instantly, the thought of going all the way to Buffalo with this guy seemed like the stupidest idea ever, and I wanted nothing more than to go back to the cabin. It didn't matter that I'd be in a heap of shit. Borrowing Morley's motorcycle was one thing. Stealing an innocent old lady's van was something else entirely. Especially now with the question of the blood and the missing knife.

"Can you take me back?" I said, trying to keep my voice steady.

"What? Where?"

"The cabin."

He ignored me.

I stared out the side window, descending into panic as I tried to come up with a compelling reason for him to take me back. But we'd been on the road for a while, and it didn't seem likely that I could convince him to turn back now. It was at that moment I saw a road sign that confused me. It said: Port Raven: 21 miles, which meant we were going in the opposite direction on the I5—north instead of south—which also meant we would be back at the cabin in less than fifteen minutes if we made a left at the next exit. I was instantly relieved. Didn't even care how much shit I would be in.

But when he didn't take the exit, my panic started rising again.

"Aren't we going back to the cabin?" I said.

He didn't answer.

"Hey, did you hear me?"

Nothing.

"Where are we going?"

"Fuck, kid! Change of plans."

"What does that mean? What happened to Buffalo?"

"Relax. We're going to Canada."

"What? Why?" I shrieked.

"Trust me, wouldja? We'll get to Buffalo. We'll be less conspicuous if we go through Canada."

"How are we going to get past the border without passports?" I said.

He shook his head as if it was a minor issue.

"Look. It would be so easy for you to take me back to the cabin right now. We're so close I could literally walk there! Just pull over at the next rest stop, and I'll get out."

Gus turned and stared at me, enraged. Over his shoulder, I saw the car beside us—a white Avalon like my mom's—drift into our lane, as if the driver hadn't seen us, but Gus didn't notice. I grabbed the wheel and wrenched it to the right. Gus over-corrected and swerved into the Avalon, bounced off it, then fishtailed when he tried to correct the other way. I screamed and grabbed the oh-shit handle as the van's wheels hit the shoulder.

I clamped my eyes shut. The van tipped. It rolled once, twice—

Chapter Fifteen

WEDNESDAY, 6:47 A.M.

I barrelled down the stairs to Sparkles's crumpled body. His face was pointed to the sky, his eyes wide and unseeing. His lips as dark as the retreating night. I shook him anyway. He was ice cold.

"Sparkles!" I yelled, as if that would revive him. "Morley! Help!"

With my gaze transfixed on Sparkles's gracelessly bent neck, I vaguely heard footsteps running down the stairs behind me.

"What the hell?" It was Jarett. He crouched down next to me and put two fingers to Sparkles's neck, checking for a pulse, though it was painfully obvious he wasn't going to find one.

"Do you know him?" Jarett said, standing up.

My mouth opened then closed. I did know him, but not as well as Morley did. They'd been neighbors for almost ten years.

"What's going on?" I heard Morley say from the top of the stairs. When Jarett and I parted to show him the gruesome scene, he hurried down the stairs to join us. Rose had come out onto the deck behind him and clapped her hand over her mouth, as if to stifle a scream.

"I'm sorry, sweetie," I said to Morley. "But he's dead."

"Yeah, I can see that," he said, his leather riding gear creaking as he crouched down and balanced himself on two stairs.

I locked my eyes on Jarett's. "Do you think Gus had something to do with this?"

"It sure looks like it. But it's not his usual MO."

"What about the innocent old lady in Everett? Was that his usual MO?"

Jarett shrugged. "He's obviously gone rogue."

"Fuck!"

"We're wasting time," Jarett said. "Morley, are you ready to go? We can deal with, uh, what was his name?"

"Sparkles," I said, much to Jarett's amusement. I couldn't blame him for chuckling. The whole scene was bizarre. The only thing missing was a monkey and an organ grinder.

". . . we can deal with Sparkles while you're gone," Jarett finished.

"It can wait until I get back."

Jarett looked at the twisted body dubiously.

"Morley's right," I said. "Remember, he'll only be gone four and a half minutes."

"Shouldn't we call the police?" Rose squeaked out.

"I *am* the police," Jarett said, searching Sparkles's pockets, producing a grimy orange radio-station lanyard with a dozen keys at the end of it. "And we don't need any more eyes on this problem."

I started up the stairs. "I agree. This whole thing has already gone way off the rails."

A few moments later, we were assembled in the living room, where Morley was pacing back and forth with his hand over his mouth. It was the first sign of worry he'd shown the whole time.

"We'll load him into the Range Rover and take him home," he said. "Then put him at the bottom of his stairs in his living room. Make it look like it happened there. We won't be seen. All the summer people are gone."

I nodded mechanically. "That's exactly where his cousin will find him in a couple of weeks. At the bottom of his stairs with a broken neck."

"I hate to do that to the poor guy, but it's the only option." He looked at Jarett. "What time did you last see Gus?"

"I got up to go to the bathroom around midnight. He was definitely here then."

"Please be careful," I said, kissing Morley on the cheek. He held the back of my head, keeping me there a moment longer. I threw my arms around him and hugged tight.

When we parted, Morley scooped a glittery orange helmet off the coffee table and slipped it over his head. "You'll need to turn around for the next part," he said to Rose and Jarett, who reluctantly complied.

Morley grasped the talisman between his fingers and zipped up his leather jacket. "Driveway, 819 Chapman Road, Port Raven, September 11, 2019."

And he was gone.

"You can turn around now."

"Crazy!" Jarett said, swooping over to the empty spot, waving his hand around in it. Rose gasped and grabbed the back of the couch to steady herself.

I smiled wearily. "Yeah, it's pretty freaking mind-blowing."

Rose let out a big breath. "Well, if I wasn't convinced before, I am now."

I laughed, then stopped myself when I remembered poor Sparkles at the bottom of the stairs. "I'm going to find a tarp to spread out in the Land Rover."

"I'll come help you," Jarett said.

Rose unglued herself from the back of the couch and

came around to the front, sitting down heavily. "You say Morley will be coming back to this very spot?"

"Yep. In about four and a half minutes."

"Okay, good. I've got my front-row seat."

Once Jarett and I were in the garage, I got him to pull a blue plastic tarp down from the top of the stainless-steel shelving. "Are you okay?" he said.

"What? Oh yeah, I'm fine. You mean because of Sparkles?"

He nodded as the garage door squeaked closed behind us.

"I didn't really know him. Morley did, though. Thanks for asking."

Jarett smiled. I popped the Land Rover's back hatch, and I watched Jarett spread out the tarp in the soft morning light. There was that stupid feeling again.

"That should do it," he said, turning without warning, bumping into me. We locked eyes. I quickly looked away and pushed the button to lower the hatch door, then scuttled toward the house. "Morley should be back soon."

It wasn't just me. Jarett felt it, too.

As I stepped into the house, I scolded myself for even thinking such a thing. Morley was going to be dead in two days, for shit's sake.

"Hope we didn't miss the show!" Jarett said, following behind me. Without even seeing him, I could hear a smirk in his voice. Like he was enjoying our moment of . . . whatever it was. I couldn't wait to get inside.

"Any minute now," Rose said, studying the spot on the floor where she'd last seen Morley.

Jarett and I walked up next to her when Morley popped into the spot he'd left vacant four and a half minutes before. After he peeled off his helmet, we all asked a variation of the same question at the same time. "Did you find them?"

Morley ran his hand through his hair and lowered himself unsteadily to the loveseat, motioning us to sit as well.

"You want the good news or the bad news first?" he said.

"How about you start with the good news?" Rose said from the couch, speaking for the rest of us.

"All right. I can probably cover it in thirty seconds," Morley said. I sat down next to him, and Jarett took the wing-back chair across from us.

"They didn't kill Sparkles. At least, not on purpose. Gus had a scuffle with him and pushed him away, more in self-defense than anything. I don't think he meant to push him down the stairs." Morley shook his head as he studied a spot on the floor at his feet. "Poor guy was just trying to protect my property."

I rubbed his back. "I'm so sorry."

"Me too. He was one of those people you sort of take for granted, you know?"

Jarett cleared his throat. "No disrespect, but isn't it odd that he was poking around your cabin in the middle of the night?"

Morley gave Jarett a look that made me wince. I put my hand on his knee. A warning. "That's how it works here at Sandalwood," I said to Jarett. "Sparkles looked after things."

Morley hadn't taken his gaze away from Jarett. "Sparkles was also a raging insomniac. Did his rounds when he got bored at all hours of the night. His poking around was a service to the community."

Jarett's mouth opened to respond, but I cut him off. "That's a relief. Sparkles's death was an accident. Were you able to follow Lainie and Gus?"

"Yes. They're in Port Raven as we speak."

"Awesome!" I said. "So, they didn't go to Buffalo after all."

"Maybe that was their initial plan, but for some reason, they changed their minds. They got as far as Everett, then turned around. But I don't think they were planning on coming back here. To the cabin."

I narrowed my gaze at him.

"They blazed right by the Sandalwood-Chapman Falls exit. That's where the story gets a little crazy."

"Crazy good or crazy bad?" Rose asked.

"Well," Morley said, chewing his bottom lip. "They're still alive."

"Good. 'Cuz I'm gonna kill Gus when I see him," Jarett muttered.

"You might not get the chance."

"What do you mean by that?" I said.

"While they were still in Everett, they used my bank cards to drain a couple of ATMs, then had a meal at a sleazy diner, then traded the Goldwing in for a late nineties Dodge Caravan at the north end of the city. They took it from someone's house."

"Alice Robertson's," Jarett said. "The murdered grandmother."

Morley winced. "I followed them to the highway—south on the I5 for about ten minutes and just before they reached the 405, they changed course and headed back this way."

"That makes no sense," I said.

"No. It's all very strange—even stranger when they sailed right past the Sandalwood-Chapman Falls exit."

"Where did they go after that?" I asked.

He took a breath and clutched my hand. "I'm sorry, but there's no delicate way to say this."

"Spit it out!"

"Shortly after they passed the exit, their van went out of control and swerved off the highway."

My mouth fell open. I felt like I might throw up.

Morley said quickly, "It's not as bad as you think."

I tried to speak but couldn't.

"They crashed?" Jarett said, his eyes going wide.

"Yes, unfortunately. From what I could tell, Gus was probably distracted. Bumped into another car before losing control altogether. The van rolled maybe five or six times, and I actually saw Gus fly out of the vehicle. He landed about twenty feet away."

"Oh, shit!" Jarett said. "Is he dead?"

Morley glanced at him impatiently. "I pulled over to see what I could find out."

"Was Lainie okay?" I said, finally finding my voice.

"I checked Gus first. He was unconscious but had a pulse. A weak one. But it was there."

"What about Lainie?" I shouted, practically jumping on Morley.

He rubbed my hand. "She was still strapped into her seatbelt, but she was in and out of consciousness. She had lacerations to her face, a pretty nasty bump on her forehead—probably from her head hitting the dashboard considering there was no airbag—and she might have fractured her arm. But her vitals were good. I didn't want to risk extracting her from the vehicle. Stayed with her as long as I could—until I heard the ambulances coming. Then I had to make myself scarce."

"So, you just left them?" Jarett said.

Morley sighed irritably, looking at Jarett out of the corner of his eye. "No, I didn't *just leave them.* I waited a little way down the highway, then followed them to the hospital. They were taken to St. Bart's."

"Did you go in?" Rose said.

Morley shook his head. "Didn't want to chance it. I know too many people at St. Bart's."

"Why would that be a problem?" Rose asked, still new to the finer details of time travel.

"I was in a timeblink," Morley said. "Remember, if I'd had physical contact with a colleague in the past, that person wouldn't be able to see or hear me in a timeblink."

"If they can't see you, why would it matter?"

"It would be fine if I were invisible to *everyone*, but think about how it would look if a group of my colleagues stopped to chat, and only some of them could see me."

Rose's eyebrows lifted almost comically. "Oh. It would look like they were talking to thin air."

Morley smiled.

"We have to go see Lainie," I said, getting impatient.

Morley frowned. "Not a good idea."

"Why not? We know where she is. I need to find out if she's okay!"

"Don't you think it would be a little suspect if you showed up at the hospital out of the blue asking to see her?"

I moaned. "So, what do we do then?"

"We wait until the hospital contacts us."

"That could take forever! How will they even know to call us? Oh no! I hope she has the sense not to tell them who she is. The last thing we need is someone calling her mom. And my dad! He's still alive in this timeline."

Morley rubbed my knee and said, "She's a smart girl. I think she'll figure it out."

I barely heard him. "Can you imagine?" I said. "*Hey, Julie and Cyril, your fifteen-year-old daughter is in the Port Raven Hospital*— to which they would say, *That's impossible. Both our daughters are sitting right here—in Buffalo, New York.*"

"Let's not get worked up about it until we know more," Morley said.

Jarett nodded. "I agree. We should wait. It will be better if we don't bring attention to the whole thing."

I said to Morley, "But if Gus is as bad off as you say he is, we should probably kick that skydiving plan into high gear and go straight to the hospital. If he dies, we'll be stuck in 2019 for good."

Morley rubbed his chin. "We can't rush it. So much needs to happen before we get to that point. First, we need to get the skydiving gear. Then you two need to learn how to use it. Then we need to figure out how we're going to get all the gear into the hospital, and that's even *if* Lainie and Gus are in any condition to use it. And if they are, will they even cooperate with us?"

I groaned. "This is a disaster. But we need to do *something*. Rose, any chance we can grab that equipment today?"

"Of course. I'll need an extra pair of hands, though."

"I'll come. Gotta keep occupied or I'll go nuts. You said two o'clock, right?"

"Yes. There won't be a soul in the gear room between two and three. Steve takes his lunch religiously when the team is out on a dive."

"Will there be enough gear left for all of us?"

"Plenty. We only need three tandem rigs, a couple of harnesses, and some goggles. I won't bother with helmets. We'll have enough to keep track of."

"Why three tandem rigs? I'm going solo," I said.

"For ease of teaching. Less room for error if everything's the same."

"Okay. In the meantime, let's cross our fingers that Lainie is well enough to share Morley's contact information with the hospital staff. And nothing more."

"That's our best hope," Morley said. "Most of the staff know me and would contact me right away."

Jarret stood up. "Even if she's not talking, it shouldn't be too long before the motorbike and credit cards are traced back to you. Are you coming to help me with Sprinkles, Dr. Morley?" he said, heading for the deck door. Morley shook his head at me as if to say, "What a clown," and followed Jarett anyway. "Right behind you, Officer Coop."

Chapter Sixteen

WEDNESDAY, NOON

Lainie

A bright rectangle of light flickered above me, unfamiliar. The room blurred in and out of focus.

My mouth was so dry, like it was coated with flour, and when I tried to lick my lips, my jaw throbbed. There was a sharp metallic taste. Blood.

And then I vaguely remembered a tumbling sensation. The sound of crunching metal. My head knocking against something hard. Morley's face hovering over me—a hallucination?

I reached up to inspect my face, finding a bulky fiberglass cast on my arm that started in the middle of my left palm and ended just below my elbow. As I laid it back down, a jolt of pain zipped from my shoulder to the tips of my fingers.

Oh no. I was in the hospital.

I'd been in an accident.

With Gus.

I lifted my other arm, surprised to see an IV line taped there. It seemed like a lot of fuss for a broken arm. Probably precautionary. When I examined my face, I found a fabric bandage taped to my forehead. It didn't hurt when I touched it. The rest of my face seemed okay, though my birthmark was pulsing, as it often did when I was stressed out.

A woman about my mom's age wearing baby-pink scrubs and a messy bun appeared next to me.

"Well, there's a good sign," the woman—the nurse—said as she pulled a blood pressure cuff off the wall and fastened it around my uninjured arm. "How are we feeling?"

I closed my eyes.

"I'm Josie, and I'll be looking after you for the next few hours. What's your name, dear?" I heard her say as she pumped up the cuff.

Even in my fog, I knew I shouldn't say anything. Especially the part about being a time-traveler from the year 2024. Better keep that under wraps.

Where was Gus?

Josie seemed to read my mind. "Your friend is in the next room. He's not in good shape, I'm sorry to say. Is he a boyfriend? Your brother?"

I opened my eyes groggily to look out the small window to where the sun was high in the sky. I must have been unconscious for hours.

"Well, if you're not going to tell me, Detective Douglas will probably get it out of you. I'll send him in when I'm done here."

My heart raced. Detective Douglas? Why were the police involved?

And then I nodded to myself, assured. Of course. Police always attended accident scenes.

After Josie gave me a drink of water from a bendy straw in a paper cup, she left, and a hefty middle-aged man dressed in a business suit strolled into the room. He approached the bed and gave me a warm smile. I noticed a metal chair behind him, but he didn't pull it over to sit down.

"Hello, miss. I'm Detective Douglas, but you can call me Sam."

I blinked at him vacantly a few times. My brain fog was finally lifting, but I wasn't about to tell him that.

"You know, you're lucky to be here right now. That was a pretty nasty accident you had this morning. Do you even know where you are, kiddo?"

I turned my head away from him. A sparrow hopped from branch to branch on a gnarled oak tree outside the window.

"How about your friend? The driver?"

I moved my gaze to the buzzing light in the ceiling, saying nothing.

In my peripheral vision, I saw the detective pull a notepad out of the inside of his suit jacket. "In case you didn't know, you're in Port Raven. St. Bart's Hospital. Maybe we can start with your parents' phone number? At least let them know where you are?"

Port Raven. The furthest point from Buffalo in the whole country. I closed my eyes and pretended to sleep, determined not to move until I heard him leave.

"Look, you're in a bit of trouble here, miss. Things will go better if you cooperate. Can you tell me who your friend is? He's clinging to life in the next room, and we need to notify his family."

Oh, Gus.

When I didn't open my eyes, I heard the man grunt and walk away. Before he reached the door, he delivered a final piece of disturbing news. "At any rate, you're both under police guard for suspected homicide. Let me know when you want to talk. I've stationed one of my officers right outside your room."

My heart dropped as he disappeared through the door.

Homicide?

My mind flew back to Morley's cabin and the guy at the bottom of the stairs. But it was self-defense! I had to tell the detective what happened. That the dude—a total stranger—had barged his way onto the deck and harassed us and then tried to grab Gus. And that we panicked and split when he took a tumble down the stairs. I would tell him we didn't know he was dead.

"Wait!" I yelled, scrambling to sit up. A searing pain jolted me in the middle of my forehead, and I sunk back into the pillow. "Wait!" I called again, but he was already gone.

Gasping and dizzy, I made to get up and follow him, but one of my legs jerked to a stop as I tried to swing it over the edge of the bed.

"What the—?"

When I tore the covers off, I found a black nylon restraint attached to my left ankle.

I took a few deep breaths, thinking it was probably for the best that the cop hadn't heard me call out. Silence was best until I could figure out what the hell was going on.

Nausea swept through my belly and into my throat. I flopped my head back on the pillow and pulled the lightweight blanket back over my legs. Homicide!

I had to talk to Gus. I had to make sure our stories lined up. It didn't matter that all of it was true—if even if a tiny part of his story differed from mine, we'd be sunk. Our biggest mistake had been leaving the scene at the cabin. Damn it! I should've ditched my stupid plan the moment that dude confronted us on the deck.

But it was too late now.

I simply had to get into the next room and talk to Gus.

Chapter Seventeen

THURSDAY MORNING

Lainie

My eyes fluttered open reluctantly. Outside, a strip of neon orange sunlight glowed over a children's park next to the hospital, tricking me into thinking the day was winding down, but the longer I watched it, the more I realized the sky was growing brighter, not darker. I couldn't believe I'd been asleep for over fourteen hours.

Why hadn't Syd come for me? Great. One more person in my life that didn't give a shit about me.

But before I got too pissy about the whole thing, it occurred to me that in order for Syd to find me, I would need to reveal my identity to that cop. But no way was I about to do that. At least not yet.

Now was the time for plans. Huge, impossible plans. But were they really that impossible for a time traveler? Was it crazy to believe that no matter what I did from now on I would be invincible? I mean, I'd survived a plane crash without a scratch and a car rollover with only a broken wrist and a few bruises. That had to count for something.

If there was any hope of getting myself out of this mess,

though, I needed to get a plan going. I scanned the room. To my right was a narrow cupboard, roughly the size of my locker at school. I hoped my black canvas bag—and with any luck, its contents—would be stored there.

As I shimmied over to investigate, the restraint around my ankle stopped me dead.

Right. *That.*

Just then, a plump, middle-aged nurse with a permanent-looking scowl on her face pushed through the door. "Oh good, you're awake."

She pulled the blood pressure cuff off the wall behind me and wrapped it around my arm. I didn't protest. Now was not the time for action.

"So, Miss Doe. Have we found our voice yet?" she said as she pumped up the cuff and looked at her watch. "Things will go much smoother if you tell us who you are."

I turned my focus back to the window where the magical orange sunrise had already dissolved into a bland yellow sky.

"Suit yourself. I'm here to get you healthy enough to leave, not to solve your problems."

I pretended not to hear her.

"All done. Oh, before I leave, are you on any regular medications? Birth control? Asthma meds?"

I probably should've told her I was on Fluxipram, but I wasn't about to admit that when I was being blamed for someone's murder. It would be wise to paint a picture of flawless mental health.

The moment the nurse left, I sat up and assessed the restraint on my foot. Thankfully, it was made of neoprene or nylon rather than metal, probably for patient comfort. Easy enough to cut through. I glanced at the storage cupboard, so close yet so far from my reach. It hardly mattered. My knife was gone. Probably ever since Gus and I grabbed the minivan in Everett.

I sank back into the pillow, surprised at my crushing

exhaustion after fourteen hours of sleep, but my body obviously needed it.

About an hour later, I woke up to find an uninspiring breakfast laid out on a wheeled cart next to the bed. I took a bite of the toast, finding it cold and soggy from the butter. As I choked down three bites, the food-service clerk rolled his towering stainless-steel cart into the room to collect my tray. When he reached for it, I snatched up the plastic knife. The clerk narrowed his eyes but said nothing, then began organizing trays on his cart, somewhat unnecessarily, I thought, like he was waiting to see what I did with my "weapon." I smiled at him sweetly. He gave me a tight smile back.

As I tucked the knife under my pillow, the door swung open, and the same cop, or rather, *detective*, from the day before strode into the room looking every bit as self-assured as a man who'd just won the lottery. But I was aware of something beneath the surface: desperation. He needed my cooperation.

"Hello, Miss Doe, remember me? Detective Douglas? Sam?" he said, smiling, sliding a metal chair over and making himself comfortable on it. His face reminded me of the actor from that old movie my mom watches every Valentine's Day. *Overboard.* Kirk Russell, I think. Or maybe Kurt. But this guy was heavier than the actor and he had a short haircut instead of a long, wavy mop.

I didn't return his smile.

Sam clasped his hands in his lap and raised his eyebrows at the lingering food clerk. "Need something, sport?"

The clerk glanced at me and bit his bottom lip. Shit. He was going to rat me out about the knife.

After he shifted from foot to foot a half a dozen times, he finally said, "No, sir," and pushed his cart toward the door.

"Weird dude," Sam said when we were alone. He leaned forward in his chair. "Look. I know lots of kids like you. I get your pain. Your loss."

I pulled the thin white blanket up to my chin. It smelled faintly of bleach.

"But most of all, I know that kids like you get caught up in the craziest shit, simply from being in the wrong place at the wrong time. With the wrong people."

He waited for me to react, but I resisted.

"You want the truth? I really don't want to bring you in," he said, shaking his head regretfully. "Because even if you didn't murder anyone, people never look at you the same way again."

Bile surged into my throat at the word *murder*.

"But the way things are looking, I may have no other choice."

All of a sudden, I couldn't get air into my lungs. Even when I sat up. Even when I tried to take a drink of water. The more I gasped for air, the quicker and shallower my breaths became.

Sam unhurriedly leaned over and opened the bedside table drawer. Then, as if he'd done it a million times before, he withdrew a narrow paper bag, the kind you find on planes for air sickness, and handed it to me. "Breathe into this," he said.

I did what he said, watching him out of the corner of my eye as I gulped for air.

He just sat there. Staring at me. No doubt judging me based on my hair color and piercings and my choice of makeup. Most people do. They used to judge me for my birthmark. I don't know what's worse.

"It's your choice, kid," he said when my breathing became less labored. "You can give me the information I need now, or you can force me to do it the long, convoluted way. But just so you know—I won't be happy about it. And when I'm not happy, you won't be happy, because it means plastering a photo of your banged-up face all over cyberspace."

I didn't give a rat's ass about my face, but I did wonder what problems the publicity would create for a time traveler.

"What do you want, then?" I said, pulling the bag away from my mouth.

The chair squeaked as he leaned closer. "Honestly? I don't believe you're capable of murder."

I stared him down. "No shit."

"But your friend in the next room. He's another story. I get you want to protect him, but in the process, you might land yourself in some pretty deep doo-doo. Prison even."

He let that sink in a moment or two. "Can we start with your name?"

I crossed my arms in front of me, which wasn't easy with a cast on one of them and an IV-line in the other. All my instincts told me to keep quiet. That it would be better if this cop didn't know who I was. Or who Gus was.

My broken arm throbbed in its new position across my chest, but I fought the urge to move it, certain the cop would read it as fear or panic. Or guilt. Fortunately, I didn't have to think about it too long. There was a gentle knock on the door followed by a young Black nurse pushing a cart full of vials and ominous-looking needles into the room. I cringed. Needles didn't bother me, but I wondered if a sample of my blood might somehow betray me.

"Grand Central Station in here, hey?" Sam said, then turned his attention to the nurse. "Do you really have to do that now?"

"Doctor's orders, sir," she said.

"All right. Get on with it."

She rolled her cart to the far side of the bed, and I allowed her to apply a tourniquet to my bicep as Sam sat back and watched.

"Can we get in touch with your parents?" he said while the nurse fussed with my arm. "I'm sure they're worried about you."

An image of my dad's face flooded my vision. And all the memories. How he'd soothed me after a tumble off my tricycle when I was little and how he'd cheered me along at my dance and piano recitals. How, a few short months ago when I turned fifteen, he'd taken me to an empty parking lot in his fire-orange Q8 and taught me the basics of driving. I'd told him getting my licence was a waste of time when ride sharing was as easy as ordering a pizza, but he'd insisted I would thank him later. I should have paid more attention to his coaching. Maybe then I could have driven *myself* to Buffalo and I wouldn't be in this mess.

Sam gave me a searching look as he pulled a cell phone out of a pocket in his jacket. "How about we do a quick video call to let your parents know you're okay?"

"Parent," I said bitterly. "My dad died a few weeks ago."

"I'm sorry," Sam said, rather genuinely, I thought.

When the nurse finished taking my blood and set to organizing her cart, I flopped my hand open in front of Sam. He gave me his phone, and I reluctantly punched in my mom's number, bracing myself. She was going to blow a gasket when she found out I was being held in the hospital for suspected murder. My broken wrist and mangled face would be secondary problems in comparison. I handed the phone back to Sam. "Good luck with that," I said.

"Your mom?" he said as the phone started ringing.

"Yeah."

"Her name?"

"Julie. Brixton. She's in Buffalo."

After the fourth ring, my mom's puzzled voice filled the room. "Yes?" she said in her usual forthright manner.

"Hello, Mrs. Brixton. I'm Detective Sam Douglas of the Port Raven Police Department," he said. "I have a young lady here who's gotten herself into a bit of trouble. Do you have a daughter?"

There was silence on the other end of the phone for a moment. "How do you know my name?"

Sam fished a wallet out of his pocket and flipped it open to his picture ID and held it up to the screen to prove his identity.

Before my mom had a chance to say anything, I heard another voice in the background, and tears flooded my eyes. My dad. I tried to snatch the phone from Sam's hand, but he yanked it away before I could reach it.

"Hey!" I said. "That's my dad!"

Sam's eyes narrowed. "I thought you said he died."

Shit, of course! It was 2019. How could I have forgotten my dad was still alive? It was the whole reason I was going back to Buffalo.

"What? Who's dead?" I heard my mom yell.

"No, no, Mrs. Brixton. No one's dead. I'm just trying to get to the bottom of a little mystery I have on my hands. I'm at St. Bart's Hospital in Port Raven with a young lady who claims to be your daughter."

I heard my dad say, "Port Raven?"

"Yes sir. Are you Mr. Brixton?"

"Yes, but . . ."

"Don't be alarmed. Your daughter is here at the hospital. She was a passenger in a motor vehicle accident on the I5."

To my left, I noticed the nurse shuffling vials around on her cart, stalling for time, it seemed, not unlike the food clerk had done. Everyone loves a shit-show.

"Oh no!" my dad said. "Which daughter?"

"Perhaps you can identify her for me," Sam said, turning the phone around, zeroing in on my face. "Dad!" I blurted when I saw him, tears spilling down my cheeks, stinging my cuts and scrapes. My mom was standing behind him looking both anxious and annoyed at the same time.

My dad shook his head. "I'm sorry, but that's not my daughter."

"WHAT?" I yelled at the phone. "Dad! It's me!"

But he kept talking as if he hadn't heard me. "I have five daughters. One of them went missing when she was eleven. Two of them do live in Port Raven, but they're in their thirties. And that girl is not one of them."

"Daddy! Look at my cheek!" I yelled, turning my face to show him my birthmark.

He didn't even flinch.

I glanced over my shoulder at the nurse who'd taken my blood, and immediately my dad's strange reaction made sense: He could only see her—not me. Great. It was true what I'd overheard at the cabin about being invisible to some people during a timeblink, which meant that even if I did manage to make it to Buffalo, I would be a ghost to my dad and Dee.

"And my other two daughters, Sarah and Lainie, are fourteen and ten years old, respectively. They're at school right now. I drove them there myself about two hours ago."

Apparently realizing the nurse was hovering to eavesdrop, Sam jerked his head toward the door at her. After she clumsily packed up and scooted out of the room, Sam turned his attention back to my parents on the phone. "So, she's definitely not your daughter."

"Not unless I adopted her when I was sleepwalking or something. How about you, Jules?" I heard him say to my mom. "Do you have a daughter you never told me about?"

I heard my mom cluck her tongue.

"Okay, then. Sorry to have bothered you. I still may contact you if something crops up. This gal seems pretty convinced you two are her parents."

"How odd. I wish we could help. She looks like a nice kid."

Sam said goodbye and tucked the phone back into his pocket as the last trace of his calm, comforting manner vanished. "All right. You'd be wise to stop jerking me around. Murder is no joke. You're gonna tell me your name. NOW."

"You won't believe me."

"Why would you lie? I'm gonna find out one way or another."

I licked my lips, finding a new gash I hadn't noticed before. "It's Lainie."

Sam shook his head irritably. "Well, that's a co-inky-dink, isn't it?"

I shrugged.

"All right, *Lainie* . . . Lainie Brixton, I'm assuming?"

I shrugged again.

"I don't know what to do with you."

As if to stop himself from throwing a tantrum right in front of me, he got up from his chair and stalked over to the window. "Here it comes. Fall. Best season of the year. Don't you love all the pretty leaves? The smell of rain on warm pavement? The cooler nights? Halloween parties? Thanksgiving around the corner?" He pivoted to face me. "I hope you get to experience those things again, Lainie Brixton. Instead of watching them on TV from a prison cell."

Just as I opened my mouth to tell him it wasn't our fault, that Gus had pushed the guy away in self-defense, the door swung open again, and a scrawny young cop wearing a wrinkled uniform walked into the room and approached Sam without looking at me. He produced a plastic bag containing a mud-caked cell phone, which I recognized as Morley's.

"Found it at the MVA site. Sorry we missed it on the first sweep, sir."

Sam snatched the phone from the cop's hand and brought it over to me. "Yours?"

I nodded.

"Thanks, Cash. You can go."

Sam moistened a paper towel at the sink and sat back down. After he cleaned the dried mud off the phone, I heard it ping to life. Luckily for him—not so much for me—Morley had deleted the password to make it easier for me to use, saving Sam the trouble of trying to hack into it.

"It's about time something went my way today," he said, navigating the various screens before finding one that made his eyebrows go up. "Interesting. Says here the phone belongs to a Dr. Morley Scott. Someone you know?"

He eyed me for a reaction, and when I didn't give it to him, he kept talking. "Oddly, we've determined this Dr. Scott might be tied to this crime somehow, but we haven't been able to find him for questioning."

I thought back to the crumpled guy at the bottom of the stairs and wondered if Morley—and the rest of them—had taken off when they found him. It made sense. Syd was so paranoid about being exposed as a time traveler that she probably rounded everyone up and split. Either way, it seemed the cops were investigating Morley for the guy's death. And my heart nearly broke in two.

"But we haven't quite zeroed in on how he's connected to the murder."

"It was self-defense, okay?" I blurted. "We didn't mean to do it!"

Sam's eyes went wide, registering equal parts surprise and self-satisfaction. "Come now, Lainie. Self-defense? You don't have to cover up your boyfriend's bad behavior."

"He's not my boyfriend. And I'm not covering anything up. We were provoked."

Sam rolled his eyes. "The woman was eighty-two years old, for God's sake. She was hardly a threat."

"*Woman?*"

"Yes, woman. Alice Robertson. Who did you think I was talking about?"

I looked at him blankly.

"Don't play dumb. It's not going to work. You were pulled from her demolished van."

Once again, bile bubbled into my throat.

"He said it was a friend's van!"

"*He*, as in your comatose friend next door? What's his name?"

"Cody," I said, surprising myself. It was the name of my first crush back in grade school.

"Cody what?"

"I don't know. I just met him a couple days ago. In the city."

Sam nodded. "See? Telling the truth is so much easier than trying to make up wild stories to protect your friend."

He obviously didn't know about the dead guy at the cabin. Or maybe he did and just hadn't sprung it on me yet.

"At any rate, Dr. Scott's phone also lists a "Cabin landline." Since we haven't been able to locate him at his primary residence, what say we try this one?"

I held my breath while he typed in the number.

Chapter Eighteen

THURSDAY, NOON

It was just after noon when the phone rang in Morley's kitchen, startling everyone, especially me, since it was the first time I'd ever heard the ancient device ring in all my time at the cabin. We were on a lunch break from Rose's accelerated skydiving lessons, which Jarett and I had been immersed in almost nonstop since four o'clock yesterday afternoon. I was happy about the reprieve. There was a lot to learn.

"Maybe it's the hospital," Morley said, jumping up from his chair.

Through the archway in the dining room, we saw him pick up the phone.

"Dr. Scott speaking," he said, waiting a moment or two before responding, "Yes, Detective Douglas. How can I help?"

He punched a button on the handset, then drew a finger to his lips to warn us to keep quiet as we all gathered around. A deep, authoritative voice came on the line.

"I'm investigating a suspected auto theft, a motor vehicle accident, and a homicide, all of which seem to be related to each other. We're currently holding a young couple in connection with it, and your phone was in their possession. We've also found a motorcycle registered to your name."

Morley said, "Are they being held at the police station? The young couple?"

"No, they're here at St. Bart's. The young lady claims her name is Lainie Brixton, but when we video conferenced her parents in Buffalo, they claimed not to recognize her. She's said little else, other than that her friend's name is Cody. But that's all I've got right now. Do you know these kids?"

"Are they okay?" Morley said, avoiding the detective's question, casting a panicked look at me.

"Lainie is being kept for observation. She sustained a significant head injury, but it looks like she'll be fine. Her friend, Cody, on the other hand, is touch-and-go right now. Do you know them?" he asked again. "Or are they just random motorbike thieves?"

"I don't know the young man, but Lainie is my niece," Morley said, shrugging at me, flustered, as if he regretted the lie instantly.

"Well, we're finally getting somewhere."

"I'd better come and see her."

"Funny, I was just about to suggest the same thing."

An hour later, Morley and I met up with Detective Douglas in the main lobby of the hospital where Morley introduced me as his assistant, Janice. I suppose I looked like a Janice in the cropped brunette wig and horn-rimmed glasses we'd picked up on the way—a necessary disguise to keep my identity hidden from both the detective and the security cameras.

While we rode the elevator up to the second floor to see Lainie, the detective filled Morley in on what his "niece" had been up to the last twenty-four hours, ending with her potential involvement in Alice Robertson's murder.

"There's no way she had anything to do with it," Morley said. "Sure, she might have 'borrowed' my bike to go on a joyride with her friend, but beyond that, I would bet my life she's innocent."

"I tend to agree with you. But the only halfway useful information she's provided so far is that Cody told her the van belonged to a friend of his. Not an innocent grandmother."

When he let us into Lainie's room a few minutes later, my stomach turned. I certainly had not been prepared for the seriousness of her condition. She was only sleeping, but her pallor and absolute stillness made it seem like she was hovering near death's door. There was a large square bandage on her forehead, and her birthmark was barely distinguishable among all the bruises and cuts on the rest of her face. One arm was encased in a fiberglass cast. The other was hooked up to an IV line. Her hair was a tangled green mess that stuck out in all directions, and when we approached the bed, she smelled terrible, like she hadn't showered in a week. If I didn't know her better, I would've pegged her for a heroin-addicted street kid, and my heart ached for her.

Morley jostled her shoulder, and her eyes sprang open. She gave me a quick confused look before turning her head toward the window. Good. She was playing along with my disguise and keeping her mouth shut, too. The last thing I needed was her blurting out my name in front of the cop.

"I'll step outside for a few minutes to give you some privacy," the cop said.

"Thanks for bringing us up to speed, Detective Douglas."

"Please, call me Sam."

"Okay, Sam," Morley said. "Do you mind if I check on this Cody fellow next door? If I were his dad, I'd want someone looking out for him, no matter what he's done. I can give him a quick examination at the same time."

"Of course. He's probably a bit older than any of your patients, though."

"I follow most of my kids until they're twenty-five."

"Oh? Is that so? Do most pediatricians do that?"

"It's a matter of preference. Some stop at twenty-one. And sometimes it's the patient who breaks up with us first."

"Well, I'll be. You learn something new every day."

"I'll go see him now and let my niece wake up a little more. Janice, do you mind waiting here?" Morley said, winking at me out of Sam's line of sight.

"Sure thing, boss."

Once the men left and the door whispered shut, I said to Lainie, "Thanks for not saying anything. The more anonymity we have, the better. It's why we left Jarett at the cabin, even though he wanted to come and see Gus for himself."

Lainie turned her head and looked me in the eye. "I suppose you're gonna yell at me."

"Now that you mention it—what the fuck were you thinking?"

Her eyes went wide. She opened her mouth to respond but changed her mind.

"Listen, I get you wanted to see your dad," I said. "I miss him too."

"No, you don't."

"Pardon me?"

"I heard what you said to Kendall."

I waited an uncomfortable length of time before I couldn't stand it any longer. "Feel like filling me in?"

"Yeah. You said—and I quote: 'I can't wait to get that fucking funeral over with and be done with this side of family for good.'"

I winced. She'd heard the conversation correctly, though she seemed to have taken it a little out of context. All I meant was that I wanted to go home to my own bed and . . . No. That's not true. I meant exactly what I'd said. I was desperate for closure. To be rid of Julie and Sarah. And Lainie.

"So?" I said.

"So? He was the sweetest, kindest man in the world! How could you talk about him that way?"

I sat down on the cold metal chair next to the bed and opened my mouth to state my side of the story, then stopped. Now was not the time to dig a deeper hole with Lainie. That fight was for another day, not when I was supposed to be posing as her emotional support animal. Besides, she already knew my history with my dad and how he'd left me dangling in the wind at my time of greatest need. At least, I was pretty sure she did.

"I'm sorry you overheard that. I was blowing off steam."

"He was the only good thing left in my life!" she belted out. "He was the only one who didn't judge me. Even when I dyed my hair. And got my piercings. Now I have NOTHING!"

I reached out and put my hand on her arm, surprised that she didn't bat it away. "I know you think your mom and Sarah aren't on your side, but you should hear the awesome things they say about you when you're not around."

"That's bullshit," she said, snatching her arm away, shuddering in pain.

"No. It's not bullshit. They love you. A lot. I think they just have a tough time understanding your struggles."

"Oh, like you *do*?"

"No, I don't profess to be a Lainie Brixton expert," I said, trying to lighten the mood. "But our dad must have had a damned good reason for throwing the two of us together."

She huffed and took her focus back to the window.

"Look. We don't have much time, especially now that Gus is clinging to life. If he dies . . . it will be disastrous for the rest of us. I'm not sure if you're aware of it, Lainie, but we all need to be together to get back to 2024. Gus included. If he dies, we're screwed. We'll be stuck here forever."

She whipped her head around to face me. "And why would that be a problem? My dad is still alive right now. And Dee. We already know what's going to happen to them. We can save their lives! And *then* go back to 2024."

"I'm sorry, but it's not possible."

She stared at me evenly. "Of course, you'd say that."

"It's the truth, Lainie. I was of the same mindset as you when I first timeblinked—absolutely convinced I'd been given the power to save Morley's life. You'll just have to trust me on this. It can't be done."

"So, it's true then? Dad and Dee won't be able to see me? If I go to Buffalo?"

I nodded solemnly. "Nor will anyone else you've ever had skin-to-skin contact with. All your friends. Your teachers. Your mom and Sarah. Hell, even that cute waiter at the Raincloud Café we all went to last week. Remember when he fist-bumped you?"

Her whole body went limp with misery. I knew exactly what she was thinking: That the power was useless. More of a curse than a gift.

"Anyway, back to the issue at hand. Thanks for not telling Detective Douglas Gus's real name."

"I wouldn't normally lie to a cop, but seeing as though I'm a time traveler . . ."

"Yes. You can certainly take some liberties. He thinks my name is Janice."

"What's with the weird wig and glasses, anyway?" she said.

"I'm Morley's new admin assistant, don't you know?" I said, batting my eyelashes.

Her eyes narrowed.

"It's for anonymity, which, unfortunately, is a virtue you lack right now."

"Sorry. The cop kept pushing me to get in touch with my parents. I should have just shut up, but I panicked."

"If it's any consolation, Morley panicked, too. He told Sam you were his niece. Mind you, it wasn't the worst lie, considering it gained us access to your room."

She nodded. "I'm sorry about all this. I wasn't thinking."

"Never mind. It could have been a lot worse. Imagine if

your folks *had* been able to see you. I'm sure they would have recognized their own daughter, even with green hair and five years older. That would've been a five-alarm disaster."

"That was freaking weird, seeing Dad like that. He was *right there*." A tear ran down her cheek, and she quickly wiped it away with her good hand.

"It's always a mind-fuck to see your loved ones alive again. I don't even do it anymore. Well, apart from Morley, of course. But I got lucky with him; we never cell-swapped in our natural time. That's the only reason I'm able to see him on my timeblinks."

"Oh! I didn't even think about that. Yeah, you're super lucky. Me, not so much," she said, rolling her eyes.

I sighed. "It's just a relief that you're okay. You look like shit, but you're going to be fine."

"I'm pretty sore, but I could definitely walk outta here."

"Best news I've heard all day," I said. "So, you're sure you didn't mention anything about timeblinking to that detective?"

"Of course not," she said. "Do you think I want to end up in the psyche ward?"

I laughed. "Point taken. Listen. Dr. Franklin said you would be here until at least Saturday. But now that I know you're going to be okay, tomorrow's the day. We're going back to 2024."

She slumped further down into her pillow. "Are you a hundred percent sure there's no way to save them? Dad and Dee?"

"Don't you think I would have saved Morley by now? Why would I leave him here to die if he didn't have to? He's Christopher's father."

It was like a light went on behind her eyes. She understood my love for Morley.

"Be ready to go at three. For the afternoon shift change."

"Why not the morning one? This place is a ghost town at seven a.m."

"There's a better chance of blending into the hustle and bustle of visitors and extra staff in the afternoon."

"How are you gonna get past the cop sitting outside my door?"

"We'll figure it out."

"Okay, fine. But I'll bet this wasn't part of your plan," she said, pulling the blanket off her legs, exposing a restraint around one ankle. "You should probably bring a knife."

"Fuck."

"I could work on getting rid of it before then," she said, reaching under her pillow, producing a white plastic knife.

"Good grief, that'll take forever. Especially with one hand in a cast."

"Got any other ideas?"

"We'll just do it when we come. I'll bring scissors."

"What if you forget? Are you going to let a small detail like that ruin our escape? Come on, Morley must be able to get his hands on something around here. A scalpel maybe? I can cut this thing off just before three."

"I . . . I don't know, Lainie. It's risky. What if someone discovers it before then?"

"What you really mean is you don't trust me."

She was right about that, but there was no denying her idea was clever. One less thing for me to worry about tomorrow.

"Ugh, all right. But only because it will save valuable time. I'll talk to Morley."

With some effort because of her swollen, split lip, she smiled.

"Don't make me regret this," I said to her playfully, though in my heart, I was dead serious.

"Um, I think I've caused you enough trouble already—starting with that big, scary guy at the cabin. I'm sure you guys already found him," she said, looking like she might cry.

I nodded solemnly.

"Did you know him?"

"Yeah. Sparkles. He lived a few doors down from Morley."

"*Sparkles?*"

"He was a good guy. Not the brightest or most tactful person in the world, though he meant well."

"I'm sorry. But he kind of attacked me and Gus."

"Kind of?"

"We were in the middle of sneaking out, and he came up and was all confrontational and wouldn't let us go. We just wanted to get out of there. And then he jumped Gus. And then Gus pushed him. It was an accident. He didn't mean to push him down the stairs. Honest! It all happened so fast. And then the guy—" She closed her eyes as if trying to block out what happened next.

I put my hand on her shoulder. "It's okay. I believe you. Sparkles was his own worst enemy. I actually had a run-in with him once."

"Y—you did?" she said, giving me an incredulous look.

"Yeah. I'll tell you about it someday."

Behind me, I heard a soft rap at the door, and Morley walked in as I turned around.

"How's our friend Cody doing?" I said.

"They weren't exaggerating when they said he was in a bad way. He's in a coma, but stable. For now. It will be a shame if he dies in this realm. His parents will never know what happened to him."

"No, no, no, he's not dying here. He can't. We need that mass-murdering asshole alive," I said, imagining what would happen if we were to be stuck here forever: I would be forced to watch Christopher grow up without me, completely incapable of interacting with him and the rest of my family until my dying day. And I would never see Morley again. Ever. He was going to die tomorrow, and I'd have to spend the rest of my life without him. Gus dying was not an option.

"It's going to be tricky getting him strapped to Rose while he's unconscious like that."

"We have no other choice," I said.

Behind me, I heard Lainie crying, and I went over to console her. "It's okay. We'll get through this. Jarett and I are getting the crash course from Ro—"

"*Mass murderer?*" she yelled, her face wet with tears. "Why? Why didn't anyone tell me?"

"I'm so sorry, Lainie. We didn't know."

Morley added, "Jarett was still working on normal protocol and wasn't allowed to divulge Gus's identity or the nature of his crimes to anyone. And he certainly didn't expect Gus to get away from him."

Lainie screeched, "I never would have freed him! It's all Jarett's fault the old lady is dead right now! And Sparkles!"

I said again, "I'm so sorry. But you can't blame Jarett. Or yourself."

A faded knot of green hair fell across Lainie's flushed face, and she shot me a sour look. "When did you find out?"

"After you took off with him."

"Come on, ladies. Let's not argue. It's done. What's important is getting all of you home before Gus's condition deteriorates."

I was thankful for Morley's intervention. "Okay, first things first. We need you to get some industrial-strength scissors. Or a knife."

He cocked his head at me, and I whipped Lainie's blanket off her legs to show him our challenge. "Right. That's unfortunate," he said, crossing his arms. "Oh, you mean *now*?"

"Yes, now," I said. "We're going to leave the scissors with Lainie, and she's going to cut the restraint off just before we arrive at three o'clock tomorrow. And before you suggest I bring scissors when we come, don't bother. The more time we can save tomorrow, the better."

Once Morley went off on his mission, I reached over to

inspect the strap anchoring Lainie's ankle to a bar under the bed. It was made of nylon or polyester, like a seatbelt, and she would be able to cut through it easily with a scalpel or even a pair of angled bandage scissors.

A few minutes later, after I'd gone over the plan with Lainie one more time, Morley returned, smiling from ear to ear. He produced a small tool from his pocket that looked like cuticle scissors and held them up in front of us.

"I was expecting something more . . . impressive," I said.

"What, like a machete? Don't let the small size fool you. They're bone-cutting forceps," he said, carefully handing them to Lainie. "Watch yourself. They're sharp as heck."

Lainie examined them with interest, then snipped the plastic knife in half as if it were made of cheese. "Definitely the right choice," she said, smiling. It was a relief to see her spirits lifted.

"Okay, are we clear on what needs to be done?" I asked her.

"Yes, I'll be ready at three," she said, slipping the scissors under her pillow. "But I still don't see how you're going to get past that cop outside my door."

"Let us worry about that," I said, turning to leave. "And Lainie?"

"Yeah?" she said, brightly.

I almost said, *Don't fuck this up*, but instead gave her a thumbs up. "See you tomorrow."

Chapter Nineteen

THURSDAY, 4 P.M.

That evening, on a rare break from our skydiving lessons, Rose ushered me upstairs to my bedroom and asked me to put on *something fancy*. She was waiting for me outside my room fifteen minutes later.

"Come on, follow me," she said, grabbing my hand and leading me down the hall to her bedroom, where she sat me down and began fashioning a loose but elegant bun on top of my head.

"What's all the fuss?" I asked, hoping Morley had something to do with it.

"You'll just have to wait and find out," she said.

I was glad to have Rose in my life. I hoped she would want to continue our friendship when we got back to 2024. *If* we got back to 2024.

As if reading my mind, she said, "What do you think will happen when we land? I mean, apart from the good chance that we'll touch down in a farmer's field in Iowa. What happens after that? One of us has a broken arm, another is in a coma, and who knows what else we'll have to deal with once we get there?"

"Yeah, there's a lot to manage. And the truth is, I haven't given the *after* much thought."

"We haven't even discussed what we're going to tell the NTSB and the FAA."

"Don't forget the FBI. I'm sure they'll be interested in the story."

"And everyone else. The entire world is going to want answers. How did five people survive a fiery plane crash without so much as a scratch, especially if the rest of the passengers needed to be identified by dental records?"

"You haven't seen Lainie. Or Gus. They're definitely not getting back to 2024 without a scratch."

"They're pretty beat up, hey?"

"I almost didn't recognize Lainie."

"That's awful. But I'm glad she's okay."

"Me too. As for what happens when we get back? It's going to be complicated."

"Even more so if the plane doesn't end up crashing."

I gasped. "I hadn't even thought of that."

"For me, it's the only outcome I've been willing to entertain. I had loved ones on that plane."

"Oh, Rose."

A knock at the door interrupted us.

"Come in," Rose said.

Jarett poked his head in the door. "They're here."

"Who's here?"

Rose went to the window and invited me to join her. "Come and see, Cinderella."

Outside, thousands of tiny lights twinkled amongst the poplar trees lining the driveway on either side. I'd almost forgotten they'd been there. Morley rarely turned them on, but that wasn't the surprise. In the driveway directly below me, a man in a swanky gray suit and newsboy cap was getting out of a white limousine.

"What's going on?" I said.

"Don't fight it," Rose said, putting her arm around me and leading me out of the room. As we descended the stairs together, I spotted my smartly dressed soulmate at the bottom, holding my coat open. Rose stopped halfway, allowing me to go to Morley.

"What's going on?" I asked again when I reached the bottom.

"Date night," Morley said, slipping my arms into a coat before I even knew what was happening.

"But we still have—"

"Uh-uh," he said, grabbing my shoulders and pointing me toward the door. I glanced back at Rose.

"What about our lessons?"

"You're fine. I couldn't have asked for a more dedicated—or naturally gifted—student. *This* one, on the other hand—"

"Hey, hey! I'm trying my best," Jarett said.

"Yes, you are very trying. Now, let these two go so we can try some more. I found a great video on what to do if you start spinning out of control."

"Sounds like a barrel of fun," he said sarcastically.

I felt sorry for the guy. He was certainly much more nervous about this mission than I was.

Morley took my hand and guided me out the door to the sleek white car. I felt silly.

"This is a bit much," I said. "A limousine? Is there an occasion?" I regretted the words the moment they came out. Of course, there was an occasion. Morley's last full day of life.

"Just want to spoil my beautiful bride," he said.

"Oh, to be your bride for real. I'll just have to pretend."

Morley guided me into the car, making sure my head didn't hit the doorframe on the way. He slipped the driver a bill. "Thanks, Burt. It's perfect."

"You're welcome, sir. Enjoy the ride," he said, closing the door after Morley got in.

"Where are we going?" I said.

"It's a surprise."

"Oooh, I love surprises."

"You deserve more than this, my love. I wish things could be different for us. But I shan't dwell on what-ifs. Let's celebrate what *is*. You passed your skydiving lessons with flying colors!"

"No pun intended," I said, snuggling into his chest. He wrapped his arms around me and held me tight. I could've stayed there forever.

"I'm glad your humor is still intact. You've been so serious."

"I'm sorry."

"Don't apologize. You've had to deal with one big problem after another."

"Lainie being the biggest. I'll bet her mom will strip me of my mentoring duties when we get back."

"See? There is a silver lining in all this," Morley said, pulling a bottle of chilled faux champagne from a cooler. He popped the cork and filled two delicate glasses with the bubbles.

"To us," he said, clinking his glass on mine.

"To us. The OG timeblinkers."

The limo pulled up in front of a quaint French restaurant in the nearby village of Fairview a half an hour later. *Dominique*. I hadn't been to this little town in years. Had no reason to. But it'd done well for itself in my absence with the addition of several new dining establishments—bistros, pubs, and family restaurants—as well as adorable little book shops and boutiques that I would love to poke around in. Maybe I'd organize a girls' day out with Kendall and Isla when I got back.

"Great pick," I said as the host ushered us to a table in the window a few minutes later. I felt like a princess. "I'm glad Rose suggested I wear something special tonight, though I would have gone with a cocktail dress had I known it was going to be *this* special."

"That black sheer blouse is perfect. *You* are perfect."

"Oh, my. You're far too kind."

"No, really. I've always loved that on you."

"Why? Because you can see my lingerie underneath?"

He rolled his eyes. "Well, maybe. But also because it's elegant. And it shows off your beautiful collar bone, which, by the way, is the most exquisite backdrop for the talisman."

I reached up and took the talisman into my fingers and traced the dragonfly with my thumb. "This piece seems to go with everything."

"Do you ever take it off?"

"Only to shower," I said, taking a quick glance around me and leaning closer in. "A gal never knows when she'll need to zap to an alternate reality."

"Well, it certainly came in handy on that plane," Morley said as a lanky young man with acne along his jaw approached our table to tell us about the specials. He took our drink order before scurrying away.

"Sometimes I wonder if I made a mistake zapping here."

"You'd rather have stayed on the plane?"

"No, I mean there were plenty of other days I could have chosen. But no, I had to come here and bother you when you could have been spending your last days in quiet reflection."

He reached across the table and took my hands. "Syd. How many times have I told you: I'm honored you chose this week to come."

"Even with a whole gaggle of other people?"

"Even with the gaggle. It's been a wonderful distraction. I've barely had time to worry about tomorrow." He kissed my knuckles so tenderly I almost melted in my seat.

We sat for a few minutes engaged in light chitchat, never letting go of each other's hands.

"Ahem," came a voice, pulling me out of the fairy tale. "Sorry to interrupt, but do you have any questions about the menu?" our server said, setting our drinks on the table. A martini for Morley. A cranberry soda for me.

We dropped our hands and encouraged him to give us his recommendations, which were exactly what I would have ordered myself: steamed mussels and a charcuterie board for both of us to start, and sole meunière for my main course. Morley decided on the Cassoulet, which sounded delicious if it weren't for the duck-leg part.

When our server retreated and allowed us to get back to our conversation, Morley said, "As for tomorrow, have you thought about what's going to happen after the plane crashes? After you and your gaggle touch down nowhere near the crash site?"

"We were chatting about that earlier. We're going to make our way back to Chicago and simply feign amnesia."

"All five of you?"

I leaned back in my chair. "How else are we going to explain it?"

Morley sat back, too, shaking his head. "I don't know. But you're going to have fun watching the authorities try to figure out what really happened. The possibilities would make great headlines in the tabloids: *Five Passengers from Doomed Flight 444 Abducted by Aliens, Subjected to Chilling Experiments* or how about *Flight 444 Survivors Admit to Taking Mind-Altering Drugs, Can't Account for Whereabouts for Twelve Hours.*"

I smiled at his attempt to allay my worries. "Damn it, Morley, this is exactly what you and I have been so careful not to let happen. Bringing attention to ourselves. Exposing that time travel is real."

He grimaced. "It could mean the downfall of civilization."

"Thanks for that."

"I'm not blaming you. You went into survival mode on that plane. I would have done the same thing."

"Are we worrying unnecessarily? If the government—or even average Joes like us—gets a hold of the power, would it even *have* an effect on civilization? We've tried to change events in both the past and future and discovered it's not possible."

"Or is it? What do you and I really know about the scope of its power, anyway? That's one thing I struggled with in med school, right until my residency. And beyond. That as much as I'd learned about the human condition, it was just the tip of the iceberg. I'm still just a mortal with a bunch of letters after my name."

I smirked. "You mean you're not God's gift to humanity?"

"Sorry to burst your bubble. No." He took a sip of his martini and set it down. "Some of my colleagues might believe they're divine beings, but they're deluding themselves. That's what I'm saying about timeblinking. How much do we really know? And what about Collette? The talisman belonged to her first. Had she been aware of its power?"

"Wouldn't she have told you?"

"I like to think she would have. But who knows? Maybe she was just as cautious about it as we are."

"You said she got the talisman from her grandmother. Maybe grannie knew about the power but didn't tell her."

"Or I'm the first one to discover it. All I know for sure is that the moment I went to the future and watched myself die, I stopped experimenting with it."

I reached across the table and took his hands. "I'll do everything I can to keep the power secret. With any luck, the rest of my gang will do the same."

"Sounds like you're worried about it."

"Only a little. They're all reasonable people. Surely, they wouldn't want to be responsible for bringing down civilization.

Even Lainie. But Gus. He's the wildcard. If he regains consciousness, he could blow the whole thing apart."

"He's a convicted murderer. Do you really think the NTSB would believe his crazy allegations that you're all time travelers?"

I sighed. "What other explanation makes any sense?"

"For you and me, nothing makes more sense. But for someone trying to figure out how five people got on a plane that crashed and ended up nowhere near it, I'm pretty sure time travel wouldn't be on the short list."

"Which reminds me, Rose brought up an angle I hadn't considered before. What if the plane didn't crash? What if it made an emergency landing or got out of the turbulence and stabilized?"

Morley raised his eyebrows.

I explained the obvious: that there would be hundreds of witnesses who could attest to five people vanishing mid-flight. "At least if the plane crashes, it could be argued that we never got on it in the first place."

"Oh boy. That is a conundrum."

I forced a smile, wishing I hadn't quit drinking years ago. A glass of wine would help calm my jangling nerves.

"I've been so focussed on getting us all back in one piece that I've been neglecting the more pressing issue: all the shit that's going to come *after* we get back in one piece."

"That's the spirit, my love. Switching your vernacular from *if* you get back to *when*. Having faith in the outcome is half the battle, one that I preach to my little patients' families all the time. It seems to help."

He picked up his martini and took a healthy sip. It was nice to see him enjoying his favorite cocktail on his last full day alive. Tomorrow at this time, he will be sitting at The Merryport Pub chatting with my 2019 self like any normal day. And then he'll walk outside where a maniac hellbent on killing his ex-girlfriend and her lover will run him down.

"You look so serious," he said to me now, pulling me back to the present. As present as it could be.

"Oh, Morley. I don't want tomorrow to come."

He laughed. "How do you propose to stop it?"

"I need some air," I said, standing up.

"Are you okay?"

"Yes," I said. "Don't worry. I'll just be a few minutes. Oh, can I borrow a credit card?"

"Uh. Sure?" he said, fetching one from his wallet. "This one has lots of room on it. Unless you're planning on buying a Ferrari."

"Nothing that extravagant."

Outside the restaurant, couples strolled arm in arm, cozied up next to each other in the blustery night. My heart ached. I folded my arms across my chest, annoyed that I'd forgotten my coat in the restaurant. It didn't matter, though. The store I was looking for was three doors down. *Nicolas Martin*. I'd heard lots about it before and noticed it when we got out of the limo. I braced myself against the swirling wind and hurried down the street.

The bell over the door tinkled merrily as I stepped inside the cozy shop where the air was laced with cinnamon, vanilla, and patchouli. I weaved through display tables of home décor knickknacks, candles, hand-milled soaps, and greeting cards and approached the clerk behind the huge glass display case at the center of the store. Exactly what I was looking for.

"Hi," she said, smiling. "May I help you?"

I scanned the jewelry in the case and pointed to a plain men's band. "May I see that ring?"

"It's an exquisite piece," she said, retrieving the ring and handing it to me. "Eighteen karat white gold. Made by a local designer, Grant Snowdon. It's engraved inside, see?"

"Oh, I didn't notice," I said, tipping the ring to read the inscription:

To live in hearts we leave behind is not to die.

I gasped.

"Beautiful sentiment, isn't it? But for a very specific buyer, I'm finding." She extended her hand, expecting me to give it back, but instead I took a closer look.

"Where did the saying come from?"

"Thomas Campbell, a Scottish poet. It's from *Hallowed Ground*, written in 1825."

"I'll take it."

The clerk's eyes narrowed. "You will?"

I handed her the ring along with Morley's credit card. "You seem surprised."

"People generally take more time to decide on such a significant purchase."

"I knew right away it was the one." It would be hard to explain that I'd ended up in her shop by the pull of outside forces rather than by conscious choice. I'd barely given it a thought. But here I was.

"I assume it's a gift? We do offer free resizing if it's not right."

"I'm sure it will fit him perfectly," I said, willing to bet my life it would fit one of his fingers just fine. Even if it didn't, he would only be wearing it for twenty-four hours.

"All right, let me just find the box," she said, pulling a drawer open underneath the cabinet. "You know, that ring has been sitting in my shop for close to five years. I'd given up hope of ever selling it, and to be honest, I'm a little sad to see it go."

"It will be well taken care of," I said, not knowing if that was true. I'd never seen the ring again after Morley died.

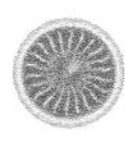

Outside *Dominique*, I stopped just shy of the window when I spied Morley inside. He'd pulled out his reading glasses and was studying the wine list intently, as though it were any normal Thursday night. As though he had all the time in the world to decide what wine would go best with duck and white beans. I sniffled and wiped a tear from my cheek. "Get your shit together, Syd," I said, eager to get inside the warm restaurant.

As if Morley had heard me, he looked up, caught my eye, and smiled.

"He's a handsome fellow," I heard a woman say, barely audible over the howling wind. She was standing in the restaurant's entryway, buttoning up a gray camel-hair coat and tucking a strand of shoulder-length brunette hair behind her ear. She looked vaguely familiar, but a daintily patterned silk scarf covered the lower half of her face, so I couldn't be sure.

"Is he yours or are you just window shopping?" she said.

When I realized she was talking to me, I said, "He's mine, yes."

"Lucky you. He looks like a nice guy."

"He is," I said, and then impulsively added, "I'm proposing to him tonight."

Her eyebrows went up. People can't resist a good love story. "Oh, congratulations! I'm always secretly jealous when the woman does the asking. I wish I'd had the courage back in the day, but I'm a hopeless romantic and had to wait him out. We would have been married four years sooner if I'd overseen the operation."

I laughed. "At least you got married. I have no idea if he's going to say yes."

"Are you kidding? Look at you? Young, beautiful. Full of bright-eyed optimism."

"I'm sorry, but do we know each other?"

She shook her head and pulled her scarf a little higher on her face. "I don't think so."

I wasn't convinced but didn't bother asking if she'd ever been to The Merryport. Nine times out of ten, when someone familiar crosses my path, that's where I've seen them before.

"I should get in there," I said, nodding toward Morley.

"Of course!" she said, stepping aside. "If you see my husband, can you ask him to hurry? It's freezing out here."

"Sure, what does he look like?"

"Much like your fiancé-to-be. Dark, wavy hair sprinkled with gray. Ruggedly handsome. About my age."

"Will do," I said as I opened the door. A rush of warm air and savory smells hit my face.

"Good luck with your proposal."

"Thank you!"

My tummy fluttered as I slid into my chair a moment later and scanned the small space for a man who looked like Morley sitting alone. But there was no one fitting that description. He was probably in the restroom.

Before I could give it another thought, our server appeared out of nowhere with our appetizers, gave a brief description of each of the items on the charcuterie board, then made a stealthy departure.

"Well, he's efficient," I said.

"He's certainly got some skills. Especially for someone so young. It would be a shame if he didn't pursue this as a permanent career."

"That's interesting coming from you."

"You mean someone with fifteen years of education under his belt? Listen, education isn't always the be-all, end-all. Who would fill all these hospitality jobs? They're just as important as careers in engineering or medicine or law. More important, I would argue."

I smiled. "Well, as a gal who's made a decent career out of bartending, I'd have to agree."

He picked up his drink and held it in front of us. "Cheers to that."

"Anyway, I'm sorry about leaving you sitting here alone," I said.

"It's all right, you weren't gone long."

"I would have been back sooner but was held up by a chatty woman outside the restaurant. She looked familiar. Probably a Merryport customer."

"Hm. I didn't see her."

"She was snuggled into the alcove to stay out of the wind. You wouldn't believe how brutal it's gotten out there," I said, steering the conversation away from the details of my conversation with the mystery woman.

"What was your big emergency purchase, anyway?" he said.

"Aren't we the nosy Nellie?"

He laughed. Probably thought I'd needed some feminine products or something because he dropped the subject and gestured to the steaming bowl of mussels. "Let's eat before they get cold."

My gut was full of butterflies, and it fluttered at the very thought of food. But I didn't want to ruin our dinner, so I spooned a couple of mussels onto my plate. After my first bite, my appetite returned with a vengeance, and we'd soon devoured the mussels and most of the cheeses, meats, and fancy dips on the charcuterie board, too.

An hour later, my apple-cranberry galette sat half-eaten on my plate, not because I wasn't enjoying it, but because I was so full I thought I might explode. Morley had one more mouthful of his after-dinner wine left in his glass, and I still hadn't built up the nerve to go through with my plan.

I was beginning to understand why people found proposing marriage so terrifying. But at least they didn't have the additional stress of being a time traveler. We were in a public place. There were phones—with cameras—all around us. And some people might find a woman on one knee in front of a man worth sharing to the world. So, to avoid the risk of being recorded, I'd decided to roll out the proposal quickly and quietly without drawing the attention of looky-loos.

"Shall we ask for the bill?" Morley said.

"No!" I almost yelled. "Not yet. I have something important to ask you first."

Already this was not going how I'd envisioned it. I didn't want to be rushed. Or nervous. Maybe I would wait until we got home.

As I looked up to the ceiling to gather my courage, I caught sight of the whimsical fairy lights woven into an English ivy strung around the perimeter of the room. My gaze lingered there for a moment before I closed my eyes and allowed the comforting smells of meaty stews, roasted chicken, and nutmeg-infused pastries to surround me. A lively, yet dreamy blend of saxophone and piano played over the soft chatter of other diners, mostly couples, and I imagined the two of us were in Paris for a romantic holiday filled with food, culture, and mind-blowing sex.

When I opened my eyes, all my anxiety was gone. My jitters had been replaced with a certainty I'd never felt my entire life. I took a quick glance around the room and reached across the table and took both of Morley's hands in mine.

"Oh, Morley. I have never loved anyone as deeply as I love you. My heart is full when we're together. Complete. I can't even imagine growing old without you."

He looked to be on the verge of tears, but I kept going.

"You've given me so much. A precious son. The gift of timeblinking. A love that will last forever, even if we can't spend our lives together as a normal couple."

"Fate has certainly dealt us a cruel hand," he said wistfully.

"But I've thought of a way to honor our love for each other."

I pulled the small jewel-green box from my purse and

flipped the lid open in front of him. His eyes went wide, but he sat and waited for me to say what needed to be said.

"Morley Scott. I love you. So much. Will you marry me?"

He placed a hand on my wrist—the crooked wrist from my childhood accident, which seemed to signal that he accepted me, flaws and all, and after what felt like seventeen minutes but was likely only milliseconds, he answered.

"Oh, sweetheart," he began cautiously. I stiffened and took a quick glance around the room. Fortunately, no one seemed interested in what was going on at our table. My focus dropped to my plate where the ice cream from my dessert had melted into a cheerless white puddle. I held my breath.

He stroked my knuckles. "I love you with all my heart. You know I do. The moment we met, I knew you were going to be a huge part of my life."

Oh, no. Was he really about to turn me down? My eyes darted to the window where I half expected to find the woman in the camel-hair coat laughing at my foolishness.

He went on. "I'm flattered—and delighted—that you want to seal our commitment to each other this way. But it's not possible."

I couldn't speak. A tear sped down my cheek. I wiped it away.

Morley squeezed my hand. "It wouldn't be fair to you."

"Screw that," I said. "What's the real reason?"

"I mean it. Think about how you're going to feel when you return to 2024."

I rolled my eyes. "I'm not going to stop loving you when I go back."

He sighed. "Of course not. But let's say you get involved with someone else. Like Jarett."

"Screw that!" I said again, louder. "Jarett? What the fuck, Morley?" I scanned the room. The music and conversation were just loud enough to cover my voice, and no one even batted an eye.

"Hypothetically speaking, of course. I don't really think you'll hitch your wagon to that doofus." He smiled apologetically.

"Look, I'm asking you on a purely symbolic level. According to the laws of this state, we can't even *get* married. You have to wait three full days after applying for a license. No exceptions."

This information came from the clerk at *Nicolas Martin*, who'd asked me what my plans were for the ring. I'd told her I was proposing to my soulmate tonight, and that I was hoping to find someone to perform the nuptials tomorrow.

He cocked his head. "So . . . what's the point of—"

"The point is that I will be officially engaged to the father of my son."

I almost added *Is that too much to ask?* but kept it to myself.

"Oh, Syd. I'm sorry. More than anything, I want you to be happy. But you can't be hanging onto some sad old ghost from your past."

"Sad old ghost?"

"Okay, maybe that was a little dramatic. But you're not thinking this through. At least if we keep things status quo, you're free to live your life as you please. With no guilt. No complications.

"Complications? There's the doctor coming out in you. I don't give a rat's ass about complications. What I want is you. I want to celebrate our love, and I want you to take this damn ring and stop being so fucking analytical about it!"

I pulled the shiny band out of the box, grabbed his ring finger, and slipped it on. It was a perfect fit.

He held his hand up and inspected the ring, obviously liking what he saw. My heart flipped thinking ahead to the moment he would read the inscription on the inside.

"I'll ask you again," I said, taking his hands down so I could see his face. "Will you marry me?"

"Are you sure you want to do this?" he said, gently, raising his brows.

I nodded fiercely.

"A hundred percent?" he said, now torturing me.

"For goodness' sake, Morley. Yes!"

He stood and came to my side of the table, then bent down on one knee. "In that case, Sydney Brixton, I accept your proposal. With all my heart."

I laughed through tears, completely aware of why he'd chosen those words and why he couldn't say, "Yes, I'll marry you." Because it wasn't possible. We'd have to settle with an everlasting engagement.

"I love you," he said, kissing the back of my hand tenderly. The couple at the next table raised their wine glasses toward us, and soon the whole restaurant was clapping and cheering. Not a phone was raised in our direction.

Morley stood and pulled me from my chair, wrapping me in his arms. When the excitement of the diners died down, he kissed me passionately, sparking a fresh round of applause and hooting and hollering.

When we finally pulled ourselves away from each other, he announced to everyone in the room, "We're engaged! And I'm the happiest man alive."

Chapter Twenty

FRIDAY, 7 A.M.

Lainie

Ever since Dee died, no one has expected me to do the right thing. Why would I start now? Someone's dear old grandma was dead. Sparkles was dead. Syd and Morley probably hated me. I was in a shit-ton of trouble with the police, and it was all my fault. I had to disappear.

As I pulled the IV line out of my arm, I made a mental list of places I could go. Surely the first place the cops would look for me would be in Buffalo, so that option was out. At least for now. Besides, considering all the trouble I'd caused, did I even deserve to see my dad and Dee again? Even if they couldn't see *me*?

One thing was certain: I had no intention of going back to 2024 with Syd. As for her bullshit story that we all need to be together to go back, does she think I'm stupid? I know she's just covering her own ass, afraid to face my mom if she turned up without me. Sure, my mom would blow a hairy fit for the TV cameras and probably threaten to sue Syd. But when the doors were shut, and it was just my mom and Stoopid Sarah sitting around the kitchen table, their chats wouldn't be about how much they missed me. They'd be about Sarah's outfit choice for her upcoming guest appearance on the Erin Daniels show. Erin fucking Daniels. Sarah's rising stardom made me think of that OLP song from a few years back: *Stop Making Stupid People Famous*.

I can't recall when Mom and Sarah's animosity toward me started, but it had reached epic levels after Dee's suicide—a time I was so mentally fragile I needed medication to keep me from going down that same road. How hard would it have been to comfort me instead of cutting me down?

A few months ago, for instance, as I sat minding my own business reading a book on the couch, Sarah rushed past me on her way to a friend's house. Right before she closed the door, she paused to wish me a pleasant trip. When I told her I wasn't going anywhere, she said, "Well, there's the understatement of the century." If she'd thought to ask about the book in my hands instead of laughing hysterically and slamming the door behind her, she would have learned I was reading *Like Water for Chocolate*. It was probably for the best. She would've sneered at my "boring" reading choice and rolled her eyes when I told her it was the Spanish version.

As for my mom, it's weird, but she always seemed kind of jealous of my relationship with my dad. Not in a gross, sexual way, of course, but I often turned to my dad whenever I had an issue at school or with friends, and the only time I went running to my mom instead of him was the day I had my first period (for obvious reasons). Yeah. My dad was the gentler, kinder half of that marriage. Always had time for my problems. On the other hand, I know my mom loves me—she's my mother, after all—but I wonder: is she even aware of how differently she treats me from Sarah?

Who knows? Maybe she'll reflect on all that when I've disappeared from her life for good.

As the dusty clock above the door ticked over to seven a.m., I was free from my restraint and fully clothed. By good fortune, the cops had left all my possessions in the patient cabinet. I took one more futile look in my bag for my medication, hoping I'd missed it the first ten times, but of course it wasn't there. I'd have to figure out how to get my hands on some later. Or just take my chances. So far, I didn't feel much different. A little headachy and tired, but that was probably from the accident rather than quitting my meds cold turkey.

On my way to the door, I stopped to study my reflection in the mirror above the sink. Ugh. Despite my best efforts, I still looked like an assault victim. I *had* managed to camouflage the worst of the angry-looking bruises on my face with my new fancy makeup, but I wasn't fooling anyone. It was nasty.

At least I'd remembered my black beanie, which was a bonus for a time traveler with neon green hair and a big, ugly bandage on her forehead. I briefly considered removing my facial piercings, but my shiny new topaz looked super hot with the eyebrow bar, so I decided to leave them both in.

All I had to do now was crack the door and watch for the cop to get involved in a conversation with a nurse or go for coffee or a pee break. Morley had been quite certain that it was rookie cops who got assigned to babysitting duty in these situations and didn't expect any problems during our escape. Besides, the guy knew I was tied up. He knew Gus was in a coma or whatever. He probably couldn't wait to go home and sleep or play combat video games or other dumb stuff rookie cops get up to in their free time.

When I opened the door a half an inch, I was surprised by how much I could see: Nurses' station B and a glowing Exit sign at the end of the hall. I even had a clear view of the cop outside my door, and I couldn't believe my luck. It was a young cop—a woman—and she was fast asleep! Snoring like a trucker. On top of that, the nurses' station was deserted.

I didn't hesitate. Hiked my canvas bag on my shoulder, pulled the door open, and strode right past the snoring cop. Right past Gus's room. My heart was drumming so hard I thought it would wake up the cop, but I kept going—careful to walk, not run—like I had every right to be in that hallway. For all anyone knew, I was a kid who'd been visiting her dying grandfather in his last hours on Earth, but I didn't have to worry about that because I didn't encounter a single person until I reached the front entrance. There, a rickety, gray-haired night guard was handing off his duties to the morning shift, a woman who looked to be Latina and in her mid-thirties. My mom always told me to respect people in positions of authority, being especially mindful of the female ones. In her opinion, they always had the most to prove.

"G'morning," I said, confidently to the two of them as they watched me pass by their podium.

I spotted a glassed-in bus stop a few yards from the front door and willed myself not to break into a sprint. Beyond the bus stop was a neon orange Lamborghini parked across the street. Otherwise, the place looked deserted.

"Good morning," the woman said. "Have a spill?"

"What?" I said, turning to face her.

She pointed to the cast on my arm.

"Oh! Yeah. Skiing accident." *Shit.* That was dumb.

"Skiing? Where the heck can you ski in the middle of September?"

I stared at her blankly, though my mind was whirring with possible responses. But nothing would come. She raised an eyebrow suspiciously at me, waiting. I was screwed.

"Traveling, were you?" she said, taking two steps toward me.

"No," I said, searching my brain feverishly.

When she pulled her phone out of her pocket, I blurted, "Waterskiing! At Sandalwood Lake."

Her eyes narrowed.

"I shouldn't have gone for one last blast around the lake, but the weather has been so amazing. Couldn't resist."

I hoped she didn't know that only small, personal watercraft and outboard boats were permitted on Sandalwood Lake. Not speedboats.

The old guy said, "Well, I hope you heal quick, dear!"

"Thanks. Me too. I've already messed up this year's piano program," I said, lifting my injured arm, wincing in pain.

"Awe, sorry to hear that," he said, while the woman looked down her nose at me as if to say *Sure you play piano, you punk.*

"Do you have a ride home?" the man said, obviously much more concerned for my well-being than the woman was.

"Nah. I'm hopping the bus."

He flashed me a look not unlike the ones I'd received from total strangers at my dad's funeral. Pity. I had a fleeting stab of panic he was about to offer me a ride, but he said, "Well, take care of yourself, dear."

I smiled and scurried through the doors, aware of his cohort's gaze on my back. Once I'd reached the bus stop, I took a seat on the bench and positioned myself sideways so that I could keep an eye on them. My mom had been right. The female guard was like a hawk, watching my every move. I had to get out of there.

At that moment, like a life raft floating toward a drowning person, a yellow cab rolled past the Lamborghini and into the circular driveway, about twenty feet away from me. I pretended not to notice and busied myself looking for some cash in my bag, not really expecting to find any. But when my hand landed on the wad of bills under a pair of leggings at the bottom, I nearly screamed. Morley's cash! I couldn't believe I'd missed it earlier when I'd been digging around for my meds. I decided to take it as a good omen.

My joy was cut short when I suddenly remembered the cop outside my room. Had she woken up and discovered me missing? All the money in the world wouldn't stop her from raising the alarm.

Just as I was gathering my nerve to make a run for the

taxi, a black SUV roared into the driveway and screeched to a stop outside the front doors. Two men tumbled out in a panic. The man from the passenger side raced toward the entrance yelling, "Help us! My brother's been stabbed!" As he rushed through the doors, the SUV's driver threw the back door open and pulled a limp and bloodied man out of the vehicle.

It was my chance. Before I could change my mind, I sprang to my feet and dashed toward the idling taxi. When I banged on the window with my cast, the driver jumped, obviously engrossed in the shit-show in front of him. He hitched his thumb to the back door, urging me to get in.

"You sure came at the right time," I said, jumping into the back seat, gasping when my broken arm took the brunt of my weight. And then it occurred to me I had no drugs to numb the pain.

"Where y'going?" the driver said, pulling away from the curb.

When I caught my breath enough to speak, I said, "To paradise."

Chapter Twenty-One

FRIDAY, 7 A.M.

It was dawn at Sandalwood Lake, but the day was so bleak even the sparrows hadn't come out to greet it. Gunmetal-gray clouds clung to the heavens, casting a dull, colorless cloak over the lake while powerful gusts lashed at the highest pine branches and hissed through their needles. It wasn't yet raining, but because I'd already lived through this day, I knew the deluge was coming. With a vengeance.

The weather didn't deter Rose from hustling us two protégés out to the deck to practice—for the thousandth time—how to get into our skydiving gear quickly. Time would be of the essence when we arrived at Gus's hospital room later today, and I was happy to have this time to get the sequence perfect. Jarett had finally passed the theory component of our studies last night while Morley and I were at dinner, though he seemed no less nervous for the effort.

As Rose handed me my rig, I caught sight of Morley—my fiancé!—putting away the last of the breakfast dishes in his cozy, warm kitchen. My heart threatened to break into a million pieces. Morley would take his last breath later today, and there wasn't a damned thing I could do about it.

"All right, let's see if we can't break your previous records. But remember. Quality over speed."

"Ooh, can't wait to win *again!*" I said, smiling wickedly at Jarett. I'd beaten him at a ratio of three to one since we'd started competing for the best time.

"Show off," he said, rolling his eyes.

"Enough trash-talking. This is serious stuff," Rose reminded us. She held up the timer Morley had given her and waited for us to get our rigs into the optimum position.

Every time we'd gone through this exercise, I kept a solitary vision at the forefront of my mind: Christopher. He was my whole world, and thinking about his sweet little face kept me laser focused on the task at hand. I wondered if Jarett's chances of beating me might have been increased if he, too, had had a child to go home to.

When we'd organized our rigs to our satisfaction, Rose started the countdown. "Ready? Three . . . two . . . one, GO!"

I wriggled into the leg straps and whipped the container—which was essentially an industrial-strength backpack holding the parachute—onto my shoulders. Next, I fastened the chest strap and double checked its integrity. Both Rose and the endless instructional videos she'd shown us stressed how important it was to get this part right. Fuck it up, and you could slip out of your rig in mid-flight.

I heard Rose say, "Leave it loose, Jarett. Always tighten the chest strap last."

"Shit!" he said, fiddling with the strap, costing him precious time.

While he was correcting his error, I was already onto tightening my leg straps, storing the loose ends in the flap, and adjusting my chest strap to the perfect tension.

"Done!" I yelled.

"Damn it!" Jarett said, having just finished tightening his leg straps.

Rose came over and checked the quality of my connections. "What's this?" she said when she inspected my leg straps. I looked down and immediately spotted her concern. My left strap was flipped.

"Oops!"

"Oops is right!" Jarett said. "Guess I won that one."

Rose gave him the thumbs up after inspecting his connections. "You sure did. Okay, take them off, and we'll go again. Better luck next time, Sydney Scott."

Despite my embarrassing loss, I grinned from ear to ear. *Sydney Scott* had a lovely ring to it.

While we stripped off our rigs, Rose threw out a pop question, which she'd been known to do throughout our training. "Jarett: What's the little pilot chute you deploy right at the beginning of freefall?"

"Easy. The *drogue*."

"Very good. Syd: What are the three functions of the drogue?"

Jarett got the easy question, I noticed. But it didn't matter. I knew my stuff. "To slow the tandem team down, to stabilize their position in the air, and to pull the main canopy out of the rig."

"Excellent," Rose said. "And what happens if the drogue fails?"

"No droguey, no floaty," Jarett answered, using Rose's lighthearted, yet grim little catch phrase.

"That's right. No droguey, no floaty."

"And if it fails, that's when you pull the reserve chute," I said.

"You two are superstars. Best students I've ever trained."

"Aren't we the *only* students you've ever trained?" Jarett said.

Rose winked. "A minor technicality."

As a cluster of dry leaves let loose from a birch tree and swirled past us in the wind, I said to Rose, "I'm glad you'll be there to help us at go-time."

"Who said I'll be helping? I'm going to have my hands full getting Gus into his harness and attaching him to my own rig."

Hearing this, Jarett gave Rose a worried look. "What if we pass out from lack of oxygen because we're too high up?"

Rose sighed. "We've gone over this. We were definitely no higher than eighteen thousand feet when we left."

"According to what? The crappy little entertainment system on the plane?"

"We'll have to put our faith in it, I'm afraid. Besides, if you recall, the plane was descending pretty damned fast when we zapped off of it."

Jarett wasn't convinced. "Okay, then. What happens if we're too low? What if we can't open our chutes in time?"

"Even if we're at five thousand feet, there'll still be plenty of time to deploy," Rose said reassuringly. "Remember the video I showed you about that tandem team who deployed at twelve hundred feet? I think we're good."

Jarett's shoulders slumped.

"Hey, what happened to that fearless traveler I met a few days ago?" I said, play-punching his arm. "What happened to Mr. I-fly-so-often-I-don't-get-scared?"

"We were on a plane. Not freefalling to Earth under a thin nylon sheet."

Rose said, "Granted, the situation isn't ideal, but you're going to have to trust that the Timeblinker's Accelerated Skydiving Course has given you all the skills necessary for a safe jump."

I laughed. "That's badass. I can see it now: TASC: Wimps Need Not Apply."

"Easy for you to make jokes," Jarett said. "You're flying solo."

"Would you like me to take Lainie for you? Because I'd be happy to if you're *that* worried about it."

"What, and have you mocking me about it forever? No thanks. I'll figure it out."

"Come on, guys. We have work to do," Rose said irritably.

"Look, I'm terrified of heights," Jarett blurted. "There. I said it. I'm terrified I'll pass out from sheer terror before I even get the chance to pull the 'chute."

"Have you been paying attention at all during these sessions?" Rose said.

"Yeah, sure. Don't panic, keep your eyes open, and pray like hell."

"That's not what I said, at least not the praying part. But it wouldn't hurt, come to think of it." She crossed her arms. "Are we going to have to redo all the theory? Because if that's the case, we probably shouldn't attempt this jump today."

I scowled at Jarett. "We can't wait another day. Not with Gus hanging on by a thread! Not without Morley here to help us."

"Do you really think I'm doing this on purpose? It's a life-long phobia," he said, glaring back.

I felt sorry for him. He had one of the scariest jobs on the planet, but here he was, paralyzed by a fear that probably fell into the category of the top five phobias of all time, and in fact, made my fear of spiders seem rather silly.

I took a small breath. "Look, I get it, you're afraid. We all are. But have you thought about the consequences of *not* going through with it? You said your parents are still alive and that you're close with your brothers. And their kids. Do you really want to spend every Christmas from now on without them? And miss going to your nieces' and nephews' graduations and weddings? Not to mention the pain you'll cause all of them when you die in this realm, because they won't even have your remains to bring them closure? It will be like you disappeared from the planet without a trace. And as someone who has gone through that with my own family, I know what it's like, and I would never wish that kind of agony on anyone. Especially if I knew I had the chance to prevent it."

Jarett's gaze went to the treetops, where he seemed to be searching for an answer. I shook my head in disbelief. Was his fear of heights really more powerful than the need to be with his loved ones? Or to stop me from being with mine?

I tried a different tactic. "If you prevent me from holding my son in my arms again, you're gonna discover a whole new kind of phobia: the fear of being stalked by an irate, bereaved mother for the rest of your life."

Out of the corner of my eye, I saw Rose wipe a tear from her cheek. Shit. Eli. How could I be so insensitive? I flashed her an apologetic look, which she dismissed with a smile and a nod. "If you were smart," she said to Jarett, "you'd avoid contracting Sydaphobia at all costs."

He groaned and rolled his eyes at me. "Don't worry. You had me at Christmas."

I gave him a quick appreciative smile as Rose handed us our rigs and started the timer.

Chapter Twenty-Two

FRIDAY, 7:45 A.M.

Lainie

"Paradise?" the taxi driver said. "Is that a new restaurant or something?"

"No. Harborfront Towers." I noticed his eyebrows rise in the rear-view mirror. "I don't know the address, though."

"That's okay, miss. I know the place."

He was probably wondering what a beat-up punk like me would be doing at a fancy condo overlooking the harbor, which truly was a slice of paradise. Little did he know that I'd had a bit of luck on Wednesday morning when I grabbed Morley's credit cards from his wallet and later discovered the key card among them. Now I had easy access to the condo's main door and was almost certain Syd's birthdate would gain me entry to the unit itself. If not, I'd have to rethink my plan, which really wasn't much of a plan at all, if I was being honest with myself. I just needed a quiet place to think. And maybe find some powerful painkillers.

As the city rushed by my window, I wondered if I could restart my life here. Port Raven 2019 had a distinct small-town vibe to it, with only three movie theatres, two hospitals, and a ton of family-style restaurants. It was slowly being revived, though. Even during my family's last visit here in 2023, my dad mentioned a building boom had started, causing a flurry of old warehouses and department stores to be repurposed as upscale micro-lofts. He'd described the tiny three-hundred-square-foot units as "ridiculously expensive, even for Port Raven," but he was glad the city was growing up. He said it had been set in its old ways too long and that it was one of the reasons he'd given up on it and moved to Buffalo. That, and because it's where my mom lived.

When we arrived at the Towers—which was in fact only one building and hardly a tower at all with only eighteen floors—I paid the driver cash, then slipped him an extra fifty. "You didn't see me."

He nodded vigorously, probably thankful for the extra money, but he also might have assumed I was fleeing some sort of domestic abuse situation. A mashed face and broken arm had its advantages.

When I let myself into the building, the lobby was bustling with smartly dressed businesspeople leaving for work. I kept my head down as I made my way to the elevator, where the door dinged open and a group of passengers spilled out. None of them seemed to notice me. I briefly wondered if I'd somehow become invisible in this parallel dimension until I stepped inside the elevator and caught sight of my reflection in the mirrored walls. I looked awful. Worse than awful. Maybe it was the bright halogen pot lights, but my hastily applied makeup seemed to accentuate all the scrapes and bruises rather than conceal them. The fact that no one even gave me a second glance said a lot about the world I live in.

As the elevator doors began sliding shut, a hand appeared in the gap, forcing them open, and an elegant middle-aged woman with shoulder-length brown hair hurried inside. I recognized her black crocodile ankle boots as belonging to one of the passengers that had just exited. My pulse quickened.

Maybe people were a little more observant than I'd given them credit for.

"Forgot my lunch," she said, reaching to hit the eighteenth-floor button, surprised to see it had already been pressed. There were only four penthouse units. During my two previous visits—once a few days ago, and once in 2023 when we were in town for my dad's birthday—I hadn't met any of the neighbors.

"I can't afford another meal out this month. My husband will kill me."

I gave the woman a tight-lipped smile, wincing when the gash on my lip broke open. Noticing this, she fished a packet of tissues out of her purse and handed them to me, pointing to her own lip by way of explaining. "It's bleeding."

Not wanting to make a scene, I reached up to take a tissue, but she pushed the whole pack into my hand and said, "No, no. Take it. I have lots."

"Thanks," I said.

As we rode up, she asked me if everything was okay.

I gave her the same bullshit waterskiing story I'd told the security guards at the hospital.

"Who are you here to see?" she said, catching me short. "Alison Beatty in 1801?"

"My uncle. Morley. I forget the unit number. The one at the end facing the harbor."

"I know Dr. Scott well. Didn't know he had a niece. Huh, the things you learn in a day," she said, more surprised than doubtful, it seemed.

When the doors parted on the eighteenth floor, I dashed out and headed down the hall. "Thanks for these," I said, holding up the packet of tissues.

"Glad to help. I hope you feel better soon," she said, pausing in front of the elevator doors as they scraped shut. She was watching me, possibly aware that my "uncle" wasn't home.

I punched Syd's birthday into the keypad, praying Morley was as predictable with his passwords as he'd been previously. But I was met with a series of red flashing lights and a soft beeping noise. The readout said INVALID CODE.

Trying to keep calm, I tried again, thinking I'd mistyped the number. The red lights flashed again. The beeping was a little louder this time. Quicker.

"I hope he didn't change his code and forget to tell me," I said, laughing nervously.

Out of the corner of my eye, I watched the woman start digging through her purse. Probably for her cellphone to call the cops.

Breathe, idiot. You got this. And then, as my finger hovered over the keypad, I realized my mistake: I'd been typing in 10-10-86 instead of 10-10-87. Slowly, deliberately—acutely aware that a third mistake might lock me out for good—I typed in the numbers.

The keypad glowed green, and I heard a click.

I turned to the woman. "That was close. Entered the number wrong. Twice!"

She stopped poking around in her purse and let out a small breath. "Good thing you figured it out. I was about to give Dr. Scott a call for you."

What a busybody. Just what I needed—Morley finding out I was here.

"Lucky we didn't have to bother him. He's trying to unwind at his cabin for a few days."

Her shoulders relaxed. "Good for him. I always tell him he should get out there more often."

When I closed the door behind me, my knees went weak. I hadn't realized how tense I'd been. On quivery legs, I turned to look through the peephole. Not too surprisingly, I saw the woman press the elevator button instead of going to her apartment to get her lunch, confirming I wasn't as invisible as I'd imagined. Or hoped.

I kicked off my shoes and padded over to the floor-to-ceiling windows where thick, gray clouds hung level with Morley's rooftop deck. A light rain had started in the time it took me to let myself into the apartment, and I was glad to be warm and dry, watching lively streaks of water zipping down the glass.

When a stabbing pain coursed through my injured arm, I began a search for painkillers that Morley—the doctor—would surely have in good supply. But I was wrong. Apart from the usual soap and shaving cream and toothpaste, I found only a freakishly excessive amount of toilet paper in each of the three bathrooms. I laughed despite my pain. Maybe he'd timeblinked to 2020 and saw the chaos unfolding all over the world and stocked up. He would've done that for Syd.

Hoping he kept his drugs in the kitchen like my grandma used to do, I opened every cupboard in there too, finding only a few cans of tomato soup, a box of cereal, and a package of oatmeal cookies. There was one TV dinner in the freezer, which would come in handy later. I hoped it wasn't freezer burnt.

I ripped open the package of cookies and scarfed five of them back like a starving dog, wondering why Morley's cupboards were so bare. Then it hit me: he'd probably been getting rid of stuff ahead of his upcoming accident at the pub. Oh, no. Morley was going to die.

Tonight.

Shit. Two more people gone—Sparkles and now Morley—with a possible third on the horizon: Gus. I didn't know any of them very well, but I'd been around Morley enough to care what happened to him. He's like the super cool uncle who would let you get away with murder.

Gus is the evil cousin who would actually go through with it.

I pushed back an urge to throw up when I remembered

what he'd done to that poor old lady and how he'd killed other people before.

I could have been next.

Feeling exhausted and a little sorry for myself, I shuffled to the couch and crawled under the fuzziest, softest wool blanket I'd ever touched and fell asleep immediately.

According to the clock on the mantle, I'd been asleep for three hours, and it took me a bunch of bleary blinks to remember where I was: Syd's condo in the city, which was technically still Morley's condo in this timeline.

Morley's empty, drab, neutral-toned condo.

When my family visited that summer, I remember how welcoming and homey it had felt. Toys were strewn over the floor and coloring books lay open on the coffee table next to broken crayons and half-empty cups of orange juice and milk.

By then, Syd had covered the dreary gray walls with a coat of warm white paint that reminded me of French vanilla ice cream. Above the hutch in the dining room, she'd hung what looked like a discount-store print of a sunflower garden set against a vibrant blue sky. It had lifted my spirits immediately. The walls in Christopher's room were just as cheery, with bunny and puppy posters taped up alongside the crayon scribblings of a toddler who didn't know the difference between paper and drywall yet. Syd had made no apologies for the scribbles, saying only that she didn't have the heart to paint over them.

Half asleep, I shuffled toward the patio, which was separated from the living area by a bank of massive glass doors—the kind that telescope into each other. As I reached for the door, my mind flooded with a memory of that summer visit when the day had been warm and Syd pushed all the glass panels open to create one giant living space.

The kids were splashing around in the hot tub and some sort of jazzy music was playing in the background. At the time, I thought the music choice was pretentious, but in retrospect, it fit the setting and the mood of the day. I remember my dad being blown away by the apartment. He couldn't stop talking about it when we got home, too. But what stuck with me most was his utter joy when Syd—having heard about his barbecuing skills from my mom—asked him to cook a meal for all of us in the fancy outdoor kitchen. Yeah, it had been a great day. I'd really enjoyed myself. Too bad I'd never admitted it to my dad.

As if to punish me, when I slid one of the panels open now, an icy spray of rain blasted me in the face. But it was just what I needed to pull me back to the present and chase off the dregs of sleep.

In my bare feet, I darted under the covered section of the patio and made my way to the edge where a waist-high concrete planter box ran along the entire perimeter of the deck. I wondered why the builder hadn't installed a glass-paneled railing there instead, which would have allowed spectacular views of the harbor and city. But just as quickly as that thought surfaced, it disappeared. Keeping forty feet of glass clean in Port Raven's drizzly climate would be a nightmare.

Out on the harbor, rolling whitecaps battered little commuter ferries tethered to the dock, their scheduled trips obviously having been cancelled because of the turbulent weather. In the streets below, people dashed into alcoves to get out of the wind and rain, most of them wearing waterproof coats and carrying closed umbrellas at their sides. The brave ones who dared open their umbrellas ended up with inverted teepees thrashing around in the wind, which was amusing to watch. I didn't mind crazy weather like this. It made me feel alive.

When the bone-chilling wind and rain finally got the best of me, I went back inside. The temperature in the condo wasn't that much warmer, but I had no energy to figure out the heating system. Instead, I lowered myself to the couch and pulled the cozy blanket back over my shoulders.

My arm pain had worsened to epic levels, and I briefly considered going out to look for a pharmacy but decided it was too risky. The cops would be looking for me by now. I would go out when it got dark. Maybe I'd just keep going afterwards. Maybe hit the bus station and jump on a random Greyhound and start my life over in a completely different place. I could live in a teen shelter until I found a job and made enough money to rent an apartment with a roommate or two.

But for now, I was stuck at Morley's chilly condo. It wasn't just physically cold. It was utterly lifeless. As though it were mourning Morley's upcoming death. I figured part of its hollow quality stemmed from the lack of Morley's personal possessions, which he'd obviously been getting rid of lately. But that wasn't all of it. The same ominous feeling had overcome me a few days ago when Syd, Morley, and I stopped in to pick up the Range Rover.

Warm morning light streamed through all the windows, and Syd and Morley were in the kitchen fixing a broken faucet while I sat right here on the couch listening to Rise Against on Morley's phone. I'd been staring at the enormous oil painting above the hutch in the dining room—the painting that Syd would eventually replace with the inexpensive sunflower print—when I was overcome with grief. And I began crying. Uncontrollably.

When Syd and Morley rushed over to find out what was wrong, I'd told them I missed my dad. It was true. I missed my dad, of course I did. But I didn't tell them the real reason because they would have thought it was stupid: the painting. I couldn't explain it, but no other work of art had ever touched me so deeply. No poem, no image. Not even a song.

And as I sat on the couch looking at it now, I was moved to tears again.

It's not even a particularly interesting image. There are no people or animals in it. There's barely any color. It's just a simple, misty lake framed by shadowy fir trees and a dull, gray sky. There's a bright red canoe adrift in the middle of the lake. The canoe is empty.

"I miss you so much, Dad," I said out loud.

A tear trickled down my cheek, and I whisked it away with my good hand. I couldn't lose my shit now, especially without access to my happy pills.

It was then that I noticed Morley's liquor collection across the room. It was housed in a big, metal, egg-shaped cabinet in steampunk style with riveted seams and a door that looked like a ship's portal. I narrowed my eyes at the attractively shaped bottles and the clear or amber-colored contents within, and my stomach dropped. The one and only time I'd experimented with drinking, it'd come with terrible consequences.

It had been a mild Friday night in May. Dee and I had just come out of the corner store with a bag of chocolate bars and soda when a car full of older boys—whom we'd recognized from our school's football team—pulled up beside us. Thanks to our nerdy ways, we weren't the most popular kids at school, so when they invited us to a party a few blocks over, we'd looked at each other with wide eyes that said, "Hell yeah!"

We'd squeezed into their little red sports car—me on one lap, Dee on another—and giggled the whole three-minute drive there.

On our arrival, we discovered it was just the five of us. The three jocks, me, and Dee.

I remember nothing past my third drink. However, I woke up in my own bed at eight o'clock the next morning with a massive headache, an overwhelming urge to vomit, and a ton of questions I was afraid to ask out loud. How had I gotten there? Did my parents know anything? How had I gotten out of my clothes and into my Poppy 17 concert tee? Where was my phone? Where the hell was Dee? Oh, no. Dee.

At eight-fifteen, my mom didn't even bother knocking before barging into my room. Her face was grim.

"Well, you're still alive," she said, without a hint of sympathy. "Get dressed and come downstairs. *Now*."

As the door slammed behind her, I jumped up and ran over to my garbage can, where I threw up all over my discarded algebra worksheets.

I'd had reason to be sick. Thanks to Dee's sister knowing where I lived, her parents had shown up on our front doorstep and were sitting quietly on the couch when I entered the living room a few minutes later. Dee hadn't come home.

I'd been just as freaked out as they were, so I spilled it all: where we'd gone, names and descriptions of the guys we'd been with, and how much we'd had to drink, which was really anybody's guess.

Dee's parents had stormed out of our house, warning me not to contact my friend ever again, effectively blaming me for the whole disaster. An hour later, they called my mom to report finding Dee at the house where I'd left her, naked and passed out in an upstairs bedroom with a boy they described as "a lecherous punk who took advantage of an innocent girl." Little did they know, finding their barely fifteen-year-old daughter in bed with a quarterback was the least of their problems.

By Monday, the lewd photos of Dee were all over social media, and I could only watch in horror as random groups of teenagers whispered and giggled whenever she walked by. The worst part was that she wouldn't even look at me. Had she just been following her parents' orders? Or did she, too, blame me for the whole terrible mess? Whatever the reason, I wasn't allowed to be a friend when my best friend needed me the most.

A week later, Dee was dead.

I vowed to never take another drink. And I'd meant it.

But now, as my wrist pulsed with a steadily worsening pain, I recalled the numbing effect of the alcohol that night. The euphoria. The feeling of not caring.

And before I even realized it, I found myself in front of the liquor cabinet reaching in.

Chapter Twenty-Three

FRIDAY, 1 P.M.

Around one o'clock, after we'd eaten lunch and were back on the deck where Rose was quizzing us on the steps to take if we started spinning during freefall, I heard the cabin's landline ring for the second time in as many days. After a few minutes, Morley poked his head outside. "I have some bad news."

"Shocking," I said sarcastically.

"You're not going to like it."

"Spit it out, hubby."

He sighed. "Lainie's gone missing."

"*What?*"

"The nurse didn't report it until about an hour ago. She'd assumed Lainie had been taken to the imaging department, considering the guard hadn't raised the alarm."

I let out a guttural roar, like a woman possessed. Morley rushed over and put his arm around my shoulder as the first fat raindrops of the day splatted on our heads. I went with him willingly toward the house.

"Why did I trust that little bitch? The nerve stranding us here forever!"

"You're not stranded. Not yet, anyway." Morley said, obviously trying to be optimistic. "The hospital's security department is reviewing the video footage as we speak. And there's an APB out on her."

"Oh no! We'll never get back to 2024 if the cops get to her first!"

Morley's face dropped. He knew it was true.

I stripped off my gear and stormed into the living room. "Damn her!"

Jarett followed me. "We could go out and look for her. There can't be too many options for a fifteen-year-old girl with no transportation or money."

"Are you serious? Where the hell would we even start looking?"

Morley patted his chest where the dragonfly pendant lay beneath his shirt. "I can find out."

"Of course!" I said.

But Morley shook his head and frowned.

"What's wrong?"

"Logistics. Half the staff at that hospital know me. The place will be swarming with people who can't see me and a lot more who *can*."

"This is a disaster."

"Not necessarily. There's a pretty good chance Lainie will come out the main door. It's the closest one to her room. I could just wait outside."

It was a good idea. The best one under the circumstances.

"But I'm using Sparkles's car," he said, heading for the hall table, where I assumed he kept a key to the dead man's car. Sure enough, he produced a fob from the drawer then ducked out of sight behind the stairs.

After we heard him recite his destination, time, and date, Rose rushed over for a peek behind the stairs. "Jumping Jupiter, I'll never get used to that."

"Why is he using Sparkles's car?" Jarett asked.

"Because Lainie would recognize his, I imagine. Although,

I don't know how inconspicuous he'll be in a bright orange Lamborghini."

Jarett chuckled and plopped down on the couch. "At least we know Sparkles won't be reporting it as stolen."

I shuddered, thinking back to Wednesday when Morley and Jarett performed the unimaginable task of depositing Sparkles's body at the bottom of his staircase.

"Hey, you. No rest for the wicked," Rose said to Jarett, holding her hand out to help him up from the couch. "We have one more module to review: Securing Your Passenger."

"Again? I've practiced that a hundred times already," he said, referring to yesterday when Rose got him to hook me onto his rig over and over until he claimed he could do it in his sleep.

"And I'm sure you'll do just fine, but it never hurts to practice."

I said, "All of this may not even matter if Morley can't find Lainie. And even if he does, it's pretty obvious she wants no part of going back to 2024."

Rose said, "Surely, once we explain the importance of going back, she'll come with us willingly."

"I wouldn't bet on it. I told her all that yesterday. She just doesn't give a shit about anything."

"Well, we're going to have to go on the assumption that she comes to her senses. Let's get back to business," Rose said, handing Jarett his rig. "Put this on and secure your passenger, sir."

"Yeah, yeah. But before that, can you remind me of the sequence once we're in Gus's room?"

Rose sighed. "All right, but this is the last time. Pay attention."

"Sure, boss."

"First, us three will put on our rigs. Then Morley will unhook Gus from the medical equipment and help me get him into his harness and secured to me. In the meantime, you and Syd will help Lainie get hooked up to you. Then, we go."

"There are a lot of moving parts to this plan," he said uneasily. "And its success hinges on Morley being able to sneak all this gear into the hospital in the first place."

"Are you kidding?" I said. "He's practically a rockstar there. He's just missing a bodyguard and the red carpet."

After Jarett had practiced loading me into his rig three times without a hitch, Morley walked into living room from the hall. His amused expression put me at ease until I realized I was still hooked to Jarett's chest.

"That looks cozy," Morley said, failing to mask his jealousy.

Over my shoulder, I said to Jarett, "Would you mind?"

"Mind what? I'm rather comfortable."

"Let me go!" I said, fumbling with the hooks at my hips. Rose came over and set me free.

Breathless, I went to Morley and gave him a kiss on the cheek, then we both sat down. The others gathered around.

"She took a taxi to my condo," he said.

"And she was able to get inside?"

"Yes. For one thing, she had the card key to my building; it was with the credit cards she took. And for another, she's quite aware of my favorite passcode."

"Couldn't you come up with something a little less obvious than my birthday?"

"Hey, don't complain. At least we know where she is now."

"Wasn't it risky for you to follow her into the building? Neighbors and all that?" Jarett said.

"Didn't have to go in. While I was sitting in Sparkles's car, I spotted her in my window."

"Are you sure it was her?" Jarett said.

"A green-haired girl in an arm cast? Yeah. I'm pretty sure it was her."

"Never mind all that. We have to go!" I shouted. "Before she leaves."

"I don't think she's going anywhere. Not right away. Technically, she's a fugitive, and she knows it. Probably trying to figure out her next move."

I wasn't convinced. "Rose, can we finish our training at the condo?"

She shrugged. "No need. I think you're both ready."

"Really?" I said.

"Yes. From here on out, it all boils down to instinct."

"Survival instinct, you mean," Jarett said.

Rose nodded.

"Well, that's good news, right?" Morley said. "At least if we're at the condo, we'll all be together—and conveniently close to the hospital."

"And The Merryport," I said.

"Yes. For my appointment with the truck."

Rose's eyes went wide. Where I'd grown used to Morley's quips about his impending demise, she was clearly shaken by it. I picked up Morley's hand and kissed his shiny new ring. "All right. Let's get this show on the road."

Chapter Twenty-Four

FRIDAY, 2:30 P.M.

Lainie

The room spun when I got up from the couch. Or wait. Maybe I was on the floor. *Shit.* I was on the floor, and I hadn't stood up at all. Why was the room whizzing around me?

"I'll never drink again!" I yelled at the blurred painting of the red canoe. "What an idiot!" Was that out loud? Or did I just think it?

Beside me lay a half-empty bottle of booze. I grabbed it and—with a great deal of effort and one eye closed—read the label. Russian vodka. Well, well. Good for me. I tried to unscrew the lid. It was stuck. "Fuckin' thing!" I said, dropping it back down beside me, surprised when it didn't break on the shiny tile floor. Then I realized I was sitting on a rug. A red, blue, gold, black, green, purp—shit, man! How many colors did this thing need? Did I just see a kangaroo in the pattern? It made no sense. It was a Persian rug. Kangaroos live in Australia. But wait, where did it go? "Where are you, Mr. Kangaroooo?" I said, becoming nauseous the more I looked at the busy pattern. Where was the bathroom?

"There's three of them, dopey dope! Swing a cat and you'll hit one!"

I started giggling. Swing a cat! That was something my grandma used to say, like, all the time. Swing a cat. Oh, she used to make me laugh. I miss you so much, Grandma.

I hiccupped.

Water. I needed water.

I rolled over to my hands and knees and used the couch to push myself to my feet. So dizzy. "Ugh! Make it stop!"

Once I was standing, I felt better. Still unsteady, but clearer in my head. "Hey, how'd *that* get there?" I said, hiccupping again. It was an empty glass on the kitchen counter. Did I use it for my drinkie-poo? Who cared, anyway. It was just what I needed.

I overfilled the glass with water from the tap and chugged it back, spilling half of it down the front of my hoodie. "Oopsie-poopsie!"

I threw the glass in the sink, and it smashed apart. "Oopsie-p—" I said, losing my balance, grabbing the edge of the counter with both hands. A jolt of pain went up my arm. I think?

"Hey, look! A cast!" I said, holding my arm up in front of me. I was just kidding. I knew I had a broken arm. Wrist, whatever. But the good news was that it didn't hurt nearly as much as before. Yay, booze! The funnest painkiller on the planet! *Funnest?* That's not even a word. I really must be drunk.

"Sit down, Lainie," I said, laughing when it came out *Shit down, Lamey*.

I wobbled over to the couch and fell back into its plush folds. HA! Plush folds. What a loser.

I closed my eyes but must have dozed, because when I looked around, the room was less blurry and my wrist pain was back.

The oil painting was clearer. The canoe seemed to be moving.

I had to find out who created that fan-fucking-tastic piece of art. I lugged my ass off the couch and went over to it, but the artist's signature was unreadable. It started with an MSt. Maybe M Stewart?

"Why ya gotta be so cryptic? Don't cha want people to know who you are?"

I got down on my knees and pulled the hutch door open and spread its contents on the floor. Geez, Morley. For a man who was downsizing, what was all this shit? Jigsaw puzzles. Binoculars. Health magazines. A medical dictionary. Crystal salt and pepper shakers from, like, the fourteenth century. And at the very back, a three-by-five photo lodged in a crack. I pried it out.

The photo showed a woman standing on a beach with Morley's arm draped around her tanned shoulders. Behind them, the brilliant blue water looked tropical, nothing like the dark, depressing waters around here. The woman wasn't Syd. It was weird to see Morley with someone else. Syd and Morley went together like peanut butter and jam.

I almost put the photo back into the cabinet before something jumped out at me about it: even though the woman in the photo was wearing giant, bug-eyed sunglasses and a floppy straw hat, she looked familiar. But from where? She was very elegant looking. Tall and slender with a flawless complexion and a sleek brown bob. Morley looked happy. Like he'd just swallowed a rainbow.

Oh wow. Was this the woman from the elevator? The one who almost busted me? It sure looked like her. But why would Morley go on a vacation with his posh neighbor? Then I remembered he'd been married before Syd met him. Oh, no! He was cheating on his wife!

No, dummy. It must *be* his wife. The one that died before

Syd and Morley ever got together. What do you call a wife that died? There must be a name for it. Not widow. Not dead wife. Well, sure, but—*late wife!* That's right. How many times had I heard my mom referring to my father as her late husband?

"Fuckin' people dying," I said, throwing the photo back into the cabinet, piling everything else on top and slamming the door shut. Why should I even bother covering my tracks? I was completely fucked, anyway. The cops were after me. Everyone I cared about was dead. I was in so much pain. Who cared if Morley was banging his neighbor at the beach? Or his wife?

With a stupid amount of effort, I got up off the floor. My wrist needed numbing again. My brain needed escape. I stumbled back to the vodka bottle, snatched it off the floor, and let myself outside. The freezing wind and rain hit me like a truck. I put my face to the sky and soaked it in. I deserved to be cold and wet. Deserved to be in pain.

With my eyes closed and the storm whirling around me, I imagined what it might be like to leave this world. It wasn't a horrible thought.

My eyes sprang open. I was so dizzy. So sick of it all.

Above me, the clouds had grown darker. Heavier. And when I spotted the empty, dreary-looking concrete planter surrounding the deck, I moved robotically toward it. There, I could be alone with my thoughts, looking out at the city going about its pointless business.

I slogged through the pooling rain and lugged myself—bottle and all—into the planter. My butt sank into the wet soil as I swung my feet around and leaned over the edge to take a look. The people below me looked like tiny ants. I closed one eye and tried to squish them between my fingers. "Squish, squish, squish," I said, trying to remember where I'd heard that phrase before.

"Agh!" I gasped when I leaned a little too close to the edge and nearly tumbled over it. As I steadied myself, a huge rush of excitement coursed through my body.

And in an instant, I knew how to make all the pain disappear.

Chapter Twenty-Five

FRIDAY, 3 P.M.

In all my years in Port Raven, I'd never seen such an intense storm, and that was saying a lot for a town with an annual rainfall of thirty-nine inches. The wind had increased to a level I was sure could have flipped a car upside down, and when I finally pulled Morley's car into the underground parking lot beneath the condo, I was glad for the shelter. Morley, Rose, and Jarett were minutes behind me, and I decided to wait for them so we could all go up to the penthouse together.

I cut the engine and slumped back in the seat, savoring the quiet.

"Damn it, Lainie," I said, wondering how she could be so selfish. I'd filled her in on the negative consequences of time-blinking yesterday, and she took off anyway. It made no sense. She had to have realized how lonely her life would be without her mom, Sarah, and her friends in it. She had to have understood what a depressing existence she was setting up for herself by staying here. How the hell did she think she was going to support herself? With Morley's credit cards?

I could understand her need to see our dad again. To see him living, breathing, telling his silly jokes. Lainie had obviously been super close with him, like I had been before the shit hit the fan—before I single-handedly destroyed our family with that one terrible decision to leave Isla alone at the park all those years ago. I squeezed my eyes shut and let that horrible truth sink in. Lainie's very existence was the direct result of that choice.

Maybe that's why my father shoved the two of us together like this. He wanted us to meet on neutral ground. Did I owe that to him? Even if I did, Lainie was making it so damned difficult.

Just as I was reaching to start the car to get some heat circulating, I heard the garage gate roll up. Morley pulled the Range Rover in next to me, and Rose hopped out of the front seat. I got out and waited for Morley and Jarett to do the same.

"All the gear's loaded up and ready to go," Rose said, patting the SUV. "I hope Morley can sneak it into the hospital undetected."

"He seems pretty sure."

"If only I had his confidence. I'm getting really nervous about this operation, now that it's getting close to go-time."

"Shhh," I said, nodding to Jarett, who'd appeared around the back of the vehicle. Rose winked and whispered, "Our little secret."

When the two men joined us, Morley said, "We'd better get up there, pronto."

He had reason to be anxious. It was already three o'clock, and we didn't even know if Lainie was going to cooperate with us. Well, I had news for her: she was coming to the hospital if I had to knock her out and drag her there myself.

Morley hurried everyone over to the elevator and punched the button repeatedly.

"You seem worried," I said.

"Is it that obvious? Lainie's on the deck. And she's pretty close to the edge."

"What? Like, how close?"

"She's sitting in the planter box. With her feet dangling over the edge. Hopefully it's nothing, but—" He pulled a pill bottle out of his pocket. "I found these back at the cabin. It's her antidepressants, and she hasn't taken them in two days now."

I gave him a worried look and stabbed at the button five or six times, like it would speed things up. "This is the slowest elevator on the planet."

Fuck. How much disaster could one teenaged girl cause? Unfortunately, I knew the answer to that, because I'd been that girl once.

In the elevator, we'd agreed to use the element of surprise. Jarett and Morley would close in on Lainie from either side and grab her before she even knew what was happening.

"Flank and seize," Jarett had said, summing it up neatly. I assumed it was a police term.

"I hope she's okay," Rose whispered as Morley eased the apartment door open and allowed us to enter. Rose needn't have kept her voice down. There was little chance Lainie could hear us over the roar of the wind and rain.

"I'm sure she's fine," Morley said, not too convincingly.

When we got to the patio doors, I let out the breath I'd been holding since we got inside. She was still there. Soaked and shivering and looking absolutely miserable. But she was still there. It was all that mattered.

"Ready?" Morley said to Jarett as he inched the door open. Jarett nodded and followed Morley into the raging storm. I was too nervous to sit around and watch, so I tailed behind them.

We moved as a group, being careful to stay out of Lainie's line of sight. As we got closer—perhaps fifteen feet away—

Morley pointed to an item propped up in the planter box next to Lainie, and my heart plummeted. It was a bottle. Booze of some sort. Maybe vodka or gin? It looked like the bottle was empty. I tore my gaze away from it to assess Lainie's condition. Between bouts of shivering, her head bobbed forward, as if she were about to nod off. Oh, no. Was she so drunk that she might pass out? We had to move fast.

As if they'd read my mind, Morley and Jarret broke from our formation and hurried toward Lainie, fanning out on either side. I rushed forward, too. It hadn't been part of the plan, but I was so worried for her. For all of us.

In my singular goal to get to Lainie, my foot caught on the leg of an overturned lounge chair, throwing me off balance. I stumbled forward and crashed to the ground.

Lainie must have heard. Her head snapped around in surprise, and both men stopped in their tracks, as if programmed with the same code. I couldn't believe it. They'd been so close. Ten steps maybe. Lainie swayed precariously without speaking, more curious than startled by our presence, it seemed.

"It's okay," I said, from my kneeling position on the deck. I reached my hand toward her, a gesture I hoped she would find reassuring. I didn't know what more to say. What do you say to a drunk, depressed teenager perched on the edge of a building eighteen floors above the street?

Morley took a step toward her. She bristled. "Stay away from me," she yelled, but her words came out slurred.

Morley obeyed.

"Lainie," Jarett said from where he stood. "We know you're in pain. It must feel like the entire universe is against you right now."

Lainie's shoulders relaxed a little, and I wondered if Jarett had undergone some sort of sensitivity training for such circumstances.

"Can you come down from there? You look cold," he said, stretching his hand out toward her.

Lainie rocked her head. Streaks of black makeup flowed down her cheeks and dripped off her jaw.

Jarett persisted. "I can see you're really hurting."

Lainie burst into tears. "No shit!"

She turned away and focused on the ground below where I envisioned dog walkers, bike couriers, and businesspeople rushing around, doing their best to stay dry.

Morley took another few steps closer. Jarett followed his lead. They were within arm's reach now. "Come on, dear," Morley said. "We all care about you. And we want to help."

I cringed. Maybe she didn't want our help. Correction. She probably didn't want *my* help, even if it was our father's dying wish.

She twisted around. "I hate myself! I don't deserve to live!" she shouted.

In that moment, I no longer saw her as the annoying project my dad had forced on me. She was my sister, and she was in deep pain.

"You DO deserve to live, Lainie. I mean it. Your mom loves you very much. And your dad did, too. He was so proud of you. He was always bragging about you."

I hoped she didn't ask me to elaborate. Apart from telling me she was an honor-roll student who enjoyed spending time alone, my father had never actually spoken much about Lainie—or any members of his second family, for that matter. Maybe he thought I couldn't handle it.

Maybe he was right.

"Two people are dead because of me," she said mechanically. "Actually three, if you count Dee. I'm a horrible, horrible human being. My sister thinks I'm a waste of space. And who are you to tell me what my mom thinks? She hates me! Do you know what she said to me at the airport when I left? 'Grow up and get your act together. If you can't do it for me, then do it for the memory of your poor, dead father.'"

When she turned her attention back to the street, Morley and Jarett pounced simultaneously. Jarett seized her right arm. Morley grabbed for her left, but her cast was slick, and it slid out of his grasp. Jarett hadn't expected the sudden weight of Lainie swiveling and slipping off the edge of the planter, and he screamed as her arm slithered out of his grasp. Morley scrambled to grab her, but it was too late. Lainie had gone over the edge. I heard her scream. The sound was small and insignificant amidst the roaring storm, but it hit my soul with the force of a tsunami. I raced over—not wanting to see what happened, yet needing to know.

"Help!" came Lainie's terrified voice. We all leaned over the edge. Somehow, her hoodie had caught on one of the building's ornamental flourishes and was bunched up around her armpits. Her arms and legs flailed wildly in the sideways rain.

"Stay still!" I yelled. The hoodie was the only thing keeping her from falling eighteen floors to a certain death.

Jarett dropped to his stomach and shimmied to the edge of the planter box. He reached down and grabbed for Lainie's hand, but it was too far away. Eight or ten inches too far.

"Omigod, omigod, omigod," Lainie repeated over and over as she wriggled and thrashed about. Why couldn't she just stay still? "I promise to do better! I don't want to die!"

It sounded like she was trying to make a deal with God.

"You're not going to die," Jarett said. "But you have to try to be still."

Behind us, I heard Rose asking what she could do to help.

Morley yelled over his shoulder at her. "Bring me a sheet! NOW! From the linen closet in the hall next to the kitchen."

She was gone before Morley even finished his sentence. I assumed the idea was to get Lainie to hang onto the sheet so we could pull her up the extra ten inches. Then Jarett could reach her hand and haul her to safety. At this point, it was the *only* idea.

In the meantime, Jarett was doing a fantastic job of soothing Lainie. She'd stopped squirming but was still dangling precariously above the street while the wind and rain assaulted her from all sides. "Just another few seconds, kiddo," Jarett said. "We got you."

Watching him, my heart was no longer gripped with panic but bursting with a feeling much more powerful. I couldn't tell if it was admiration or something much deeper. I put the thought aside.

When Rose got back with the sheet, Morley got us to help him roll it into a long rope, then he tied a bulky knot at the end and passed it to Jarett, who was still sprawled out on the planter box consoling Lainie.

"All right," Morley said to me as Jarett fed the knot down to Lainie. "You, me and Rose are going to hold the other end of this sheet. Wrap it around your arms a couple of times."

I gave him a dubious look, not because I wasn't confident the three of us could hoist her up, but I was worried about Lainie herself. How was she going to hold on to the sheet with one arm in a cast, not to mention being drunk out of her mind?

Morley's voice pulled me back. "Tell Lainie to sit on the knot," he said to Jarett.

My heart lifted. Of course! The knot was meant as a seat.

After the longest ten seconds of my life, Jarett called back to us. "Okay, pull!"

Morley had taken the front position. Rose and I were behind him with the sheet wrapped around our arms. None of us hesitated. We all pulled simultaneously.

Apparently Lainie was lighter than any of us had expected, especially Morley, who stumbled backwards into me, sending all of us crashing onto the wet tiles. Miraculously, we kept our grip on the sheet, which was still taut and straining under the weight of its passenger. But I noticed another imminent problem as we scrambled to our feet. Over at the planter, despite Lainie's modest weight, Jarett appeared to be struggling to hold onto the sheet, his hips sliding dangerously close to the edge.

"Pull!" he yelled. As we did, Morley immediately slipped again on the wet tiles. Both Rose and I went down at the same time, and the sheet slithered out of my grasp. We'd all lost our hold. I could only watch with horror as it disappeared over the edge of the planter.

I screamed.

"Shit!" Jarett yelled. Morley and Rose rushed over to him. I was too dizzy to get up. Too nauseous. Lainie was gone. It was as if I'd tumbled over the edge with her.

"What should we do?" came Rose's voice as I crumpled into a ball in an inch of frigid rainwater.

"Someone, hold my legs!" Jarett yelled. Rose dashed over and took hold of his feet.

"Morley! Grab her other arm!" Jarett shouted. "Okay, Lainie. This is probably going to hurt like a son of a bitch, so take a deep breath."

What? He still had a hold of her?

I sprang to my feet and sloshed over to the planter where the three of them were working to haul Lainie to safety.

With one last tug, Morley and Jarett pulled Lainie up and over the edge where she tumbled heavily into the muddy planter box. She was drenched, shivering, and bawling loud enough to be heard over the storm, which had intensified to a crazy new level. I froze, unsure of what to do. Should I go to her? Say something comforting? Hug her? If it had been Isla or Kendall, I'd have grabbed her and hugged her and never let go.

As I stood there paralyzed with uncertainty and worried that a gust of wind would come along and whisk everyone off the edge, Morley climbed out of the planter and helped

Lainie sit up. He pushed a long green strand of hair out of her eyes and slipped his arm around her shoulders, guiding her to the ground. Jarett and Rose followed, and in that moment, I was so grateful for my little group that I broke down in tears.

Morley and Rose took Lainie toward the apartment as Jarret hurried over and drew me into his chest. I couldn't move. His embrace was so comforting I hardly cared that my cheek was resting against a giant smear of dirt on his shirt. I watched with a sort of detached curiosity as the mud ran off his clothing and pooled on the white tiles at our feet.

"Hey," Jarett said, stroking my drenched hair. "It's okay. She's fine. We're all fine."

I was too rattled to speak.

"Come on. I'm sure you don't want to spend another minute out here in this monsoon," he said, stepping back and taking my hand. "Let's go get warm and dry."

As we stepped through the door hand in hand, Morley flashed me a wounded look that nearly broke me. It had only been a fleeting glance—and completely involuntary, I'm sure—but it was as cutting as if he'd told me to fuck off and die.

I broke away from Jarett's grasp and wiped the mud off my face with the heels of my hands, knowing I couldn't afford to get sentimental now.

Lainie looked like she'd just been through a war zone. We all did. But there was no time to sit around and wallow in our shock now. I had to keep this train rolling.

Fortunately, Morley and I had a decent supply of clothes on hand that we could change into immediately. I said to Lainie and Rose, "I'll grab some blankets and put your clothes through a quick wash. Jarett, you can change into a set of Morley's scrubs as planned."

Rose followed me down the hall, and when I stopped at the linen cupboard, she said, "That was intense. Thank God Lainie's safe."

I sniffed and nodded, afraid that if I spoke, I'd start crying again.

She put a hand on my shoulder. "The plan is still on track, Syd. Everyone's okay."

As I stared at the neatly stacked linens, I realized something. I'd been so focused on my own desperate need to see Christopher again that I put very little thought into what everyone else needed. Rose had just lost her entire family, but all I kept talking about was how I couldn't wait to see mine. I'd called Jarett a spineless coward when he admitted to a debilitating fear of heights. And the worst of it: the real reason I hadn't wanted Lainie to plunge to her death was to ensure my own return to 2024.

I snatched blankets from the top shelf and handed them to Rose. But hadn't I—for a fleeting moment out there—also been a little relieved when I thought Lainie had slipped away? Yeah, I had. I'd been *that* angry with her. And with my dad. And her death would have been justice for everything they'd put me through.

Oh, man. She did not deserve that. No one did. Not even someone who may or may not have been contemplating taking her own life. For all anyone knew, she could have just been sitting out there feeling sorry for herself with no other intention than to be cold and miserable.

I could not abandon her now, no matter how desperate I was to see my son again. What if her allegations were true—that her mom and sister had cast her aside like an old pair of shoes? It didn't seem possible that Julie could be so cruel, but if Lainie truly believed her own mother had rejected her, she certainly didn't need another heartless person in her life.

I had to do better by Lainie, no matter how forced or unnatural it might feel.

Chapter Twenty-Six

FRIDAY, 6:00 P.M.

We were all gathered in the living room, warm and dry, after having showered and changed into clean clothes—Morley in his usual business-casual attire; Lainie in her black skinny jeans and hoodie with her hair tucked under a black beanie; Rose in her comfy stretch pants, blouse, and cardigan. Jarett wore the baby blue scrubs Morley had given him to help blend in with the hospital staff, and I was wearing my standby leggings and t-shirt with a mint-green cotton hoodie.

"Thanks for dinner, my good man. It really hit the spot," Jarett said after he'd polished off the last piece of pizza Morley had ordered in for us—pizza I thought we'd all be too nervous and upset to eat. But there were only little piles of crusts and discarded onions left in the three boxes on the coffee table. Even Lainie had had a good helping, which surprised me. I didn't think she would eat anything after downing half a bottle of vodka and escaping certain death—an event that seemed to have sobered her up quite nicely.

"Should we get the gear from downstairs and practice one more time?" Jarett said to Rose.

She shook her head. "Not necessary. You two have been exemplary students."

"We don't have time, anyway," I said. "After Morley helps us at the hospital, he's due at The Merryport by seven-thirty. That leaves us less than two hours for everything."

A gruesome image flashed in front of my eyes: Morley pinned to the wall of the pub by a psychopath in a pickup truck while streams of blood and rain trickled down his face. My only solace was knowing I wouldn't have to witness it all over again.

"And on that note, we should probably get a move on," Morley said.

After we'd gathered up all the pizza boxes and tidied the apartment, I noticed Rose and Lainie chatting quietly on the couch. When I joined them, Rose was saying, "so just relax and let Jarett do all the work, okay, sweetie?"

Lainie nodded hesitantly.

Hearing this, Jarett came over and knelt down in front of Lainie. "Don't worry, kiddo. I got your back."

Lainie gave him a hint of a smile. He'd had her back once already today.

Morley and I hung back while everyone else shuffled to the front door.

"Go on," I said to them. "We'll meet you at the hospital."

"Take the Range Rover. My parking pass is in the visor. Remember: Spot number 73. The covered lot at the southwest corner."

"Yep. It's all in the plan," Jarett said, grabbing the fob from the hook next to the door.

When it was just the two of us left, I took Morley's hands and laced our fingers together. We kissed urgently, then parted to study each other's faces.

"How did you manage to keep yourself so calm the night of the accident?"

He gave me a woeful look. "That's present-tense, love. As in, how *am* I keeping myself so calm tonight?"

I nodded sadly.

"Well," he said, "Look at all the distractions going on around me. I have you to thank for that. If you and your ragtag bunch hadn't been here, I might've ended up like Lainie, drowning my sorrows with a bottle of vodka in the middle of a raging storm. But here I am, sober and dry, about to sneak you and your gang—and a cartful of skydiving gear—into the hospital."

I gave him a worried look. "I just hope we're not forced to resort to Plan B."

"Plan B? I didn't know you had a backup plan in the works."

"We don't. The truth is, I don't think anyone is expecting Plan A to fail. Plan B is a matter of switching to survival mode. At that point, we do whatever it takes to get into Gus's room and out of this realm for good."

He squeezed my hands reassuringly. "You'll do fine."

"I hope so."

Morley dropped my hands and hugged me into his chest. "We probably won't get an opportunity to say a proper goodbye at the hospital, so I'll say my piece now." His deep, sexy voice vibrated through my whole body. "I love you, Syd Brixton. You are my friend and the truest love of my life, and I'm honored to serve as your lifetime fiancé."

"I love you too, Morley Scott," I whispered into his shoulder. "It's just so unfair."

He pulled away abruptly and grasped my hands, bringing them between our hearts. "Don't let this arrangement—our being engaged—keep you from living your life, missy. I mean it. You're only thirty-six."

"What if I'm perfectly happy being single?"

"I'm not saying you need a partner to be happy. Just don't be a martyr."

"But I have Christopher to think about, too. What if I end up with someone like that last asshole?"

"Don't torture yourself with the *what-ifs*."

"I can't help it."

"Okay, then. What if you end up with someone like me?"

A tear trickled down my cheek and landed on the back of my hand. Morley brought it to his lips and kissed it.

"We should get going," he said, "as much as I would love to lock the door and hide away with you forever."

It was tempting, but we both knew it wasn't possible. Some force bigger than the both of us would compel him to make his way to The Merryport, no matter what obstacle I threw in front of him.

He went over to the table next to the door and held up my wig and reading glasses. "Don't forget these."

"You're enjoying this, aren't you?" I said, putting the wig on. "Hanging out with a cute blonde one moment and a sexy brunette the next."

He winked as he opened the door. "Come on, Janice. Let's get out of here before Syd sees us together."

We only made it half a block before Morley glanced in his rear-view mirror and said, "Shit. We've got company."

My heart dropped. Morley, the unflappable children's doctor, would never swear without good reason. As I turned around to look, a volley of red and blue flashes started up behind us, bouncing off nearby buildings in the sideways rain.

"Is that for us?" I said.

"Yeah. It was waiting for us."

"What? Why?"

"I'm guessing it has something to do with your sister," he said, pulling over to the curb, switching his hazard lights on.

"One fricken disaster after another. Shit, Morley, I have no ID."

"Don't panic. We're fine," he said, keeping his gaze on the idling police cruiser. "I think it's our good buddy, Sam."

Sure enough, when the raincoat-clad cop leaned down to Morley's window, I recognized him as Detective Douglas, making me thankful for my disguise. A gush of cold air and mist whooshed inside when Morley lowered his window.

"Hello, Sam. I didn't think detectives rode around in police cruisers. What brings you to this part of town—in the middle of a raging storm, no less?" Morley said.

Sam glanced at me, unconcerned, it seemed, then fired up his flashlight in the waning evening light to survey the back seat. Finding it empty, he said, "Hello, Dr. Scott. I'll make this brief because I'm cold and wet and running out of patience with your niece. You don't happen to know of her whereabouts, do you?"

"I'm sorry, but I don't know where she is at this moment."

I was impressed by Morley's sneaky way of speaking the truth without actually speaking the truth.

"Well, we brought a taxi driver in for questioning, and after three painful hours of 'amnesia,' he finally admitted to bringing her here. The very building where you happen to hang your hat. Did you see her at all this afternoon?"

I winced. That would be a tough question to skirt.

"I did."

Sam registered only a hint of surprise. He waited a moment, then sighed loud enough to be heard over the roaring wind. "Okay. *Where* did you see her?"

"Here. At my apartment."

"Annnnd, were you planning on telling me at some point?"

Morley opened his mouth and then closed it again.

Sam went on. "Dr. Scott. Despite her probable innocence, we have not cleared your niece in connection with Alice Robertson's murder yet. You're an educated man. You should know better than to withhold information or interfere with the process."

"I'm as flabbergasted as you, Sam. Really. But she gave us the slip when we went out to pick up dinner, even after promising to stay put."

Sam's eyes wandered over to mine. "Is that so?"

I nodded.

"Hey, aren't you Dr. Scott's secretary?"

"Administrative assistant," I said, my heart jumping into my throat.

He rolled his eyes and wiped some dribbles of rain off his chin. "I don't have time to unpack *that* right now. Dr. Scott, can you please open your trunk?"

Before Morley answered, I blurted, "It doesn't work."

Sam shot me a suspicious look.

"The button. To open the trunk. It's been broken for months. I'll have to do it manually for you."

"All right," he said. "Be prepared to get wet."

Sam walked around to the back, and as I opened my door, Morley grabbed my arm. "What are you doing?" aware the trunk button wasn't broken.

"Trust me. Be ready to go," I said and hopped out.

When I joined Sam behind the car, I said, "You think his niece is in the trunk? Yikes, I hope not! That would be awkward."

"Come on," he said. "You're stalling."

When the trunk popped open, I gave Sam a brisk push and slammed the lid down on his head. He dropped like a lead weight. At that moment, I spotted his cohort in the driver's seat, gawking at me wide-eyed. I didn't wait around to find out what he was going to do about it and ran back to the car, fumbling with the rain-slicked handle before finally getting a grip on it and flinging the door open. "Go!" I yelled as I jumped in.

Morley didn't hesitate. The panic in my voice was

convincing enough. As we sped off, I took a glance behind us, and Sam was lying in a puddle on the road. The other cop was already at his side. I thought I saw him reach for his gun. "Go left!" I said. "It'll throw them off course."

"What the hell did you do back there?"

"What needed to be done."

He let out a weary sigh, and we rode in the opposite direction from the hospital for a few blocks before turning east and getting back on track.

"I didn't kill him or anything. Just threw a little wrench into his plan. He'll be fine."

"Are you crazy? You assaulted a police officer!"

"Detective."

"Semantics."

"I know, I know, it was stupid. But, fuck, Morley. I didn't see you doing anything about it."

I felt his eyes boring into the side of my head.

"Keep your eyes on the road," I said.

He huffed under his breath but did what I asked. "Why didn't you at least get me to do it? I'll be dead in two hours. You're the vulnerable one here. You could end up in jail."

"Oh, okay. Like I should have said, 'Quick! Get out and knock him unconscious!'? I'm sure you would've hopped right to it."

I could feel Morley fuming next to me; he knew he couldn't win that argument. He was a healer by nature, not a fighter.

"Just get us to the hospital," I said.

"You do realize that's the first place they'll look for us."

"It's the *last* place they'll look. What purpose would any of us have going there, especially Lainie? She ran away from it the first chance she got!"

"That's one argument, but what if they're staking it out waiting for her to visit her 'boyfriend'?"

"*Gus?*"

He was right, of course. If I'd been looking at the situation from a law enforcement perspective, I might have thought twice about coldcocking Sam and leaving him in the street. But what was done was done.

I slumped down in my seat. "We're sticking to the plan, right?"

"What choice do we have now?"

"I don't know. Aborting and trying again next week?" I said.

"That would be fine if Gus wasn't hanging on by a thread. Or if I was still alive next week to help. Or if you didn't have the cops hot on your tail for assault."

"Look, I did what needed to do to get home to *our son*. That's my *only* goal right now. Nothing else matters."

He went quiet. Good. I wasn't in the mood for conversation. I surrendered to the sound of the pounding rain and the windshield wipers flapping back and forth at their highest speed, which I found oddly comforting.

Morley, on the other hand, seemed tense. Out of the corner of my eye, I noticed him chewing on his bottom lip, checking his rear-view mirror every ten seconds. The driver's side window was fogged up from his nervous sweating. My heart stung at the unfairness of the whole situation. Here he was, trying to help me in his last two hours of life, and we were at odds with each other.

"Did we just have our first fight?" he said, as if he'd read my thoughts.

"More of a tiff than a fight. But still. Fine time for it, hey?"

"Ah, well. I'm glad we finally got it out of the way."

"So, you're not angry with me?"

He sighed. "No, of course not. I'm just wrapped up in my own thoughts."

"Oh," I said. "About your accident later tonight. I'm sorry, hon."

"Don't be sorry. I've accepted my fate. It's yours I'm worried about. I keep running the details of this mission over and over in my head."

"Mission? Ha. You make it sound like a spy film," I said, attempting to lighten the mood.

"It's more of a thriller. Let's see, how would the teaser go? *An ill-fated doctor races against time to prevent his beautiful fiancée and her fellow time travelers from being stuck in a parallel world far from the people they love.*"

"That's good. Maybe I should write a novel when I get back."

"Nah. Plot's too unbelievable. The critics would tear it apart."

"A classic case of the truth being stranger than fiction."

A few minutes later, Morley pulled the car into the covered lot at St. Bart's and found a spot three cars away from the Range Rover. "Lucky us. Dr. Fontaine is in Hawaii right now."

As we climbed out of the car, Jarett rushed over. "What took you guys so long?"

"No time to explain. We gotta get the hell outta Dodge," I said, noticing Morley inspecting his trunk lid—for blood or hair, I suspected.

"Well," he said, walking past me. "That's a first for me. Assaulting and eluding a cop."

"What?" Jarett said.

"I'll tell you later! We have to organize the gear!"

"I'll be back in a few minutes with the cart," Morley said. "Be ready. And watch for police."

Rose was busy showing Lainie how to get into a tandem harness when Jarett and I joined them at the SUV's hatch.

"You think you'll manage?" I asked Lainie.

"Sure. It reminds me of the zipline harness I used in Mexico last year."

"That's right, I remember your dad talking about that trip.

He said you could have been a zipline instructor by the end of it."

"Yeah. It was fun. We went three days in a row. Well, me and Dad did. Mom and Sarah just went one time. Actually, Sarah didn't even finish the circuit once. She totally chickened out halfway through and had to walk the whole way back with Mom."

"That's the confidence I like to hear," I said, shooting Jarett an unintended salty look. He didn't appear to notice.

"Okay, sweetie," Rose said, "Let's get you out of that harness before Morley gets back."

After Rose had checked all the gear for the third time and packed everything away, she said. "I'm impressed. We couldn't be more prepared. In fact, I can't think of one thing that could thwart this plan."

"What about the most important one?" Jarett said. "*Gus*. I hope he's still with us."

"Have a little faith," Rose said.

"I'm trying. There are just so many things that could trip us up."

"Would you quit that?" I said.

"Quit what?"

"Fussing. Suck it up and get on with it."

"Geez, sorry," he said defensively. "Guess I'm just nervous about busting through the space-time continuum or whatever. Aren't you nervous about any of this?"

Instead of trying to reassure him—*once again*—I said, "Grow some balls, will you?"

"Like you know anything about my balls," he said, without missing a beat. "But maybe someday you'll find out."

I heard Lainie groan under her breath, and I shook my head at Jarett in disgust, feeling my cheeks growing hot. I felt like a teenaged girl in the presence of the star quarterback.

Flustered, I turned to Lainie, who was eyeing me curiously. I could only guess what she was thinking: that it was disrespectful of me to flirt with another man when the supposed love of my life had two hours left to live. But was I really flirting? Jarett was the one making all the suggestive comments and flapping his ridiculously long eyelashes at me.

"Grow up," I finally said. I had no idea why I was being so snippy with him. In general, Jarett had been stepping up to the plate every time we encountered a crisis and had only faltered when he was anxious about doing something he'd never done before. Like most people would.

"Hey, hey. No fighting, kids," came Morley's voice as he pushed an enclosed metal cart toward us. "Let's get that gear loaded up. Jarett, are you ready with the diversion material?"

Jarett reached into the pockets of his scrubs and pulled out a jumble of firecrackers from one and a blue plastic lighter from the other. He tested the lighter, and it ignited on the first try. "Ready as I'll ever be," he said.

After we'd loaded everything into the cart, Rose spread her arms out to all of us. "Group hug," she said. I didn't protest, even though every nerve in my body was on high alert and the clock was ticking ever closer to our deadline.

We all huddled in.

Morley was the first to speak. "I wish you all the best of luck and a safe journey home. Oh, what I would give to find out what happens when you land."

"So, come with us," Jarett said.

"If timeblinking worked that way, I'd have tagged along with Syd to the future long before now."

Rose said, "Well, I think I can speak for the rest of us, Morley, that we appreciate all you've done for us.

"Agreed," Jarett said. "I'll never be able to look at another log cabin without thinking about you."

"Or a Goldwing," Lainie said, as a tear raced down her cheek.

"Or Christopher," I added. "I wish I could tell him how brave you were on this day. How you knew about your fate and still helped me and four strangers get back to the people we love."

"You guys are the brave ones. Not me. But I'm humbled by your kind words."

"Umm, I hate to say it, but I think we got company," Lainie said, nodding to a spot over Morley's shoulder.

Sure enough, two police cruisers had entered the parking lot at the far end.

"Damn it!" I said.

Morley raised his hands reassuringly. "Don't panic. They might not even be here for us."

"Exactly." Jarett said. "Hospitals are a cop's second home. Trust me on that one."

"At any rate, we should get a move on," Morley said, pushing the cart towards the staff entrance. "Jarett, wait three or four minutes, then head inside and do your thing. Remember: Nurse's station B. Third floor, West."

"Got it."

"What if the cop outside Gus's room doesn't budge?" Lainie said.

Jarett shook his head. "Are you kidding? Speaking from experience, if I'd heard explosions going off in a hospital, I certainly wouldn't be sitting around twiddling my thumbs. I'd be getting my ass to the source of the noise as fast as possible."

"I hope you're right. See you in there," I said as the staff doors hissed open.

We followed Morley down a long corridor where two people were waiting outside the elevators. One was a woman in her late twenties reading a chart, and the other was an older, white-haired man wearing a navy-blue suit. His lanyard identified him as Dr. Joel Banks from Pediatric Oncology.

"Well, if it isn't the elusive Dr. Scott," he said, seeing Morley. "Did you join the PGA Tour or something? Haven't seen you around here in a while."

Morley pushed the Up button and laughed. "Something like that. Just on a short sabbatical."

"Good for you! It's about time. Have you *ever* gone on holidays?" He gave me a quick, appraising look, perhaps wondering if I'd been responsible for Morley's uncharacteristic leave. I smiled and winked at him. "I've been keeping him busy at his cabin. *Very busy*, if you know what I mean."

The doctor's mouth flew open, and he turned away from me, flustered. I glanced over my shoulder at Rose and Lainie, who were doing their best to hold their laughter.

"Well, it's good to have you back, Scotty," the doctor said, clearing his throat. "Let's meet for lunch on Monday, shall we?"

Morley patted his colleague's shoulder. "Absolutely. Looking forward to it," he said as Dr. Banks and the woman boarded the elevator on the right, going down.

When it was just the four of us, Rose burst out laughing. "Ooh, Syd, the look on his face! That wig has turned you into a bit of a vixen."

Even Lainie was giggling by now. Morley, however, wasn't impressed. "All right, all right. Enough of the fun and games. We have work to do."

"Oh, come on!" Rose said as our elevator dinged and the doors slid open. "You have to admit, it was pretty funny."

"Hilarious," he said, pushing the cart into the elevator. "Lucky for me, he'll never get the chance to grill me about my steamy lakeside tryst."

By the time the elevator doors creaked open to the bustle of the third floor, our lighthearted banter had vanished. Lainie and Rose got out first, stepping aside to allow Morley and me to get ten or twenty paces ahead of them. During the planning of this operation, we'd agreed to work in pairs. Jarett, our munitions tech, was a one-man show. His timing needed to be precise, and he needed to be quick on his feet after he lit the fuse in the supply closet halfway between the elevators and the nurse's station near Gus's room.

Morley and I walked down the long hall trying not to rush, which wasn't difficult considering three separate staff members stopped to say hello to Morley—a plump, gray-haired nurse with a kind face and scuffed white sneakers; a food-service worker pushing a cart full of dirty dishes, and a gorgeous redhead with her hair pulled into a messy bun on top of her head. Her ID tag said, Dr. Anita Stevens, Radiology.

"Morley! Long time, no see. How are you?"

"Hi Anita. I'm great, thanks. Back from maternity leave, are you?"

"Yes, finally!" she said, then leaned close to his ear. "Between you and me? Motherhood's a bitch. Let's just say I'm glad to be back at work while my nanny takes care of things at home. She's been a godsend. What brings you to this wing?"

"Checking in on my neighbor's son. He was in a car accident a couple of days ago and isn't doing very well."

"How awful. Well, you're a good neighbor. Hell, you're a good person, period. Anyone who can work with kids all day —especially fussy, ailing ones like you do—is a saint in my books."

"Hardly. But thanks for the compliment."

"Anyway, good to see you, Morley. Hope your patient pulls through," she said, nodding at me, finally acknowledging my presence. I nodded back, feeling self-conscious in my ridiculous disguise.

By the time we reached Gus's room, my stomach was in knots, partly from nervous energy and partly from out-and-out panic. There were so many components to our plan. So many opportunities for error. But I couldn't let negative thoughts distract me now.

"Good afternoon," Morley said to the bored-looking cop sitting outside Gus's room.

"Hello, sir," he said, scrambling to his feet, obviously grateful for the stimulation. He was a scrawny little thing, probably no more than twenty years old. Good, a rookie. That would probably benefit us.

"We're here to do some tests on John Doe," Morley said, plucking his laminated ID pass off his chest to show the young cop.

"Oh, yeah, sure." Another good omen. Gus was obviously still alive. "And your name, ma'am?" he said, pulling an official-looking chart off a hook beside his chair.

Morley answered for me. "Oh, it's okay, she's my assistant, Janice Sandalwood," Morley said. I nearly laughed out loud at his attempt to make up a last name on the spot.

"Okay, perfect," the young cop said, unfazed. He scribbled the names down as we hurried through Gus's door with the cart.

The room was stuffy and dim, illuminated only by the dregs of the gloomy daylight and a retro-looking fluorescent bulb affixed to the wall above Gus's head. While Morley checked Gus's eyes with a penlight from his pocket, I set to work pulling the dive gear from the cart and laying it on the floor between the bed and the window to obscure it from any staff members who might pop in unannounced. I pulled off my wig and glasses and stuffed them into a plastic garbage bag hanging off the end of the bed. Morley pulled them out. "Can't leave evidence," he said, cramming them into an inside pocket in his blazer.

"How's he doing?"

"No change."

"But he's still with us. That's all that matters."

"This is all going to happen fast. I'll remove his life support the moment everyone is suited up and in position. Not a moment before. Without these supports, he'll go quick."

I stopped what I was doing to stare at Morley.

He said, "Oh. Did you think he was going to survive the trip back?"

"Yeah. Kind of."

"He will, initially. But he'll have zero capability for respiratory function after extubation."

"In English, please?"

"Once I remove his ventilator, he'll probably go within ten to fifteen minutes."

"Oh, Morley. What do we do? We can't just leave him lying in the middle of a hayfield in Iowa. Especially if by some miracle he survives!"

"He won't. Trust me."

"Well, then. We're fucked. What do we do with his body?"

I cringed. How had things gotten to where I was deciding how to dispose of a young man's remains? Granted, a young man who happened to be a mass murderer.

"Simple. Just leave him there. When he's eventually discovered, the authorities will believe he got away from Jarett at the Chicago airport and somehow made his way to Iowa."

"Jarett won't be happy about that. It means he'll have to admit that Gus gave him the slip."

"Not necessarily. You're all claiming amnesia, anyway. Jarett can deny even knowing Gus."

I nodded. "It's plausible."

"Anyway, we're probably overthinking this. The whole scientific community will b—"

Our conversation was cut short by a series of quick, successive, and extremely loud cracks. If I didn't already know what it was, I would have sworn it was gunfire.

"Shit, I'm not ready!" I said, grabbing the final rig, which was clearly identified as mine. I slung it over my shoulders, then pulled it off again, having forgotten everything I'd learned from Rose. "Aggh! I don't know how to put this on!"

"Take a breath. You're fine," Morley said, pushing the empty cart aside to make room for our incoming comrades.

"Go find out what's happening!" I said when he turned around to watch me get ready.

"Just concentrate on what you're doing. They'll be here soon."

Finally, after taking a couple of deep breaths, I recalled that I needed to start with the leg straps, and the moment I stepped into those, all Rose's teachings came flooding back to me at once.

After I'd finished adjusting the tension on my chest strap, Morley came over to inspect my handiwork.

"Impressive," he said, unzipping my hoodie a few inches. My body vibrated. He reached down into the space between my breasts ever so gently and took hold of the talisman. "But you're going to need this." I groaned when he zipped me back up and laid the talisman on the outside of my hoodie.

Just as I was contemplating taking off the rig and all my clothes and jumping on him, the door flew open and Rose and Lainie ran in. Rose was puffing and out of breath. "Cops," she said, dashing over to where we were standing behind the bed. Morley bent down to pick up her rig.

"Thanks," she said, taking the rig and nimbly sliding into it.

Lainie wasn't so composed. "Detective Douglas! He's here. He saw me!"

Rose added, "He saw us heading down the hall right before the firecrackers went off, so he knows where to find us. Let's just hope the commotion keeps him busy for a few minutes."

All at once, Jarett burst through the door.

"Everything good out there?" Rose said, hustling past me to the top of Gus's bed.

Jarett raked a hand through his hair. "All the cops are at

the supply cabinet, but they're gonna catch on pretty quick. I need my gear."

"It's here," Morley said, plucking it off the floor and tossing it to him. Jarett joined me behind the bed. Lainie followed.

"Okay," Rose said. "I'm ready for Gus. I think we're all just about ready, yes?"

"Yep," Jarett said, cinching up his last strap. It was the fastest I'd ever seen him get into his gear. He was good under pressure, it seemed.

"All right," Jarett said to Lainie after I helped her into her harness. "Face away from me, and I'll hook you in."

As Lainie stepped into position, I said to the group, "Don't forget: your rigs have to be touching your skin. Even a tiny part. You don't want to be caught on the other side without them."

Jarett was already wearing short-sleeved scrubs, so I wasn't worried about him, but I noticed that both Rose and Lainie were covered in clothing from neck to toe with only their faces and hands exposed. I said to them, "When we go, put your cheeks to your shoulders, touching your rigs. I'll count to three to give you warning." They both nodded.

Rose said, "Remember, everyone. When we go back, it'll be noisy and chaotic. And I should be honest with you. I've only done one night dive before, and it was scary as hell. Beautiful and exhilarating, but scary. The darkness will work in our favor, though. No one should spot us."

I glanced at Jarett, who looked like he was about to shit himself. "Great," he said.

"But don't panic. We should be able to see enough to steer towards a safe area."

"Should?" Lainie said. "Aren't we taking lights with us?"

Rose nodded, pointing to an unlit glowstick hanging from her rig. "Just these. We should probably activate them now.

And don't worry, Lainie. I have all the confidence in your pilot," she said, winking at Jarett.

"Okay, I'm withdrawing Gus's support," Morley said. "And then we can get him into his harness.

With a couple of brisk tugs, he pulled the ventilator out of Gus's mouth, then dragged him to the edge of the bed toward Rose. As they struggled to get him into the tandem harness, the door banged open, and Detective Douglas rushed in.

Chapter Twenty-Seven

FRIDAY, 6:45 P.M.

"What the fuck is going on here?" Sam yelled when he exploded into the room and saw all of us gathered around Gus's bed in our gear.

For a moment, no one spoke. We were all too stunned. Then Morley put his hands up and said, "We can explain. It's all good."

"All good? Your assistant slammed my head in a trunk!" he said, touching the back of his head as if to demonstrate. When he pulled his hand back around, it was smeared with blood. "Where is she?"

That was encouraging. He didn't recognize me without my disguise.

"And why would you flee the scene like that?"

"Look. Sam," Morley said. "I'll explain. It will all make sense in a minute, but please calm down."

Rose flashed me an anxious look that said, *Gus isn't in his harness yet!* What she didn't know was that it didn't matter if Gus was wearing a harness or not. He was going to die, regardless.

"Calm down? I'll ask you again. What's going on here?"

While Morley was busy trying to talk Sam off the ledge, I

mouthed to Rose, "*Let's go.*" I pointed to Gus's hand and mouthed again. "*Hold on.*"

Her eyes went wide with understanding. And horror. And just when I thought she might jam out, she laid her cheek on her rig and reached for Gus's hand. She took my hand in her other. At the same time, I felt Lainie and Jarett inching toward us, slowly, to form our human chain. One missing link, and this entire operation would collapse.

The room was silent for a moment until Gus began making these repulsive gurgling noises. I half expected him to wake up and start clawing at his throat, but he didn't move. We were losing him.

Sam's eyes widened when he spotted the ventilator lying on the bed next to Gus. "What's going on?" he said for the third time.

"I can explain," Morley said, stepping away from Gus and Rose with his hands in the air. He shuffled behind our group toward Sam. "I'm just coming over to show you something. It will answer all your questions. I promise."

A bluff to buy time, and Sam was buying it. "Make it quick."

When Morley got within a foot of Sam, I slowly reached up and took hold of the talisman, glancing left and right, hoping no one in my group had noticed. Fortunately, they hadn't. They were too focused on the business between Morley and Sam. As I opened my mouth to call out my final directions, Gus's body convulsed, startling everyone, especially Sam, who shoved Morley aside then lunged toward us.

"Lainie! Grab my wrist!" I said. As soon as Jarett had a hold of Lainie's other hand, I locked eyes with Morley who was scrambling over to stop Sam.

It was now or never. "One, two, three. *Return!*"

After a quick black flash, a cacophony of sounds filled my ears. Screaming. Crying. Praying. Freezing air whooshing all around me. In the darkness, I smelled fuel. Coffee.

But where I should have been experiencing the sensation of falling through air, I felt substance beneath me. Ahead of me, a small screen, flickering on and off. It showed a GPS map.

At once, I understood what had happened.

Chapter Twenty-Eight

THURSDAY, APRIL 11, 2024, 7:50 P.M.

We should have been falling weightlessly through the air under a billowy nylon canopy, making gentle contact with the ground a few minutes later. But instead, there was noise all around me. Screaming, moaning, shouting. Crying. A female voice repeating the same words over and over: *"Heads down. Hands on heads. Brace! Heads down. Hands on heads. Brace . . . "*

In the darkness, lights flickered haphazardly above my head, and a row of small TV screens randomly flashed on and off, displaying a GPS map with an altitude of around 12,000 feet.

We were back on the plane.

The five of us were back in our original seats on Flight 444 right before we zapped off to 2019. I was dumbfounded. How could this be happening? Had Morley and I been wrong all along, or did it simply mean that on a return timeblink, you were sent back to the last spot you touched rather than the last locat—

I didn't have time to think about that.

Leaning into the aisle, I took a panicked appraisal of my surroundings. Two strips of blue lights glowed eerily along the length of the cabin floor, and as my eyes adjusted to the low light, I was shocked to find a body lying face-down beside me. I was pretty sure it was a man, but I couldn't tell if he was dead or just unconscious. Across the aisle, Gus was slumped against the window in his blue hospital gown with his tandem harness loosely wrapped around him. He wasn't moving. Jarett was already standing, fiddling with the straps on his rig. Our rigs! I checked for mine, and sure enough it was still there, and even more of a relief: Lainie was still wearing her tandem harness.

I clambered to my feet, clutching the seat in front of me as the plane bounced erratically, losing altitude by the second. It was all I could do to stay upright. For some strange reason, I thought to grab my cell phone from the seat pocket. The bizarre things we humans do when death is staring us in the face.

As I stepped around the body in the aisle, a young woman in the seat behind Jarett caught my eye and gawked at me wide-eyed over her oxygen mask, as if she were looking at a ghost. I couldn't blame her; we'd just appeared out of thin air. Her gaze went to the rig fastened to my back. Did she know it was a parachute? Did she think I could rescue her—and the little red-haired girl bent over in the crash position next to her? Fuck! The little girl. I instantly felt like a monster leaving them behind. But what could I do? I barely had time to get my own crew off the plane. Mercifully, the woman seemed to understand there was no hope for rescue and resumed the crash position like everyone else. I had to get out of there.

Frigid air whirled about the cabin. It seemed to be coming from the front of the plane where I pictured a jagged hole ripped into the fuselage with wires thrashing in the wind and bits of insulation coming loose and shooting out into the night. I briefly thought about herding my group there. Then we could get Lainie hooked back up to Jarett and dive out of that hole to salvation. But no. We couldn't jump out of the front. We'd be sucked into the engine for sure. The back door was our only option for escape.

I glanced at Lainie. She was still in her seat, gathering personal items from the pocket in front of her. "What do we do?" she shouted.

Before I could answer, Rose shoved past Lainie into the aisle where she stepped over the body on the floor and headed to the front of the plane. There was no stopping her. She was going to her family. As she scrambled away, I was relieved to note she was also wearing her rig. Maybe we could salvage this mission after all.

"Heads down. Hands on heads. Brace! Heads down. Hands on heads. Brace, brace . . . "

The plane had stabilized somewhat in our four-and-a-half-minute absence, but it was still on a downward path—not straight down like it was before, but still angled toward the Earth. Jarett's TV screen flashed on for a brief couple of seconds, showing an altitude of about 11,500 feet, which, if I was remembering Rose's tutoring correctly, was right around the average height for a tandem jump. We had to hurry.

"I'll meet you two at the back," I said to Jarett and Lainie. "Get yourselves ready."

"Where are you going?" Jarett said, but his eyes went to Rose, who was picking her way to the front, and he understood immediately what was happening. He took hold of Gus's harness, which came off in one quick tug, then pushed past me and took off after Rose. I followed.

Lainie stumbled into the aisle. "I'm coming with you."

"No! Go to the back of the plane!" I said, pushing her away. "We'll be right there!"

"I'm not leaving without you."

"Lainie! We don't have time for this!"

"Dad would want us to stick together."

For fuck's sake. Why did she pick this moment to get all sentimental? "Come on, then. Hurry!"

Lainie and I scampered down the aisle, holding seat backs, armrests, people bent over in the crash position, and when we finally reached the front of the plane, Jarett was showing Rose the extra harness. But her eyes were vacant; even the revelation of a spare harness didn't faze her. Eli was squirming and screaming, completely inconsolable in his mother's arms. George and one of the female flight attendants were sprawled out on the floor, face down, blocking the cockpit door, which was partially ajar and definitely the source of all that cold, swirling air. What the hell was going on in there?

I took my attention to Jarett, who was busy checking George for injuries. The overhead lights were working in this part of the plane, but I wished they weren't. The flight attendant on the floor had a large part of her scalp sheared off. Blood pooled on the floor under her. When Lainie came up next to me and saw this, she bent over and spewed a gallon of puke on the floor. Another female attendant was strapped into her seat, hunched over, talking into the PA handset. *"Heads down. Hands on heads. Brace! Heads down. Brace. Brace . . . "* A male attendant had also assumed the crash position in his seat. Neither of them paid any attention to us.

"Rose! Come on, we have to go," I said.

"I can't leave him," she said, barely audible over Eli's screams and the chaos.

"Jarett!" I yelled. "Is George okay? Can you get him into the harness?" But as soon as I said it, my heart dropped. We had two tandem harnesses and three people.

As I mulled over this new conundrum, Jarett flipped George over. Half his face was smashed beyond recognition. His left eye stared right at me, lifeless. I stumbled backwards into Lainie, fighting the urge to vomit, too. She held me for a second before I tore myself away.

Jarett had two fingers on George's neck when I crawled up beside him. He shouted over my shoulder. "Rose. I'm sorry, but he's gone."

I turned my attention back to Rose. It seemed she'd already discovered George was dead, given that she wasn't trying to help him.

"We have to get Eli off this plane!" I yelled.

That was the cue she needed. She jumped to her feet quickly, as if she hadn't even been holding Eli in her arms, grabbing at random things with her free arm to keep herself upright: a handle on the wall, the male flight attendant's arm (he didn't even notice), the overturned drink cart that had obviously been the source of George's mortal wounds—and probably the flight attendant's, too.

Jarett snatched the spare harness off the floor and showed it to her again. "Rose, look! We can take Eli!"

She shook her head gravely. "It's too big. He'll fall out."

"Can't we tie some knots in it or something?" I shouted.

"I . . . I don't know," she said, looking as though she was about to pass out.

"We'll make it work somehow. Come on! We have to get to the back of the plane," I shouted, adding quickly, "We can't jump from here. Unless we want to end up in the engine."

No one hesitated. We started the uphill trek to the back of the plane—Jarett and Rose first, then me and Lainie. I saw Jarett reach up to one of the overhead bins and yank something down from it. He did the same halfway up the aisle, but the low light made it nearly impossible to see what he was taking. I wondered if he was stealing people's possessions, but why would he even think of doing such a thing? Especially now, when we were trying to escape with our lives.

Whatever he was doing didn't matter. I had to get to the rear door. But it wasn't easy with only the illuminated floor strips and brief flashes of cabin lights to guide us. I almost wished there was no light at all. At least then I wouldn't have been able to see all the terrified passengers bracing for impact. Passengers who would probably be dead in a few minutes. Damn it. The little red-haired girl. The very thought of her nearly stopped me in my tracks. Who was I to survive this thing and not her?

But there was Christopher's little cherub face swooping into my mind again. And my own will to live. I put my grief for my fellow passengers on hold and focused all my energy on putting one foot in front of the other, one hand in front of the other—pulling myself seat by seat—to the back of the plane.

Despite having a distressed toddler to deal with, Jarett and Rose were astonishingly quick and had passed the man on the floor when it was mine and Lainie's turn to climb over him. I went first and had only gone a few steps when I heard Lainie scream behind me.

I looked over my shoulder. Lainie was tugging her foot as if she'd caught it on something. Fuck! Nothing was ever easy. But when I ran back to help free her, I saw she wasn't stuck at all. The man on the floor had seized her ankle. Damn it, we didn't need this bullshit right now. I took hold of Lainie's hands and pulled. But the man's grip was firm.

I pushed Lainie to the side and stomped on the man's hand. Hard. He yelled without releasing her. He must have seen our rigs, and now he was hell bent to get off the plane—either by latching himself onto one of us or by commandeering one of our rigs.

"Let go!" I shouted, stomping on his hand again. Harder this time. The fucker was persistent. His grip was like a vise on Lainie's ankle. I wished Jarett hadn't already gone to the back of the plane, but he would never hear me calling him now.

Lainie grabbed my hands. "Pull!" she yelled, and after using every scrap of my strength to yank her away, she tumbled into me, her casted arm scraping the shit out of my face and neck on the way. I screamed in agony, but Lainie was free. I grabbed her hand and kept going.

When we reached the last row of seats before the lavatories, Jarett was busy positioning Eli chest-to-chest with his mother, rather than outward like in a normal tandem jump. Over his shoulder, at the very back of the plane, a flight attendant was strapped into her seat, bent over in the crash position. Her long brunette hair had come loose from its bun and was hanging in a tangled mess over her face. It seemed the crew had done all they could and were now bracing for the inevitable like everyone else.

Noticing Lainie and I had arrived, Jarett said to me, "Hook her up."

"Who?" I said, seeing he was busy and nowhere near ready for Lainie.

He shouted, "Lainie. You're taking her now!"

Fear flooded my veins. "What the fuck, Jarett? You take her! I'll help Rose!"

"NOW! That's an order!"

I recoiled. He was serious. It was then I noticed the spare harness lying on the floor by his feet. He wasn't using it. Instead, he'd wrapped one of the mock seat belts from a safety demo kit around Rose's torso and fastened it at Eli's back, out of reach of his wriggling arms. So that's what he'd been grabbing from the overhead bins. He was about to do the same with a second belt around Eli's middle, and, by the look of it, a third one around his legs.

I turned my attention to Lainie, who was bent over some vacant seats, peering out the window into the darkness. My heart swelled. We'd gone through so much together the last few days, and I was almost embarrassed to admit—even if just to myself—that she was growing on me. Maybe I wouldn't have to pretend to be on her side when we got back. Maybe we could be friends.

When she turned around, the terror in her eyes chilled me to the bone. It was all the motivation I needed. She was strapped into her harness, ready to go, and it was a simple matter of hooking her up to my rig instead of Jarett's. As much as the change of plans irritated me, I flew into action, thankful that Rose had insisted we all use tandem rigs, regardless of whether or not we'd be carrying a passenger.

"Come on!" I yelled, turning Lainie around so that her back was against my torso. "You're with me."

Once I'd secured her to my rig and checked all my connections, I took a quick glance at a TV to get a gauge on our altitude, but all the screens had gone black. It was anyone's guess how close to the ground we were. Two thousand feet? Five hundred? Ten?

I peered over Lainie's shoulder, past an elderly couple huddled in the crash position, to get a look outside. There, I could see a smattering of tiny lights in a nearby town, and I was surprised to find we were still quite high up. It didn't mean we could relax.

I heard Rose shout, "Are you ready to go?"

As I turned around to answer her, I caught sight of something that—if we made it out of here alive—would stick in my mind for the rest of my life: the old couple holding each other's hands. Damn. I imagined Morley and me in their place, being together at the end, neither person having to endure the pain of losing the other first, whether to cancer or old age or a plane disaster—and it gave me some solace. They wouldn't be alone at the end.

When Lainie and I scooted toward the galley, Rose stopped us for a quick gear check.

"Everything looks good. Will you know what to do?" she said, alluding to the fact that I hadn't had as much tandem training as Jarett.

"Yes," I said. "I was paying attention."

"Good. And Lainie, since you don't have goggles, try to keep your eyes closed as much as possible."

Lainie nodded.

"I'll get that door," Jarett said, stopping what he was doing to head into the galley. Lainie and I shuffled after him. He told us to stand back while he unlatched the door. I was glad he was there to do it. I didn't have the strength.

With a mighty tug on the handle and an equally big outward push, the door whooshed open, and the galley filled with icy air. The male flight attendant shot us a terrified look, then resumed the crash position. He must have lost all hope. Or maybe he thought he was dreaming. Whatever it was, he'd decided not to interfere with our operation.

"Good luck!" I yelled to Jarett as he backed away from the open door. Rose appeared behind him to deliver some final instructions.

"Aim for the center point between those two towns. Count three seconds, then deploy your drogue," she said. "Then pull the main canopy as soon as you're stable. We're plenty high enough to make a safe landing."

Every nerve was zinging. I lowered my goggles and cracked my glowstick.

But looking out into the pitch-black sky, I hesitated. It was the most unnatural feeling, knowing I was about to jump *willingly* from a height of several thousand feet with just a sheet of nylon to slow us down. Before I could ruminate on it any longer, I guided Lainie to the edge, and we stepped into the darkness.

"AYEEEEEEEE!" I yelled, trying to make it sound like I was having fun, but in truth, I was terrified. Lainie was screaming too, but it was almost impossible to hear her with the turbulent wind whipping past my ears.

By some stroke of luck or skill I didn't know I possessed, we'd tipped out of the plane in the correct position: face down, perfectly horizontal to the Earth. It surprised me that my stomach didn't drop like it might on a rollercoaster or a zipline. The sensation was more like landing on a giant, fluffy pillow, and after a few seconds of freefall, I found my terror giving way to something much more pleasant: a huge rush of adrenaline.

In my excitement, I nearly forgot to deploy the drogue, but when I pulled on the handle, nothing happened.

Trying not to panic, I tried again.

Again, nothing.

My mind whirled. All I could remember from our training was Rose's catch phrase: "No droguey, no floaty."

In other words, if the drogue failed, the main canopy couldn't deploy, either.

I yanked the handle again, harder, thinking I just wasn't using enough force, but nothing happened. It was truly jammed.

"Shit, shit, shit!"

We were gathering speed. Without the drogue to slow us down and keep us in belly-to-Earth position, we were essentially fucked.

I reached for the handle of the reserve chute but couldn't remember where it was located. The left side at the bottom? Right side, chest level? *Fuck!* My hands went to all the places I thought it might be. I couldn't find it.

Just then—probably from my panicked movements—our position shifted, and we began to spin, slowly at first, and then faster.

Around and around we went until soon we were spinning like a top.

I had to do something. Anything to regain control.

I closed my eyes for a moment, desperately trying to remember what Rose had taught us about recovering from a spin. But my mind was utterly blank.

Faster and faster we whirled. I was disoriented. Beyond dizzy. And because of the darkness, I had no idea how high we were.

I finally located the reserve-chute handle: chest level, left side. But we had to be stable before I could pull it or we risked the lines twisting up.

"Fuck!"

Then something clicked in my scattered mind. *Relax.*

Rose had emphasized it so often I'd thought she was neurotic, but the moment I put it into practice, all the other tricks started flowing back to me. *Raise your arms and legs. Point your toes. Arch. Breathe.*

When I got Lainie to do the same, the spinning miraculously slowed—not completely, but enough. It was our chance.

I yanked the reserve-chute handle.

My neck snapped forward, and we jerked upward.

I looked up just as the canopy finished opening, and my body went limp with relief.

"Omigod," Lainie yelled breathlessly. "That was fricken *insane.*"

I tested the lines, surprised at how well the back-up canopy responded to my small corrections. I worked to keep us more or less centered between the twinkling lights of the two small towns, as Rose had instructed. Now that I was getting the hang of things, I was fairly confident I'd be able to steer us toward open land once we were close enough to see it.

"You're doing great," Lainie said through chattering teeth.

"Look at the plane," I said, pulling on the left line to get a better view.

We watched its haunting silhouette disappear into the night, its exterior lights blinking feebly, like a last-ditch call for help. I thought of Rose's husband and the little red-haired girl and the old couple hunched over, holding hands. A tear popped out, which promptly flew away into the night.

We floated silently for maybe half a minute before Lainie yelled, "I think I see a clear spot down there, maybe a field."

I tugged on the toggle to steer toward it. "Yeah. I think you're right."

With a sudden shift, we floated toward the big, black void she'd pointed out, which I was praying was a soft, grassy meadow. Trees and buildings were not acceptable landing pads.

Once I could make out the ground, I pulled on the toggles and flared the chute as Rose had trained me, and we began slowing. I'd forgotten to remind Lainie to lift her legs, but she was doing it already. When we were maybe fifteen feet off the ground—I couldn't gauge our height very well in the darkness—I spotted a problem. A huge one.

"Shit!" I yelled, trying frantically to correct our course. But it was too late.

We plunged into water. Cold, dark—*deep*—water. I don't know how far down we went (ten feet maybe?) but we were strapped to-fucking-*gether* and sinking to the bottom of what I assumed was a pond or small lake.

A cluster of bubbles escaped my mouth, my nose. I pictured them rushing to the surface and releasing my screams.

This could NOT be the end of things. We'd come too far.

But even as those thoughts surfaced, we sank deeper. And the deeper we got, the more panicked our movements became.

Think, Syd!

Fuck! We hadn't even considered a water landing! Why? Surely there were lakes in Iowa. And rivers. Didn't the Mississippi run through it?

I could feel Lainie struggling as I grappled with the parachute's lines, which were floating down around us, hopelessly tangling as I tried to push them away.

When Lainie convulsed, it gave me the flash of clarity I needed. In order for us to get free from each other, we'd have to stop our frenzied thrashing and calm the fuck down—Rose's *relax* mantra all over again. It was a tall order when you're sinking into a watery abyss in a cluster of snarled strings, but we had to relax. Without doing that, we were as good as dead.

There are four points of connection between the skydiving student and the instructor: one *quick ejector snap* at each shoulder, and one at each hip. I remember Rose saying that it takes less than three seconds to unhook a student from the instructor's harness, but that was obviously much easier to do on a clear Sunday afternoon, not in the dark of night, twelve feet underwater.

It would do no good to ponder the absolute injustice of it. We'd come too far and accomplished so much already. No, it wasn't fair, but now was the time for action, not self-pity. As I reached up to find the two hooks joining Lainie and me at the shoulders, my sneakers hit something solid. We'd reached the bottom.

While I grappled with the shoulder hooks, I felt Lainie fussing at her hips. Good. She was working on releasing the lower hooks. Her bulky cast and the darkness and the water would make the task more difficult, but not impossible.

After I finally released the upper hooks and hoped that Lainie had done the same at her hips, I tried to propel myself upward but was stopped. We were still attached. Lainie was having trouble with the hook at her left hip, no doubt because of her cast.

Another cold glug of water flowed into my nostrils. I thought of Christopher. Always Christopher. My sweet, sweet boy. Laughing. Running. Having the time of his life. I imagined him tripping and falling with no one there to comfort him. My baby was going to grow up without a mother. Or a father.

Fuck, no! I couldn't let that happen. I seized Lainie's arm and threw it aside. More water flowed into my lungs. *NO!* It felt like minutes had passed, but I knew it had only been seconds. Precious, precious seconds. Finally, my fingers landed on the hook, and I unlatched it in one frantic click.

Finally, Lainie broke free.

I kicked my legs as hard as they would go, but it wasn't easy with the gear on my back and the lines getting in my way. More water flooded into my mouth. I kicked harder. I didn't know where Lainie was. It was so dark. Had she made it?

One last thrust, and I broke the surface, gasping for air under the canopy, which I frantically pushed away. I was surprised by how quickly I'd reached the top and how shallow the water had been—deep enough to have killed us, had we still been hooked together, but no more than maybe ten feet. I heard Lainie splashing around a few feet away.

"Omigod. Are you okay?" I said, breathing hard.

Between heaving gasps, she reported she was fine, but exhausted. We both were. Lainie must have been particularly tired after her run-in with a vodka bottle and throwing up all over the plane. Not to mention swimming with a waterlogged cast on her arm.

We still didn't know where we'd landed—a pond? A lake? A wastewater catchment? Dragging the canopy behind me, I paddled over to Lainie and looped her good arm around my shoulder, then started toward the shore. She tensed for a moment before surrendering and letting her body go loose.

I unhooked my glowstick from my rig and held it up in front of me. The rig was so heavy. I briefly considered dumping it but then remembered that I couldn't. I couldn't risk abandoning it for any Joe Blow to find. We had to dispose of all our gear properly.

"Where are we?" Lainie asked.

"I don't know. A lake maybe. I think I can see the edge," I said, pointing the light stick ahead of us, but I almost didn't care. We were alive. That's all that mattered.

But of course, it wasn't all that mattered. Where was everyone else?

And in the next thought: Where was the talisman?

I choked back a scream. The last time I'd seen it was back in the hospital room when I'd used it for our return timeblink. A lot had happened since then.

I let go of Lainie and groped at my neck, but where I was

sure I would find the treasured piece, I was met with cold, bare skin.

"No, no, no, no!" I cried.

"What's wrong?"

"My talisman! It's gone!"

"Are you sure?" she said, genuinely concerned, though she couldn't know how important it was that I find it. "Maybe it's inside your shirt."

Oh, how I wanted to believe that. And why wouldn't I? Nearly every time I'd lost it before, that's where it had ended up.

"Let's just get to shore. Can you make it on your own?"

"I think so," Lainie said, shuddering from the cold. Great. All we needed now was for one of us—or both—to succumb to hypothermia.

To distract myself from our compounding difficulties, I focused on the vast sky where millions of stars glittered like diamonds. It made me feel small and insignificant, as if my problems—my very existence—hardly mattered. So why, at the same time, did I feel my problems *were* the entire universe?

It was then I noticed a small light speeding through the sky. It couldn't have been the plane. That was long gone. A shooting star, maybe? Should I make a wish? It was hurtling toward the Earth at an astonishing speed.

Lainie blurted, "That's them!"

It wasn't a shooting star at all, but one of our fellow skydivers, and the light was coming from the glowstick as they came in for a landing maybe half a mile out.

"We have to wave them down!" I said, kicking my legs wildly to get to shore. Lainie followed.

A few moments later, I dragged the canopy through a thick stand of bulrushes and helped Lainie out of the water. Once we were standing on the muddy bank together, I handed Lainie the glowstick and told her to wave it in the air.

Soaked and shivering, I released my rig and dumped it on

the ground, then unzipped my hoodie and began digging around for the talisman in my shirt, my bra, the hem of my leggings. My hair. And then the hoodie. But the only thing I found was the cell phone I'd grabbed off the plane. It was obviously destroyed. I didn't even care. The talisman wasn't there.

Lainie was busy loosening the straps on her harness when I said, "Can you have a look for my necklace in your clothes? Maybe it came off during the jump and got tangled up there."

"Sure," she said. "It really must mean something to you, huh? Was it a gift from Morley?"

I nodded solemnly. "He gave it to me a few minutes before he died."

"Whoa. That's so sad."

She didn't know the half of it. Without the talisman, I would never see Morley again.

"Is that why you hold it whenever you timeblink? For comfort?"

Uh oh. She'd noticed. But she didn't appear to suspect it was the very *mechanism* of timeblinking. "I, uh . . . yes. Didn't think it was that obvious."

She gave me a pained smile and set to work inspecting her clothes for the missing talisman. A head-to-toe search turned up only a second ruined cell phone and a small bundle of waterlogged cash she'd pulled from the waistband of her black skinny jeans—the money she'd stolen from Morley. She gave me a sheepish look and tried to hand it to me. I was instantly overcome with grief. If we'd stayed in 2019, Morley would be taking his last breaths right now and wouldn't need such trivial things as money. When I ignored Lainie's offer, she self-consciously tucked the cash into her hoodie pocket.

"Damn it!" I yelled at the sky. "I have to find that talisman!"

Lainie put her hand on my shoulder, a tender gesture that caught me off guard. "It could have come off anywhere.

Maybe on the plane. Or in there," she said, tilting her head to the lake. I turned to look at it. Now that we were on higher ground, I saw it was, in fact, just a large pond, maybe a hundred feet across and fifty feet wide. Not huge, but big enough. If that's where the talisman had ended up, it might as well have been the Pacific Ocean.

I felt myself slither away from Lainie's hand and collapse to the ground.

Chapter Twenty-Nine

THURSDAY, APRIL 11, 2024, 8:13 P.M.

When I opened my eyes, Rose was crouched over me against a backdrop of shimmering stars. She'd bundled Eli in her soft blue cardigan, and the little guy was sleeping peacefully on her left shoulder. I smiled. Jarett's improvised harness had done its job.

With her free hand, Rose pushed a clump of wet hair back from my face, and I scrambled to sit up. After I got my bearings, Lainie helped me to my feet.

"How did you get here so fast?" I said to Rose through chattering teeth.

"Lainie flagged me down while you were passed out."

"How long was I out?"

"Fifteen minutes, maybe a bit more."

"Are you okay?" Rose said, bouncing her knees gently to keep Eli asleep.

"Never mind me. How is he?" I said, rubbing the little guy's back.

"Screamed bloody murder the whole way down, but everything held."

"I'm so glad he's safe."

"Thanks to Jarett's quick thinking."

"Where is he, anyway?" I said, scanning the dark field.

"I'm not sure. He insisted we jump first—you know, the women and children thing."

"Well shit, this doesn't make things easy. We didn't bank on losing a team member along the way," I said, gasping when I remembered something else we'd lost: the talisman.

As if she'd read my mind, Rose said, "Lainie told me about your necklace. I'm sorry. I know it was special to you."

The moonlight was bright enough to illuminate the sympathetic look on her face. And something else. Dried tears. She'd lost something precious, too. It was then I decided there was nothing I could do about the talisman. Not right now, anyway. I bent down and began collecting the gear.

"We'll have to bring this with us," I said.

"Where are we going?" Lainie said, helping me gather everything up with her good hand.

"I'm not sure. First, we'll have to figure out where Jarett got to."

"Sounds like a lot of walking," she said, looking around the vast field in the moonlight. "Can't we just leave this stuff here?"

"No," I said, stopping short of telling her the original plan, which was for me to dispose of all the gear back in 2019. But of course, that was impossible now. We'd have to ditch it somewhere else and hope no one decided to investigate where it came from.

"How are we going to find Jarett?" Rose said.

"No idea. Did he even jump? Maybe he chickened out and decided to take his chances on the plane."

"Well, if that's the case, I hope it lands safely."

"Me too. But he'll have a lot of explaining to do if it does."

Once we'd bundled up my canopy and I'd described my disastrous first skydiving experience to a dumbstruck (but extremely proud) Rose, I slung the rig over my shoulder, and we set off through the grassy field toward one of the small towns. The night was mild, but with our cold, wet clothing clinging to us, Lainie and I were both shivering like a couple of scared Chihuahuas.

"So, this is Iowa," I said, not even realizing I'd spoken out loud.

"Really?" Lainie said.

"Yes, according to the last reading on the GPS. Speaking of which," I said, impulsively grabbing for my phone but remembering it had been destroyed in the lake. "Oh, right. My phone drowned."

"Yeah, mine too," Lainie said, producing her phone from her hoodie pocket, trying it anyway. "Yep. Dead."

As she made to lob it into the dark field, I seized her arm.

"Evidence," I said.

"Why is it so important to keep our time traveling secret?" she said, putting the phone back in her pocket. "We'd be freaking famous if people found out we were the world's first time travelers."

"I've got news for you. We're going to be famous, anyway."

"We are?"

"It's not every day five people show up alive and well after a devastating plane crash, especially since the security cameras will prove we boarded said plane in Chicago."

Lainie looked off toward the horizon where the plane was no longer visible. "So, how are we going to explain everything?"

"I don't know, but we're all going to have to agree on something pretty quick. Hey Rose. You didn't happen to grab your phone from the plane, did you?"

"Oh! Yes!" she said, as if she'd completely forgotten. She reached into her shirt and produced a gold bejeweled device from inside her bra, then entered her password and handed it to me while we walked.

"Perfect. At least we'll be able to get a gauge on our location. I'd try phoning Jarett, but I have no idea what his number is."

"He's a Seattle cop," Lainie said. "Shouldn't be too hard to track him down."

"No, but that would mean making phone calls to one or more precincts, and the last thing we need to do is bring attention to him. And us."

"It may be our only option," Rose said.

As I called up the map app, I stopped in my tracks. Lainie and Rose stopped, too.

"I'm calling my sister," I said, punching in her number and putting the phone on speaker. "She knows about time-blinking—the basics, anyway. Like you guys. Maybe she can help us."

Kendall picked up after the first ring. "Hello?" she said suspiciously, probably because she didn't recognize Rose's number.

"Kenny! It's Syd . . . I. We—"

"Oh, thank goodness you're okay! I just heard the news." She sounded frantic.

"Wait. How did you hear already?"

"Your friend just called me. Is it true? Your plane crashed?"

"My friend? What friend?"

"He said he was on the same flight as you. Jared, I think?"

"What the hell? Jarett? How did he get in touch with you?"

"He said he knew I was a wedding photographer and tracked me down online. I literally just got off the phone with him. I gave him your number."

"Well, that's not going to work. My phone drowned in an Iowa swamp."

"Pardon me?" she said.

"But wait a minute. You have Jarett's number on your phone now. Can you send it to this one?"

"What's going on, Syd? This Jarett person didn't give me any information except to say that you and Lainie were okay."

"Did he tell you we timeblinked?"

"No! What's going on?"

Good. Jarett was keeping his mouth shut. What happened on Flight 444 stayed on Flight 444.

"Look, all I can say right now is that our plane ran into trouble, and we were told to brace for a crash landing."

"Omigosh, Syd!"

"But we timeblinked off the plane before that happened. And now that we're back, we need to find Jarett. We need to get back to Chicago and tell a convincing lie about how we all ended up back at the airport completely unscathed."

"Oh, man," she said. "This is nuts."

"I know. But it's the only way. Deny everything. If anyone asks, just say the last time you had any contact with me and Lainie was at the Buffalo airport, okay?"

"Yes. Of course."

Kendall understood the importance of keeping time-blinking under wraps.

"One more thing. We're all going to have amnesia."

"All? Who else is with you?"

"There are five of us. But one's a toddler who thankfully hasn't learned to talk yet."

"Umm, just a thought, but won't that seem fishy? All of you having amnesia at the same time? And how do you propose to sneak five people back into the Chicago airport? There are security cameras all over the place."

"You got any better ideas?"

"It's just so far-fetched," she said, wearily.

"Yeah, but it's a helluva lot more plausible than the truth. Can you imagine? 'Hey, we're a bunch of time travelers who zapped off the plane right before it crashed. Now, if you'll step aside, we'll be on our way.'"

"Okay. Obviously, the truth isn't an option. But what if you all just insisted you never got on the plane to begin with? The security cameras will tell a different story, of course, but technology isn't always perfect. It's certainly more believable than group amnesia."

"I don't know, Kenny," I said. "Modern security equipment is pretty failsafe. And the techies will insist there's nothing wrong with it."

"Regardless of which version you go with, you'd all better be darned good storytellers. What if you're asked to submit to a lie-detector test?"

My sister was obviously thinking clearer than any of us. I'd not considered that possibility.

"Can they even do that?" Rose said. "We aren't criminals, for goodness' sake!"

I shook my head, wishing we'd given this part of the plan more thought. The one shining light in the whole mess was that I was still the only member of this group who knew *how* timeblinking worked. Or at least how it *used* to work now that the talisman was gone and timeblinking was no longer possible.

"Maybe Jarett will have some ideas," Lainie said, trying to be helpful. "About the lie-detector thing."

"No matter what you decide, the authorities are going to be watching you guys like hawks."

"I know. It's a shit show. The very last resort would be for us to disappear until it all blows over, but where would we go? And for how long?"

"I could reserve a hotel for you in my name and—"

Lainie gasped. "Wait! What if we just stayed here?"

"Here?" I said. "As in, Iowa?"

"As in *right here*, where we're standing. Think about it. We could all say everything was going along fine until the plane started having problems, and the next thing we knew, the five of us were on the ground in the middle of nowhere. We can use Rose's phone to call the police, so it doesn't look like we're trying to cover anything up."

I let that digest for a moment. It was a great idea. Why complicate things if we didn't have to? It would certainly be easier than trying to make our way back to the airport undetected and then telling virtually the same story—that we had no clue how we got there. And bonus, no security cameras to track our movements.

"Yes!" came Kendall's tinny voice on the phone. "It's a fantastic idea. Your only lie will be the part where you didn't know *how* you ended up in the field, which actually won't be too far from the truth."

I nodded. "All right, I like it. But we have some logistics to work out first. In the meantime, I'll need Jarett's number."

Chapter Thirty

THURSDAY, APRIL 11, 2024, 9:17 P.M.

About fifteen minutes later, we were standing next to a long, flat gravel road with our gear at our feet, waiting for Jarett to arrive. When I'd talked to him on Rose's phone, he said he'd landed in a field not too far from a service station where he'd found a minivan with its key handily hidden in the wheel well. "Gotta love small towns," he'd said before telling me to stay put and that he'd be there shortly.

"It probably went against every fiber of his law-abiding being to commit grand theft auto," Lainie said.

Despite my crushing worry about the talisman, I laughed.

"He's one of the good guys," Rose said.

I nodded. "He is. Though I'd been thinking the opposite when he forced me to take our lovely Miss Lainie on the jump. I thought he'd chickened out, to be honest, and that he was using you and Eli as an excuse."

"You shouldn't be so hard on him," Rose said in the darkness, rocking Eli back and forth. "He seems to like you. A lot."

"He sure does," Lainie said, playfully.

"Hey, hey! Have you forgotten he ditched you on the plane at your time of greatest need?"

"Yeah, but *you* didn't."

I smiled awkwardly at her. "Do you want to phone your mom and Sarah to let them know you're okay?"

"Not yet. Let them think I'm dead for a little while."

"Come on, Lainie. You don't mean th—"

"Hopefully that's Jarett now," Rose said, nodding down the dark road at a vehicle way off in the distance. It was coming from the direction of Waverly, which we'd learned was a small town 125 miles northeast of Des Moines, where Jarett said he'd touched down. Soon, a rusted minivan pulled up to our group and the hazard lights flashed to life. The engine was still running when the driver climbed out, which I was relieved to see was Jarett.

But as I bent down to gather up the gear, the other door popped open. "What the hell?" I said.

Jarett hurried around to help a wobbly passenger out of the van.

"Who's *that*?" Lainie said.

When Jarett and the second person shuffled over, I said, "You're kidding me."

"Hello, *Janice*," the passenger said to me with a hint of contempt in his voice, but mostly, it sounded like amusement.

"Well, fuck," I said. "Detective Douglas."

"Please. Call me Sam. Oh look, if it isn't the elusive Lainie Brixton. Looks like I've finally tracked you down."

Lainie's eyes went wide.

I shook my head in disbelief. "How did y—"

"Found him on the plane," Jarett said. "The unconscious guy in the aisle?"

My mind flew back to the plane and then to the hospital room where Sam had lunged at us just before we zapped out. "But that was a return timeblink."

"You've obviously never had a tagalong before," Jarett said.

I shook my head woozily as Sam looked at us up and

down. "What happened to you two, anyway? You look like a couple of drowned rats."

When we didn't answer, he took off his jacket and held it out to Lainie. "Here, kiddo. Take this before you freeze to death."

She gave him a small smile and accepted the coat.

"Why did you bring *him*?" I said, shooting Jarett an annoyed look.

"Now, now. Be nice."

"I'm too tired to be nice. Why'd you bring him?"

He sighed. "Right after Rose and Eli jumped, and I was about to do the same, our friend Sam here stumbled into the galley. I was utterly shocked to see him."

"No shit."

"Anyway, I remembered the extra harness and decided right then and there to bring him with me. I couldn't leave him behind. He was there because of us, after all."

I couldn't argue with him about that.

"Plus, he's a fellow officer. You never leave a comrade behind. Please don't be angry."

Damn, I wanted to be angry. But how? He'd saved someone's life. I just hoped that *someone* would be able to keep his mouth shut like the rest of us. Gus had been our only wildcard before.

I glanced over the men's shoulders to the beat-up minivan behind them. "You're going to have to ditch that piece of junk."

"What do you mean? How else are we getting to Chicago?"

"We're not going to Chicago."

"What? Why not?"

"That plan's been scrapped," I said, nodding in Sam's direction. "How much does he know?"

"Everything."

I blinked at Jarett irritably.

"I had to tell him. All of it. Right from our initial time-blink to the five days we spent in Port Raven, and all the way to the moment he crashed our party in Gus's room and ended up on Flight 444."

I shook my head, more in defeat than anger. "Great."

"I had to tell him," he said again. "For obvious reasons."

"You should have left him on the plane. No offense, Sam."

"None taken."

Jarett said, "Okay, Madame Timeblink, I thought you wanted to keep this thing under wraps. Think about it. If I'd left him on the plane, how would his remains at the crash site be explained? Or worse, if the plane doesn't end up crashing—"

Sam cut in. "If I'd survived, I would have blown the lid off this whole thing. I would have told the investigators about how you all—how *we* all—beamed out of the hospital room and ended up on the plane, no matter how batshit crazy it would have made me look."

I said, "So, does this mean you're not going to tell anyone what happened?"

He let out a small breath. "For the time being, no. I tend to agree with Officer Coop here—it would be best to keep things on the down low."

"Well, thank you," I said. "For seeing the big picture."

"I'm not saying we should keep it hush forever. What if humankind can use this power to undo some of its biggest mistakes?"

"That's not how it works," I said. "But we don't have time to get into that right now. Right now, we have to figure out where we're going to dump this equipm—Holy shit."

"What?" Jarett said.

"We have a freaking built-in solution to all our problems. And I have you to thank for it."

"You're welcome. What did I do?"

Just then, Eli started fussing.

"He's probably hungry," Rose said, bouncing the little guy more vigorously on her hip, trying to keep him happy.

"There's a baby seat in the van," Jarett said, somewhat impatiently. "Maybe there's food in there, too."

Rose headed toward the idling vehicle. "I'll have a look. At the very least, I'll be able to keep him warm in there."

I had an urge to follow her to the warm vehicle but stayed put. "Lainie, why don't you join her? You look like you're about to pass out from the cold."

"It's okay. The last time I missed a group meeting, it didn't turn out very well for me."

"Fair," I said, turning my attention to Jarett, "As I was saying, you might have inadvertently solved all our problems —by saving Sam's life."

"Well, that's an abrupt change of heart. A minute ago, you were advocating for his death in a fiery crash."

I ignored him and turned to Sam. "I don't know if you're the luckiest or the *un*luckiest guy on the planet."

"I've been wondering that myself."

"The good news is that you're still alive. The bad news . . . I think you're stuck in 2024 for good."

"What do you mean, you *think?*"

"Buddy," Jarett said. "Most people would kill for this opportunity. Think about it. You've traveled five years into the future and haven't aged a day. Not to mention, you get to skip the whole fricken pandemic."

"Pandemic?"

Jarett's mouth fell open. "Ha! You *are* the luckiest man on the planet."

"Pandemic?" Sam said again. "Like in the movies? You guys are pulling my leg."

People never ceased to surprise me. Here was a guy who accepted the whole time-travel thing without question but was dubious about a worldwide health crisis.

"I wish we were joking, but the truth is, the world kinda

sucked for a while there. You'll find out soon enough. Right now, we have some logistics to iron out before we call the cops."

The two men exchanged amused looks with each other.

"Yeah, yeah, I know. You *are* the cops. But not the ones we need. You'll have to put your badges aside for the next little while and think more like criminals if we're going to sweet talk our way out of this disaster. I wouldn't be surprised if we end up being investigated for our potential involvement in the crash of Flight 444."

"*If* it crashes," Sam put in.

"You were on that plane," I said. "Do you really think it landed safely?"

He shrugged.

"Okay, Sam. Again, lucky you . . . you've got wheels," I said, pointing to the minivan, "And now, you also have an assignment." I hoisted up my rig, which had been sitting at my feet the whole time.

"Do tell," Sam said.

"I'm sure Jarett filled you in on the problem with this gear."

"He did."

"Well, it will be your job to dispose of it. I don't care where it ends up—just nowhere near here."

"Since when did you become my boss?" he said.

"Since I've had a ton of experience with timeblinking, and you should probably trust me. Were you hoping to go back to Port Raven?"

"Of course. I do live there."

"*Did*," Jarett said. "You *did* live there. In 2019. Remember, it's 2024 now."

He raked a hand through his close-cropped hair. I felt sorry for him standing there in his suit pants and black socks, his rumpled dress shirt, half-untucked. He reminded me of a character from one of those debt commercials. A man who'd just lost everything. In fact, he probably had. And it was my duty to warn him about it.

"If you think your biggest problem is explaining your whereabouts for the last five years, think again." I looked at Jarett. "Did you tell him about the skin thing?"

He shook his head.

The coward. He said he'd told Sam everything about timeblinking, but he left out the most important—and devastating—part.

"Did you have a family in 2019?" I said, carefully.

"Yes, I . . . I *do*. A wife, three kids. Four, six, and nine years old. Wait a minute," he said, stopping to calculate. "Nine, eleven, and fourt—shit. I have a fourteen-year-old daughter."

Both Jarett and Lainie shot me uneasy glances.

"Well," I said, dreading what I was about to tell him but equally keen to rip the bandage off quickly. "Timeblinking comes with a very specific set of rules, as Jarett explained to you already. But he left out one of the unfortunate side effects."

"Side effects? Damn. Am I going to grow a third eye?"

"If only it was that simple. No. The problem is that your family won't be able to see, hear, or touch you. Ever again. You're essentially a ghost to them now."

Even in the darkness, I could see Sam's face drain of color. After a few moments, he said, "You're shitting me, right?"

I shook my head solemnly. "In fact, *anyone* you've ever had skin-to-skin contact with falls into this same category."

"So, what do I do? I've come into contact with half the people of Port Raven."

Jarett said, "I hate to say it, friend, but you should probably start fresh somewhere else. We can help you with whatever you need. Just let us know."

"I don't want to start somewhere fresh!" He started pacing back and forth. "My family needs me. I need them!"

His pain was almost palpable. I'd just spent the last week

trying to avoid the exact same fate. Fuck. Why did he come back with us?

"I'm so sorry, Sam. Truly. I wish things could be different."

He walked away from the group in the opposite direction of the van and disappeared into the darkness. We all exchanged worried looks when he broke into loud, uninhibited sobbing.

Lainie whispered, "That's the saddest sound I've ever heard."

"Hits you right in the gut," Jarett said.

"We're witnessing what could have happened to all of us if Gus had died and stranded us in 2019."

"It would have been all my fault, too," Lainie said. "I am so sorry."

Surprising myself, I rubbed her shoulder. "You weren't thinking properly. You saw a way to be reunited with your dad and you took it."

After a few minutes—minutes we didn't really have to waste—Sam came back to the group, wiping his eyes. "So, what, I go start over somewhere else and let everyone believe I just took off? Like some loser deadbeat dad? God, my poor family. My parents. Fuck! Are my parents even still alive?"

I pressed my lips together and shrugged apologetically.

His sadness had already given way to anger. "This is a fucking nightmare."

Time was ticking, but I didn't want to pressure him. Not only had I just dealt him the most devastating news, but I'd also cold cocked him, accidentally dragged him into a different time realm, and expressed my wish to leave him behind on a crashing plane. He had every reason to be pissed.

He shook his head dejectedly. "Oh, Lizzy."

"Like Jarett said, we'll help you get set up wherever you go."

"You sure there's no way for me to go back? To 2019?"

I nodded. "But here's the deal. Once this shitstorm dies down, I'll come and find you and see if we can't figure out something together," I said, knowing full well it would be impossible. Especially without the talisman.

He nodded absently.

"You should really be on your way," I said as gently as possible.

He turned and shuffled toward the van. My heart broke for him. I'd treated him terribly.

Jarett grabbed Rose's rig off the road, and the three of us —Jarett, Lainie, and I—followed Sam to the vehicle where Rose was hopping out with her agitated little boy.

Sam said, "Hope there's gas in the tank. I seem to have lost my wallet. And my shoes."

Jarett bent down and removed his canvas slip-ons and handed them to his comrade.

"Thanks. That's *one* of my problems solved," he said, sliding into his new shoes, which appeared to fit him well enough.

"Hey, Jarett," I said. "Did you grab your wallet from the plane?"

"No, it was too dark. Couldn't find it. Rose? What about you?"

"Sorry, no. I'm amazed I even had the presence of mind to rescue my phone."

Lainie cleared her throat and cast me a brief, guilty look before pulling a wad of wet bills out of her pocket. Of course. The money she'd stolen from Morley. "You could probably make it all the way to Mexico with this."

Sam raised his brows. "Well, well. Look at you, saving my butt, kiddo. Thanks. But Mexico is off the table for someone with no passport. Or even a driver's license."

"Where do you think you'll end up?" she said, handing him the money.

"I don't really know. Probably a big city. New York,

maybe. Where no one would notice a sad loner setting up shop."

Good. At least he was thinking ahead.

"For the record," Lainie said, "Gus told me it was his friend's house. He made me wait outside. I didn't know he killed that old lady until you told me."

Sam looked at Lainie sideways. "Why didn't you say so?"

"I was scared you wouldn't believe me. But, for real, I had nothing to do with it. I could never do something so terrible."

Despite his profound grief, he winked at her. "I already knew you were probably innocent. This old, seasoned detective has a bit of a sixth sense about these things. But thanks for clearing it up."

A few minutes later, as our little group huddled together at the side of the road (two of us still damp and shivering and another trying to console an increasingly agitated toddler), Sam rolled the van to a stop and lowered the window. "Good luck with everything. I'll be watching the news. Can't wait to hear how it all turns out."

"Me too," I said. "Make sure you call Jarett in a couple of days—after the hoopla dies down a little—and we'll help you get set up."

He smiled weakly and drove away. When I could no longer see his taillights, I rubbed my hands together and said, "Okay, Let's find out what good liars we are, shall we?"

Chapter Thirty-One

SATURDAY, AUGUST 24, 2024

"There she is, my hero!" Rose said when I swung the cabin's front door open to let her in. My dopey old labradoodle, Jinx, sniffed at Eli in her arms before retreating to his bed in the corner of the living room.

"Cute pup," Rose said, setting Eli down next to Christopher. She spread out her arms and pulled me in for an extra long hug. I didn't resist. We hadn't seen each other since April 12, the day *The 444 Five* ended up in an Iowa cornfield claiming to have no memory of how they got there.

When we finally unwrapped our arms from each other, I said, "Stop with the hero stuff already. It'll go to my head."

"Got it, boss," she said, winking.

As she and Christopher introduced themselves to each other, I bent down to Eli's level and said, "Hi, cutie pie. You've certainly grown in the last four months."

"*Baxzadoo*," he said, making a goofy face at me before locking his eyes on Christopher. The two of them began sizing each other up as if neither of them had seen another child before.

Rose took a quick scan of her surroundings. "The place hasn't changed a bit."

I leaned into her ear and whispered, "Remember the *Pact.*"

She nodded quickly and whispered back, "Sorry. I got excited."

The *Iowa Pact,* as we'd dubbed it the night we returned from 2019, specifically forbade us to talk about timeblinking anywhere but a wide-open space. Like a park. Or a cornfield.

"Plus," I said, still in her ear, "Isla doesn't know anything. She thinks I only met you on that flight four months ago."

Rose smiled playfully. "You *did.*"

I smiled back at my friend. Yes, Rose was my friend, probably for life, given what we'd been through together.

"Anyway, it's lovely here," she said. "So peaceful."

"Are you kidding? It's a damned zoo with all the kids running around the place. They're down at the beach right now. Would Eli be brave enough to venture down there with this little man?" I said, ruffling Christopher's hair.

"Listen, this kid fears nothing. Especially other people. He's been known to take over whole conversations at parties."

"Oh? He's talking now?"

She laughed. "If you can call it that. He has his own language. People are always looking to me for translation, but sadly, even I can't help."

"We'll consider it a blessing," I said. Rose nodded. When the authorities gave up trying to get answers from the adults of *The 444 Five,* they'd turned their attention to Eli, hoping to get an unfiltered account of the events leading up to our exit, or at least one small clue. But he'd proved completely useless with his incoherent babbling. I wondered if, with age, he would remember enough details for it to become a problem.

Christopher held out his hand to Eli. "Do you want to make sandcastles?"

"*Sqicsleshds,*" Eli answered and took Christopher's hand without so much as a glance back at his mother.

"Told you. I think he gets his social streak from his father. God rest his soul."

As the two boys scurried toward the back door, I yelled, "Be careful on the stairs!"

"We will!"

When we were alone, Rose said, "Have you heard any news about your dragonfly necklace?"

I shook my head gloomily. "My bi-weekly emails to the NTSB and FAA always get the same stock reply: *Our investigation is ongoing, and we are unable to release personal items to the victims' families or your group until the final report has been published.*"

"Oh, Syd." She reached out and rubbed my arm. "I know how important that necklace was to you."

No, she didn't. She believed the talisman was merely a piece of jewelry—a sentimental keepsake from my dead fiancé—not the holy grail of timeblinking.

I sighed. "What's worse is that their investigation could take years to finish, thanks to us. The bastards. *Your group*, they say. Talking about us like we're terrorists. Like somehow we were responsible for the disaster. And all the deaths."

"Don't let it get to you, Syd. They've already determined the cause of the crash."

"Sure, that's what their preliminary reports say. But do you really think they'll ever be convinced of our complete innocence? We survived without a scratch while a hundred and twenty-two people were incinerated."

Rose winced.

"Sorry. I just get so angry when I think about the whole thing," I said. "Anyway, enough of that. Come on. I'll get you some lemonade and introduce you to the troops."

"Has everyone arrived already?" Rose said, following me into the kitchen.

"Yep, you're the last of the misfits."

She glanced over her shoulders before she lowered her voice and said, "How's your friend, Jarett?"

I gave her a curious look. "He's your friend too, lady. And he's fine. Great, actually. He's put in for a transfer to the Port Raven Police Department."

"Oh? Did he get tired of all that driving to visit you?"

"Gosh, no. It has nothing to do with me. He got wooed by the charm of Port Raven after he spent those five days here. Just couldn't get enough of it."

"Don't you mean he couldn't get enough of *you*?"

"Rose!" I said. "Don't be ridiculous. We're friends. He wanted a job with more work-life balance, and the Seattle gig wasn't giving him that."

"Okay, girl. You just keep telling yourself that story."

I rolled my eyes at her, then pulled the jug of lemonade out of the fridge. "Besides, it has more to do with Sam. The two of them are huge golf and fishing fanatics, and Jarett's been out from Seattle almost every Sunday to do one or the other with his new buddy. Much to Lizzy's chagrin."

"Lizzy. That's Sam's wife, right?"

I nodded.

"I still can't believe Sam's luck with that whole thing," Rose said, being purposely vague—observing the rules of the *Iowa Pact*.

But I knew what she meant about Sam's luck. Not only did he bypass the whole pandemic, but he also discovered he was completely immune to the invisibility phenomenon of time-blinking.

It happened after he drove away from us in the cornfield, after we'd told him he would be a ghost to his family forever. He was a detective, after all, and it was his nature to keep digging, even when all the facts had supposedly been laid on the table. That's why, instead of heading to New York to start a whole new life as we'd instructed him to do, he drove straight back to Port Raven. He needed proof our allegations were true.

And as he stood in a downpour peering into the kitchen

that had undergone a major renovation in the five years he'd been gone, Lizzy appeared in the window. She was drying a plate and talking to someone on her cell phone when she spotted him. He watched the plate slip out of her hand and smash on the floor. Before he could decide what to do (*run? hide?*), Lizzy was already outside. When she got to him, she slapped him across the face, then threw her arms around him and hugged him until he could barely breathe.

That woman was a saint. She'd never wavered from her belief that her husband hadn't left of his own free will. Not in the whole five years. This, despite the only information she'd had to go on was that he'd disappeared from a hospital room along with two unidentified car accident survivors and two other mysterious people who'd been in the room at the same time. Morley had also been there, of course, but he'd simply slipped out of the room after our departure, then drove to The Merryport where he was killed an hour later. And therefore, unavailable for comment.

When Sam explained his AWOL status to Lizzy as being necessary for the family's safety—that he'd spent the entire time in a witness protection program—she took it as absolute truth. Even when he told her he would need to tell everyone else it was a "terrible lapse in judgement." Essentially, he was setting himself up to look like a deadbeat dad that deserted his young family for five years—and asking Lizzy to go along with the story. She did so without question, which seemed to help Sam's standing in the department. If Lizzy was willing to forgive Sam for his indiscretion (a probable extramarital affair in their eyes), it would have to be good enough for them.

As for Sam's good fortune of being visible to his family, I had to assume it was a result of his piggybacking on a return blink—a revelation that's been nagging at me ever since.

"So, is Sam coming?" Rose asked, pulling me from my thoughts.

"No, he's busy every Saturday with his kids. I didn't want to bother him."

"That's too bad. I would have liked to get to know him. At least I'll get to see Jarett and Lainie. Lainie did come, right?"

"Yes, she got here last week. I think she was a little homesick for good ol' Sandalwood Lake."

"I know how she feels," Rose said nostalgically.

"Speak of the devil," I said, spotting Lainie running up the deck stairs. She burst through the French doors and dashed into the kitchen.

"Rose!" she said, throwing her arms around my stunned friend, who hugged her back tentatively.

When they parted, Rose looked Lainie up and down and said, "Who the heck is *this* movie star?"

I'd forgotten Rose hadn't seen Lainie since the night of our return timeblink. Since Lainie's transformation.

Gone was the green hair, the thick makeup, and the eyebrow piercing we'd come to accept as a part of Lainie's very essence, pleasantly replaced by a toned-down version of the girl. More polished.

"Movie star? Me?" she said to Rose. "Ha! Do you need glasses?"

"I don't think so, girl. I mean, your green hair was fun, but *this?*" she said, caressing Lainie's long, smooth chestnut locks, "this is next level!"

"Awe. You're making me blush," Lainie said, batting her naturally thick eyelashes.

Rose laughed.

"Oh! I almost forgot why I came in here. To get a juice box for Eli. Is he allowed?"

"Of course, dear. But be forewarned. He won't leave you alone now. He's like a golden retriever puppy . . . give him a treat, and you're his friend for life."

Lainie giggled. "That's okay. He's the sweetest." She

pulled the fridge open and grabbed a box of juice before running outside.

"And that's the new Lainie," I said. "Her mom wasn't too excited about putting her back on a plane, but I reminded her that the rest of us have flown in the meantime with no problem."

"You can't blame her for being worried."

"I think she was more worried about Lainie's request to visit me, to be honest, or should I say *suspicious*, considering Lainie wanted nothing to do with me before all this."

"Well, it's wonderful you've worked things out with her," Rose said. "Your dad must've had some crazy intuition, throwing the two of you together like that."

"Indeed, he did," I said.

Indeed, he did.

Twenty minutes later, all the adults—Rose, Jarett, me, and my three sisters (yes, including Lainie)—were gathered under the huge offset umbrella I'd installed last summer, some of us sipping lemonade, some of us wine, some beer, depending on who it was, while the kids splashed around at the water's edge in the late-summer sun. Finn was showing Eli how to fill a green plastic fish mold with wet sand while Kendall's twins, Connor and Devin, posed as toddler herders when the younger boys strayed too far from the group.

"Your boys are so sweet," Rose said to Kendall.

"They know how to turn on the charm when it suits them. But honestly, sometimes they lack the brains God gave them," Kendall said, suddenly springing from her chair, dashing over to the railing. "Dev! Pay attention! Christopher's in the bushes again!" she yelled, as if to illustrate her point.

While Kendall played drill sergeant with the kids, Isla poured the last of the lemonade into Rose's glass and set the jug on the table. Noticing Jarett's gaze on the empty jug, she apologized and offered to go make more, but he held up his beer. "I'm good with this for now, thanks," he said.

"Actually," Jarett said, raising his beer a little higher, "I'd like to propose a toast. To *The 444 Five*."

"Hear, hear," Rose said, lifting her glass.

Kendall hurried to the table and picked up her wine. "Cheers to that." She put her free hand on her hip. "*The 444 Five!* Who started that, anyway? Surely, they could have come up with something easier to say?"

"Like what? *The Row 22 Renegades*?" I said.

"Or *The Sandalwood Survivors*?" Lainie added.

Everyone laughed except Isla. "What does Sandalwood have to do with the crash?"

Lainie shrank back in her seat, realizing her mistake immediately. I gave her the smallest shake of my head, a warning to keep quiet.

Because of Isla's blissful ignorance about timeblinking, she of course didn't know that *The 444 Five* had once spent several days here at Sandalwood Lake trying to figure out a way back to 2024. And I intended to keep it that way. Forever. Isla's twenty years in captivity had had devastating effects on her emotional state—even now, five years after her and Finn's rescue—and I simply could not hit her with the mind-fuck that was timeblinking.

Kendall, however, had had other ideas in the immediate aftermath of the crash, before our little group had been found safe in the cornfield and all the news outlets were reporting the crash as "one of the most devastating air disasters in recent history." Hearing this, Isla had spiralled into deep shock. And understandably so. She believed Lainie and I had just been reduced to a pile of ashes. Kendall couldn't bear to see Isla in such pain and was on the verge of spilling the beans when I called them from the Waterloo hospital where our little band of timeblinkers had been taken for observation.

At first, Isla wouldn't accept that it was really me talking to her, but after I mentioned the time when, as kids, we'd gone to the corner store and stolen a package of Skittles (which we later threw in the garbage, too wracked with guilt to eat), she knew it was me on the other end of the phone. The news of our survival had been all she needed, and I was relieved, if not surprised, that she hadn't questioned me about it since. She even went as far as turning off the TV whenever there was a story running about *The 444 Five*. Maybe she thought the spell would be broken if she knew the truth.

And now, she was sitting back, patiently waiting for Lainie to explain why our group should be called *The Sandalwood Survivors*.

"Uhhhh . . . " Lainie said, catching my eye.

"Because," I said, drawing out the last syllable, combing my brain for a plausible answer. *Any* answer. "Because we all chatted about it on the plane. Yeah. And before I knew it, I'd invited our new friends out for a visit."

Isla nodded, apparently buying the story. "Hm, I like it. Okay, from now on, you'll be known as *The Sandalwood Survivors*."

The rest of us laughed stiffly.

"I'll call the news networks tomorrow," Jarett said, winking at me.

"I'm kinda out of the loop about everything." Lainie said, quickly changing the subject. "My mom banned me from following the news because of my nightmares. Has there been anything new?"

Jarett said, "Apart from the flight being one catastrophic mishap after another? How much have you heard?"

"Just that a cockpit window was torn off in all the turbulence and that the captain got sucked halfway out the window, and his feet got wedged in the control wheel. That's why the plane was flying so crazily. I also heard that some of the crew members came in and tried to keep the captain from getting sucked all the way out and that the co-pilot had trouble getting the plane under control before it finally went down."

"Actually, he did manage to regain control," Jarett said. "After we . . . you know, *left*, he attempted to land in a field, but he wasn't expecting an old grain elevator to be in his direct path, and one of the wings clipped it, and the plane cartwheeled."

"And exploded," Lainie said, shuddering. "I knew that, but why did the window come off in the first place? Was it really because of turbulence?"

"The preliminary report attributed it to human error," Rose said. "One of the aircraft technicians replaced that window the night before, but he used bolts that were a fraction of an inch too small."

"0.026 inches, to be exact," Jarett said, shaking his head.

I raised my eyebrows at him.

"I'm good with numbers. Especially ones that could have potentially killed me."

Lainie said, "It's just so freaky. That poor pilot. And all those people. I mean, that could have been *us*."

Kendall, who was sitting next to her, rubbed her back. "It wasn't your time, sweetie. And the nightmares will go away soon."

"I hope so."

Isla said, "Hey, isn't this supposed to be a happy gathering? To celebrate your survival?"

Lainie managed a small smile, and when no one spoke, Isla picked up her glass of lemonade and tapped the side of it with a spoon she'd taken from the sugar bowl. Once she had everyone's attention, she said, "Well, I'd like to propose a toast of my own."

I just about jumped out of my flip-flops. My shy, reserved twin normally didn't like to draw attention to herself, so I grabbed my glass and held it in front of me, eager to hear what she had to say.

She cleared her throat once everyone had their glasses in hand. "We'll probably never know what bizarre, mysterious force spared you all from the crash, but whatever it was, I, for one, hope it protects you the rest of your lives."

Jarett said, "To bizarre, mysterious forces that can't be explained."

"Divine forces," Rose said, winking at me.

Isla held her glass high. "To all of you," she said as the doorbell rang inside the house.

"That must be Brett with the steaks and hot dogs," Kendall said, heading to the door. "He's early, but that's fantastic because he said he wouldn't be able to make it until four."

When she'd disappeared into the house, I said, "That's odd. Why wouldn't he just come in?"

"Maybe the door's locked," Lainie said.

"He's got a key."

Kendall emerged from the house a minute later, followed by someone I didn't recognize until he'd stepped from the shadows and onto the sunny deck.

"Sam!" I yelled, jumping to my feet, wondering which one of *The 444 Five* had invited him. Couldn't have been Jarett. We'd both agreed not to bother Sam on his sacred family day.

Jarett stood up, obviously surprised too. "Hey, buddy, come on in. Join the party," he said, patting the chair next to him.

"Can I get you a drink?" Kendall said, hovering near the door.

"Yeah, sure. I'll have water, thanks," he said, before putting a finger to his lips—a warning for the rest of us not to speak. He turned and ran his fingers around the door frame, then climbed up on a wooden box I use for storing patio cushions and unscrewed one of the pot lights. He inspected the inside of it then replaced it and slid the box under the next light, repeating the procedure three more times. At the last light, he pulled a small, wired device down, unhooked it, and dropped it in his beige chinos pocket.

We all exchanged curious glances with each other while he searched the rest of the area on and under the deck before making himself comfortable on the chair next to Jarett.

"All clear," he said, picking up his glass of water and swallowing it in two gulps.

"Um, okay?" I said.

"We can talk freely out here now, but only if the patio door's closed."

"Dare I ask what you pulled out of that light?"

"Just a bug. And I don't mean a dragonfly."

"What?" I said, though I already knew.

"How do you think I heard about your party? I gotta admit, I'm a little hurt you didn't invite me," he said, sticking his bottom lip out and batting his eyes at me.

Jarett spoke next. "Whose bugs are they? And how long have they been there?"

"FBI. About two weeks. I would have come sooner, but I just found out myself."

"FBI?" I said, stunned.

"There are bugs inside the house, too. But we gotta leave them there, or it will raise suspicion. At least they can blame a malfunctioning exterior bug on exposure."

"Why are they listening?" Isla said.

"Oh, hello," Sam said, leaping up to shake Isla's hand. "I'm Sam. And by the look of things, I'm going to assume you're Syd's twin. Nice to meet you—"

"Isla," she said, shaking his hand tentatively, probably trying to figure out who this mysterious, confident, happy-go-lucky fellow was.

"Hey sis, would you mind grabbing another case of sparkling water from the garage?" I said, eager to get her out of there, afraid that Sam might have forgotten about the *Iowa Pact*.

"Sure," she said, getting up. "Should I make up the cheese board, too?"

"Yes, perfect. That should tide us over until dinner." And it would buy the rest of us valuable time to chat with Sam about our shared history.

This was the second time I'd seen Sam since he'd driven off in a rusty minivan with Iowa plates. The first time was during my inaugural shift back at The Merryport after I'd undergone a full physical and countless interviews with police, the NTSB, the FAA, the FBI, psychiatrists, and psychics who were all trying to figure out how *The 444 Five* had gotten off that plane. Sam had shown up asking me to meet him in the town square after work. That was when he filled me in on his visibility status and the stories he'd been telling his family, friends, and co-workers.

"Bugs!" I shrieked. "See, Lainie? That's why I keep insisting we can't talk about this stuff."

Jarett said to Sam, "Wait a minute. How do you know all this? You're back at your old job at the Port Raven PD."

"I am. But I have a buddy in DC who owes me a huge favor. I contacted him on a whim when the updates on your case abruptly stopped. I mean, it was like someone turned off the tap. So, I called in a favor. He couldn't elaborate, for obvious reasons, but it was enough, and it's how I knew about this gathering."

"Damn," Jarett said. "And here we thought they'd finally given up."

"The rest of you should probably keep hush at your places, too," Sam said.

"There's a bug at my house? In Buffalo?"

"Probably several."

"Do they think we're terrorists?" I said, shaking my head, not waiting for an answer. "It makes no sense. They've already determined the cause of the crash."

"Yeah, but they still haven't figured out how the five of you got off the plane when the security cameras proved you boarded with everyone else. Sounds like they're having a field day over there trying to figure it out. What's even more baffling to them is that you were all seated in the same row. And Syd and Lainie's last-minute booking seems to be a thing of interest to them. Beyond that, my friend couldn't tell me much else."

"This is a mess. Just when I thought we could relax," I said, slumping down in my chair.

"They'll give up eventually, right?" Lainie said to Sam.

"I don't know, to be honest. This case is a first for them."

"And hopefully the last," I said. "At any rate, I'm glad your friend in DC is keeping you in the loop."

Sam shook his head. "He was already paranoid about the information he *did* give me. I'm afraid that's all I'll be getting out of him."

Just then, Connor came running up the yard toward the house, yelling my name.

"We can't find Christopher!"

I sprang out of my chair and flew down the stairs. Everyone followed me down to the beach. "Where was the last place you saw him?"

"Over there," Connor said, pointing to the path leading into the forest to the left of the property. "Devin was supposed to be watching him!"

"I was not! You were!"

"Damn it," I said, doing a head count of the other kids. They were all there.

Sam switched to detective mode. "Okay, here's what we're going to do. Lainie, I want you to stay with the little ones. The rest of us are going on a search. Connor, is it?"

"Yeah?" my nephew said, nervously.

"How long has Christopher been gone?"

"Ummmm . . . ten minutes?" he said, guessing.

"What's going on?" I heard Isla shout from the deck, having heard the commotion outside, no doubt.

"Christopher's missing!" I yelled back.

She came scurrying down the stairs to join us.

"All right. Rose and Jarett, go that way," he said, pointing down the path in the opposite direction to where Christopher had supposedly gone. "Isla, go check the front of the house. And inside it, too. I know you were just there, but he could have slipped by you. Kendall, can you check the lake? Syd and I will go this way." He started off toward the path where Connor last saw Christopher, but I stopped, suddenly woozy. I was having flashbacks to the day Isla went missing. I had to hold onto Sam for support.

"We'll find him," Sam said reassuringly. "He couldn't have gotten far."

"Aunty Syd!" Devin said, running up to me and Sam. "I just thought of something. Maybe he went for a walk with your friend."

I gave him a weary look. "All my friends were on the deck, sweetie."

"No, your other friend."

"Oh! Mrs. Barber from down the path?" I said, relieved. Mrs. Barber often invited our kids over to play when her grandchildren were there for a visit.

"No, the one I just met today. She was on the path by the fallen tree where Christopher likes to throw rocks into the lake."

The fallen tree wasn't far, and I started off down the path. Devin and Sam followed. "What was the lady's name?" I said as we walked.

"I forget."

I squeezed my lips together to keep from screaming.

Sam said, "What did she look like?"

"She had brown hair."

I wheeled around, and Devin almost plowed into me. "Long? Short? Curly? Straight?" I snapped.

He stepped back, scared by my panic. "It . . . it was straight and short. Kinda like Dante's mom's."

"Kendall!" I yelled to my sister who'd walked out to the end of the dock and was scanning the water for my . . . my little boy. "What kind of hairstyle does Dante's mom have?"

"It's a shoulder-length bob. Brunette. Why?"

"I'm sorry, Aunty Syd."

"It's okay, Dev. It just doesn't sound like anyone I know."

"Well, that's weird, because she knows you. She even told me to say hi to you."

It was all so puzzling. I couldn't think of one resident at the lake who fit that description. I was getting frantic. We were wasting time. I turned and kept walking.

"Oh! She also said you shouldn't worry about Christopher. Or something like that."

I whirled around to face him. "Devin! Think! What was her name?"

"I can't remember! I didn't think it would be such a big deal," he said, on the verge of tears.

"Oh, Dev," I said, crouching down to his level. "Please try to remember. It's really important."

"I just don't know," he said. "But she had a necklace just like yours. You know, the one with the dragonfly on it?"

"Syd, are you okay?" Sam said, his voice sounding far away.

My mouth opened, but no sound came out. As the world swam in front of me, I knew Christopher wouldn't be found anywhere near.

Or any*when* near.

DRAGONFLY: TimeBlink Book 3

With both Christopher and the talisman missing and the FBI closing in, Syd faces a mother's worst nightmare: that her son is lost forever.

Then, in a dramatic confrontation with Christopher's abductor, Syd learns some chilling news: she has unwittingly revealed the power of timeblinking to the wrong people, threatening not only Christopher's existence but also the very fate of humanity.

Can Syd undo the catastrophic ripples she has set in motion and be reunited with Christopher, or will her efforts prove futile against the inevitable flow of time?

Read ***Dragonfly***, the thrilling twisty-turny conclusion to The Syd Brixton TimeBlink Series.

Acknowledgments

Writing fiction can be a lonely endeavor. You sit at your computer for hours every day creating worlds out of thin air, crafting characters your readers will hopefully connect with, and coming up with new ways to test and torment those characters.

But in the writing of this book, and indeed the first one in this series, I never felt truly alone—not with an entire tribe of people standing behind me, cheering me on and supporting my journey. No matter how involved or peripheral their support, I am equally grateful to each and every one of them. My only regret is that I can't give them all top billing.

I'll start with my hubby, Alistair Mumford. Thank you for recognizing my passion to be creative and for bringing home the bacon while I slowly, steadily, and stubbornly strive to make a go of this thing. Your love, support, and belief in my journey mean the world to me.

To my mom-in-law, Dorothy Mumford, for always taking the time to ask how my writing is going and for your genuine interest in my life. Love you much.

To my mentors and fellow authors who have provided their invaluable advice, guidance, and free counselling during my times of greatest stress: Dawn Dugle, I met you on TikTok (!) and now I'm tickled to call you a dear friend. You took a chance on my first book and tooted your horn all over the place about it and were gracious enough to beta read *Flight 444*. You will see a lot of your clever suggestions in the pages of this book…the biggest one being a certain missing piece of jewelry (which, by the way, inspired the subplot in book three!). Thanks, buddy. You rock my world. As always, thanks to Lee Gabel, who, despite being in the throes of writing an entire three-book contemporary fantasy saga this past year, always had time for my self-publishing questions.

To my beta readers, Erin Fischer, Janet Rau, Ginny Martin, Stephanie Dunham, Dawn Dugle, and the nine strangers who signed up on Hidden Gems, thank you for your valuable feedback and suggestions. Without your blessing, I may not have been brave enough to go through with the cliffhanger at the end!

To my cousin, Mike Chutskoff, a commercial airline pilot who went through the flight sequences with a fine-tooth comb. You'll notice I fixed many of the red flags you kindly pointed out but that I took some liberties along the way. With any luck, readers with jobs in the airline industry will take those scenes with a grain of salt.

This could also be said of the skydiving references throughout the story. I'd like to thank the crew at Skydive Vancouver for helping me polish the terminology and for not rolling their eyes at the highly improbable main skydiving scene in this book.

To my administrative and creative team. Thank you for your talent and your obvious passion to your craft. You've helped me create a product that I'm proud to share with the world. To my developmental editor, Brooke Bohinc, for your keen attention to detail and your gentle way of challenging me to do better. Thanks for pointing out the flaws, plot holes, and character inconsistencies and for your lovely, encouraging notes sprinkled throughout the manuscript ("Love this!" "Hawt!" "So sweet" to name a few). To Elizabeth Mackey, who designed the kickass cover for this book—in record time and seemingly with no effort at all (though I know that's not true). Thank you for taking it to the next level. To Alison

Cairns, my website expert, who looks after all the nonsense I neither have the skill nor the patience to do myself. Thanks for your speedy, seamless, and never-ending tweaks.

To you, dear reader: I'm thrilled that you've spent a few hours getting to know Syd, Morley, and the rest of the *Flight 444* misfits. If they've entertained you, please consider leaving a review on your favorite book platform.

Finally, a colossal 747-sized thanks to those of you making connections on social media, sharing your thoughts via **MJ's Cabin Crew**, or spreading the word about this series. You're all first class in my books!

About the Author

MJ Mumford's first novel, *TimeBlink*, debuted in 2020 amidst a worldwide health crisis. It wasn't the worst timing for a book launch. At a time when many of us were scared, anxious, or bored to tears, books provided the perfect escape to less precarious worlds.

As a huge fan of time-travel thrillers, suspense novels, and simmering love stories, MJ created The Syd Brixton Time-Blink Series to blend all three genres together. *Flight 444* is the second book in the series.

When she's not dreaming up devious ways in which to torment her characters, MJ enjoys tap dancing, practicing yoga, and traveling to faraway places with her husband. Curiously, MJ never leaves home without her own trusty dragonfly talisman—an object rumored to be more than just decorative.

Hang out with MJ @mjmumfordwrites

An Invitation...

Join **MJ's Cabin Crew** for updates on new releases, book deals, contests, surveys, and a dash of time-traveling fun to brighten your inbox.

Sign up at:
https://mjmumford.com/subscribe/

Made in United States
North Haven, CT
24 February 2024